Premium Life

A Bobby Jacobi Mystery

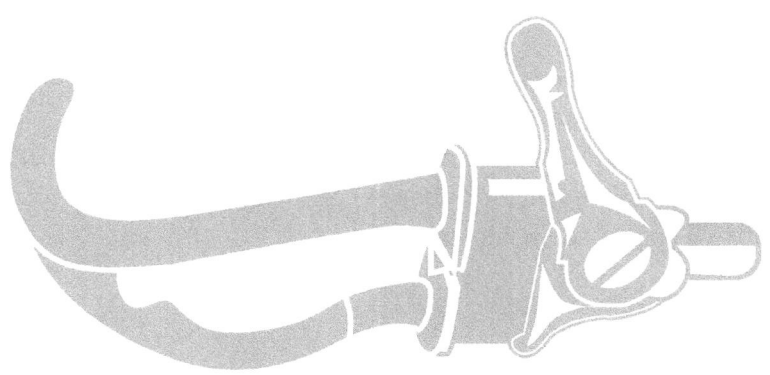

By

Thomas K. Matthews

My special thanks to The Palms at Indian Head Hotel in Borrego Springs, California. For Bobby Jacobi to be able to find comfort in the haunting night sky, the towering palms and desert winds is wonderful. So often my inspiration and serenity comes from the peaceful and nostalgic surroundings of this amazing & friendly place. ~ TM

Insurance: An ingenious modern game of chance in which the player is permitted to enjoy the comfortable conviction that he is beating the man who keeps the table.

– Ambrose Bierce

For almost seventy years the life insurance industry has been a smug sacred cow feeding the public a steady line of sacred bull.

– Ralph Nader

CHAPTER ONE

The clock on the wall read almost quitting time. I tapped my hook on the desktop, and the curved metal chimed out on the imitation wood like a metal worker beating a fender in the distance. I'd long since loosened my tie and unbuttoned my collar around my bull neck. I hate suits, but they go with the job. My chair groaned under my weight when I stood and then walked to the window. The reflection in the glass looked back at me with red-rimmed eyes. Man, I looked tired. Even my goatee looked sad and limp, so I ran my hand through the coarse hair on my chin. Good thing I'm bald or that'd be a mess as well.

Out my window, the afternoon light, subdued by fog, had an ethereal hue. I knew the Bay Bridge would be playing hide and seek for the evening commute. I've lived in San Francisco my whole life, and summer can be a schizophrenic season. One day the sky can be piercing blue and the weather hot and dry, then the high pressure will collapse, and the humidity breathes damp air that sticks shirts to backs and brings sweat to the faces of those toiling outside. The streets teem with tourists scrambling like confused ants who have lost their trail. With school only weeks away and the threat of winter on the horizon, the beaches get busy, and the wharf becomes as congested with pedestrians as cars on the Los Angeles freeways.

When the sun goes down, the fog comes in like a shroud. It rolls off the Pacific and sneaks up the bay and into the backwaters, settles into valleys where it makes halos of street lamps, and turns windshields into smeary blind spots. When we get the fog, the city experiences more traffic accidents than any other time of the year. We also see more muggings. My theory has always been that the fog hides faces, makes gloomy caverns of even open spaces, and feeds the brooding, nocturnal melancholy that can be San Francisco.

I went back to my desk, where my cup of coffee had long since gone cold. I sipped, grimaced, and pushed it away. I can drink it hot or iced, but tepid is nasty. One more time, I read through my latest case and rummaged through the clues. Then I stared at the picture of David Franklin. At first glance, it seemed to be a straightforward case, but for one critical issue, we had no body.

As an investigator, I'd seen it all, and I thrived on unraveling the stories. There is always a story, and usually one filled with lies and deception. Otherwise, they don't put the case on my desk. I dig into the convoluted events that often go back a very long time. I hope to uncover the sad history that drives someone to take action that's always resentfully desperate – not to mention illegal. Sometimes the people involved are driven by abuse, jealousy, and hatred, but mostly it comes down to simple greed. So when they do pull the trigger – so to speak – it takes someone like me to untangled the mess of emotion and motive to reveal the truth.

"David," I said, "what the hell happened to you?" Then I stared at the picture of my father on my desk. "What do you think, Pop? Got any ideas on this one?"

He only smiled back, looking sharp in his policeman's uniform. A wave of nostalgia crashed over me, and I thought of my tenure as an SFPD detective. I was once out on those streets protecting and serving so good citizens could sleep at night. That all ended when I lost the arm. Hey, shit happens.

The fog seemed to be thinning, and the late afternoon sun streamed into the office, so I went back to the window to stare and think.

As far as I'm concerned, San Francisco is the most beautiful city in the world. Many others may be cosmopolitan, ancient, and expansive, but they can't hold a candle to this place's energy, diversity, and sheer spectacle. As a cop, I knew there was plenty wrong with it. Like any other metropolitan area, there's squalor, crime, pollution, and garbage – both human and otherwise. Behind the gleaming glass and tourist destinations, the dirty underbelly of the city is alive and well. That's why I became a cop.

Actually, I became a cop because my dad and his dad were cops. Gramps walked a beat until he retired, but my father made it to detective. That meant I not only also had to make detective, but be the best damn plain clothes there was. I'd like to think I came close. Funny thing, my grandfather bragged that he never pulled his gun in the line of duty, and my dad said he did pull it but never shot it in his tenure. Not only did I pull the trigger, but I also made sure the scum on the other end was wounded or dead. Hey, they were shooting back. That's where this whole story starts.

Known for my grit and a sharp eye, I always went a step further when it came to working cases. My wife Brenda begged me to be more careful, and my partner always shook his head at me, but I knew no other way. The higher-ups loved me because they knew that to give me a case meant I'd grab it by the leg like a pissed-off pit bull. I was detective Robert Jacobi, and if a case could be solved, I did it. One of those cases put me in this office.

A scumbag snatched the daughter of a city council member who was the friend of the mayor. The kidnapper demanded a million in cash for her safe return. Pressure came down from on high to find her quickly and quietly, so I got the case.

Of course, the news leaked, and the press made up their own story because we wouldn't give them the real one. That worked in our favor, though, because they went one way while I went the right way.

I beat the streets, knocked some heads, and used everything at my disposal. The perp made a mistake like they always do. A phone trace on the last demand for the cash placed the call within a four-block grid on Oakland's shit side of town. It was the kind of place where nobody paid any attention to what anyone else was doing, but everybody seemed to know what was going on.

A snitch gave me a lead on somebody staying in an old building by the water. A dumpster filled with take-out pizza boxes proved he was right. Luckily my buddy Joe Santos from the Oakland PD made the jurisdictional problem go away, and he, my partner Paul, and I acted on the hunch.

That night we had fog as our cover, so we sneaked up on the place undetected. Joe blended in nicely in a black tactical uniform. Paul and I wore jeans and black leather jackets, with black beanies pulled over our ears. We huddled down the alley from the building. Cracks of soft light seeped from the blacked-out windows, so we knew somebody was inside. We also knew we were dealing with an amateur because of the pizza boxes. No self-respecting pro would be so dumb as to give himself away like that.

"Okay, this is what I want to do," I whispered. "Paul and I will go down the alley. Joe, go behind the building. We'll use hand signals to communicate. Press the COM on your walkie if you see a way in." I demonstrated, and the other walkies hissed quietly. "That's the signal. Two hisses mean you're in, and three means to create a distraction."

"Got it," Joe barely said.

We crept in a group until we reached the north wall. Joe pointed and disappeared around the back. Once Paul and I reached the rear roll-up doors, we could see more light seeping through the doorframe.

"I'll go around the side," I hissed, and Paul nodded. "Stay here and watch that front door."

I tiptoed along the damp wall facing the bay and grimaced at the smell of low tide. On the other side of the bay, this property would be worth a million bucks, but decay and industry had diminished this stretch to squalor. My boots made no sound on the cracked concrete steps.

I tried the knob on the front door. Locked. Careful as a burglar, I picked the old lock with a jimmy tool and carefully let myself into the empty reception area. The smell of mold, rotted wood, and urine assaulted my nose. Homelessness took its toll in the warehouse district, and this space looked like squatters had lived here for years. Fallen ceiling tiles and mouse droppings littered the floor. The soft light from the back warehouse made it possible for me to see while I quietly sneaked down the hall. I could hear the girl crying softly.

"Shut up," the kidnapper said. He sounded drunk.

My blood boiled, and my mouth tasted metallic. Anger made my heart go cold. From the shadow of the hallway, I could see the girl tied up and lying on an old mattress. The perp sat in a folding chair and drank a beer, a shotgun at his side. I inched forward with a heart of stone and eyes red as hell. The girl saw me and cried harder.

"I said shut the fuck up," the guy hissed.

I could cover the ground in a couple of seconds. All I needed was for the prick to look away. I thumbed my radio three times, and a soft hiss answered me. Then a sharp crack against a blacked-out window caught the perp's attention. He climbed out of his chair and looked toward the window. Cold gripped my heart, and a stream of sweat dripped down my face. I barely breathed.

"What is that?" The perp grabbed the shotgun and took a step in that direction. I moved like a silent monster and covered the ground between him and me in seconds. But my foot kicked an empty beer can, and he turned in surprise.

He screamed, "What the fuck?" Then he turned to shoot the girl.

There are moments in our lives that play out like a flashback from an old movie. The sound is garbled, and the scene is as drab as old paint. No matter how you review it, you know there was no other way it could have gone down. It's like watching that famous footage of the Kennedy assassination. You wish it could have been different, but the President always dies.

I came down on him with snarling rage and grabbed the barrel of his gun. My other hand got hold of his shirt collar. He pulled back, but I was too strong for him.

He stumbled and fell backward. The shotgun barrel's oiled steel slipped through my grip and aligned with my arm just as he pulled the trigger. The loud and bright blast followed by the spent cordite's acrid smell mixed with pink mist in the air. My cheek was on fire. When the perp hit the floor, I saw my left arm, or what was left of it, lying next to him. I stood frozen while the perp started to get up. Then I collapsed from shock.

"Stop, or I'll shoot!" Paul yelled, and then he did exactly that before the scumbag could get off another round.

Joe ran to my side. "Holy fuck!"

"Shit, Bobby," Paul hissed. He looked at the ragged stump that was once my left arm. It was shredded and spraying the concrete floor with gore.

Joe ran to the screaming girl while Paul used his belt to make a tourniquet. I felt like I was spinning. The sights and smells became too much for me, and I vomited. Paul held me and radioed for backup. "Officer down! Send an ambulance! I repeat, Detective Jacobi is down! Hang in there, buddy."

I could only stare at the glazed eyes of the dead kidnapper and the pool of blood forming behind his head. My bloody hand lay on the floor like a dead pink spider.

I remember saying. "Brenda's gonna' kill me."

"Not if that kills you first. Bobby, stay with me."

The ambulance ride was a blur. It's a funny thing about being badly hurt and jacked up on adrenaline. Time slows down, and the scene gets fuzzy.

They rushed me into the hospital while the girl, frightened but safe, was returned to her weeping parents. I remember the pain and the desperate sound of my partner's voice while they prepped me for surgery. I have a vague memory of the doctors and a mask dropping over my face. During the four hours in surgery, they cut away my tattered flesh and sewed a stump an inch below my left elbow.

When I woke up the next day, my room was full of cops, and Brenda sat at my side. I was happy to see that she didn't look angry. Fearful, freaked out, but not pissed.

"I'm sorry, baby," I said. Brenda smiled and stroked my brow.

"There he is," Paul said. "Welcome back. The girl is safe and back with her folks because of you. You're a hero, and they're telling everybody that. It was on the news."

"Wish I could say the same for my hand. Did they save it so I could keep it in a jar of alcohol like an appendix?" I was still high on painkillers.

"That's sick," a cop said.

Joe patted my good shoulder. "You had us worried."

The doctor came in. "Detective Jacobi, I'm Dr. Gerard. I want to explain your prognosis. You feel up for that?"

I nodded. "Sure."

"Should I make these troublemakers leave," he said, "or can they stay?"

"Let 'em stay."

"The initial blast struck you in the mid-forearm and removed the hand. It shattered the bone and tore the muscle too severely to repair. There was substantial damage to the tissue above the impact point, so we had to take off an additional part of your arm."

I looked at the gauze wrapped stump. "Jesus fucking Christ."

"Yes, well, the blast also peppered you up the arm, to the shoulder and your neck and cheek as well. Not too bad, but there will be some scarring. One of the pellets wedged too close to the joint, and removing it could have done more damage. We left it in for now and will revisit that after you heal. Any questions?"

"Just one," I said. "What the fuck do I do now?"

"Just rest."

Brenda ushered the cops out, and then she sat on the edge of my bed.

"Baby," I said, "do you got a mirror?"

"Why, Bobby?"

"I want to see my face. Do you have one?"

Brenda handed me her pocket mirror, and I looked at my reflection. Bandages covered the left side of my face, and small rose blooms stained the centers. My neck wrapped; I looked a hundred years old.

"The doctor says you'll be fine," she said.

She touched the good side of my face. I smiled at her and knew that wasn't true. Without the arm, I was off the street, left with a desk job at best.

"Give it some time," she said. "You'll heal. You're lucky you weren't killed."

A week in the hospital and some convalescing at home took care of my physical wounds. Some sessions with the department shrink helped me accept my disability, and rehab got me back on my feet. They made me whole again with a prosthetic and then amputated my purpose with forced retirement. Then they threw me a party, gave me a medal and people made speeches.

At home, things went from bad to worse. We fought, and I sulked and eventually turned to the bottle. A year later, I was drunk, lost, and divorced.

Case closed.

My old partner saved my life. He showed up one day and beat on my door until I opened it. "Holy shit Bobby, you look like hell."

"Yeah, well, I feel worse."

"Okay man, you need to get out of the house. Get dressed. We're going to get a drink. My treat, and you can't say no."

"Give me five minutes." A fast shower, two aspirin, and some mouthwash turned me into something resembling a human being. Having a drink somewhere besides the house was, at least, respectable.

"That's better," Paul said.

"Thanks. Where are we going?"

"The Blue moon, where else?"

"But that's a cop bar. I'm not a cop anymore."

"So what? Some other guys from the old days are meeting us."

We pulled up, and I imagined how good that top-shelf booze was going to taste after the rotgut I'd been drinking. Eight cops with the day off greeted me with claps and cheers.

"He lives again," Joe Santos yelled.

"What are you doing on this side of the bay?" I scolded.

They led me to a table at the back, where we all sat in a circle. A shot glass full of amber liquid and an ice-cold longneck beer waited for me. My mouth watered.

"Sit down, pal," Joe said.

Paul stood behind me with his hands on my shoulders. I gave him a suspicious shrug, and he sat beside me.

"Buddy," Joe said, "this is your last drink with us."

"Meaning what?"

Paul folded his arms. "Meaning this is an intervention, big man. Take that shot and down that beer, and then you have two options – Rehab or AA."

"You're fucking kidding, right?"

"No, we're not."

"One or the other," Joe said. "If you drink those and keep drinking, then you'll be doing it alone. We can't watch you kill yourself."

"This is bullshit," I said.

"That may be," Joe said. "But this is it. What'll it be?"

"Fuck rehab," I spat. "I'll go to meetings."

"All right," Paul said, "then let's go."

"Now?" I guessed it was my last drink, so I downed the shot.

An hour later, we sat in a church basement where Paul introduced me to a guy named Carl. He was ten years sober and head of investigations for Bayside Consolidated Insurance Corporation.

"So here's the drill, buddy," Paul said. "You need a sponsor, and Carl's a good guy. I'll leave you in his capable hands, and you guys can get to know each other."

"You're gonna' leave me here?"

"Afraid so."

I lumbered after him. "Wait. How do you know this guy?"

"Bobby, are you shitting me? Man, you're not such a great detective, after all."

"Meaning what?"

"In the five years we were partners, did you ever see me take a drink?"

So Carl became my sponsor, my friend, and eventually, my boss. He pulled some strings, schmoozed the powers that be, and taught me to apply my talents to civilian life. He gave me a purpose again. I owe him a lot.

So now, I'm a life insurance fraud investigator. It's not as sexy as being a cop, but it requires the same mindset. My police experience makes me a natural for insurance because I understand the human condition. My size and my fierce temperament are an asset too. Not many insurance investigators are six foot four with a face speckled with buckshot scars. I've had widows break down in weepy confessions, supposedly grief-stricken husbands piss themselves, and aloof extended family members suddenly point accusing fingers just at the sight of me.

I still carry a gun – a five-shot, snub-nose off-duty police .38 – and just the sight of it holstered on my belt has driven the sternest of liars to begin to stutter, lose their train of thought and weep. But despite all that, my most valuable asset is the hand or lack of it. My hook opens and closes with the same menacing gape as a snarling Doberman. Not that I wave it in people's faces. I just let it sit there, a reminder that they're facing a man who has lost a piece of himself. I've come to realize that the average person descends into some urban-myth-driven fear when confronted with that mechanical horror.

Aside from the sideshow shit, I can smell fraud like a dog smells meat. Greed is a human frailty, and I'm convinced that the day man invented insurance, a crook invented fraud. It's only natural since the idea of an ultimate payoff always brings the sneaky types looking to take advantage. I have a theory – unlike those idealists who believe that people are generally good at heart, I feel people are altogether rotten. Resisting our innate instincts to lie, cheat, and steal requires a daily desire to rise above our fundamental nature.

I know myself, and I thrive on suspicion and scrutiny. In fact, I love to wallow in my own lack of faith like a pig in the proverbial shit. And people like me are necessary. Otherwise, who would stop the unjust that wish to defraud my company and the world of money they don't deserve?

It takes all kinds, and I've seen claimants come with false injury, staged accidents, crooked doctors, and greedy chiropractors. But I leave those attacks to my colleagues and focus on life insurance fraud. That's where the big money lives. Those willing to target that vault are a special breed of criminals. On the surface, they do all they can to make their claims appear legit, but I can see through the lies.

Then there's my current case. David Franklin's story is genuinely heartbreaking and unfair – a tale straight out of the headlines. A man left work and headed for the train station. His family waited at home, but he never arrived. His wife's repeated calls to his phone attracted a passerby to the ringing sounds behind a store by the train station. There they found Franklin's car with evidence of shots fired, blood, and signs of a struggle. The preliminary police investigation concluded he was probably abducted or killed, but there was no body. The wife was traumatized, and their father's fate crushed the kids. It sounds like a cut-and-dried case, right? Well, no.

Two years ago, the Franklins got new term life, three hundred fifty grand on her and a half a million on him. Then David's business failed, so with no money and no opportunity, the stress caused him to suffer a mild stroke. With no insurance, the family suddenly faced thousands in medical bills, so they declared bankruptcy. Once David was back on his feet, he found contract work in another city. Every day he took a combined train and car ride to get to his office and back. But on that particular night, he didn't make it.

At least the wife would have the life insurance, and the kids would have enough to go to college. The settlement would help them through their grief, right? But there was one snag, the lack of his body. So it landed on my desk.

The forensic tests revealed that David had cancer, something Mrs. Franklin hadn't mentioned in her initial settlement inquiry. That sent the first red flag up for me, and I sensed some kind of deception. Not the brazen, bald-faced kind I'm so used to. This one was subtler, almost masked by the shifting fog roiling outside my window. I suspected there was an untold story beneath the whitewash of the family's grief. That's where I looked first. In ninety-nine percent of these cases, the spouse is behind the death, if indeed anyone is responsible at all.

I reviewed the news reports about David Franklin's disappearance, complete with an interview with his distraught wife. Her weepy words broadcast for the world to see.

"If anybody knows anything, please come forward. No questions asked. David has cancer, and he needs treatment." Mrs. Franklin's sadness seemed genuine, so I reread the police report and evidence until my head throbbed.

I closed the case file and scratched my chin with my hook. The clock read 6:45. My men's meeting started at eight o'clock. I locked my office, wandered to the elevators, and yawned while I descended to the first floor. I entered the vast lobby with a ding where an older man in uniform sat at the reception desk.

"Workin' late again, Bobby?"

"Yeah, Melvin. Now I'm off to face real life."

"Take care out there."

"You too."

The doors slid open, and I stepped out into the foggy night. The horn blew over the bay, and I could just make out the mist-veiled lights of Alcatraz Island. My phone beckoned me, and I smiled to see it was Gina.

"Hey, baby," I said.

"Hey back. Do you have time for a bite before your meeting? I'm just leaving the bakery."

"That sounds great. What're you up for?"

"Burgers and fries. Meet me at Henry's?"

"Be there in five."

I found Gina looking good enough to eat, so we went back to my place after dinner. I missed my meeting and promised myself I'd catch one in the morning before work.

Gina was still there when I left the next morning.

"Have a good day, lover," she cooed.

"Lock up when you leave."

"Maybe I'll stay."

I liked the sound of that.

CHAPTER TWO

After my AA meeting, I spent the morning reviewing two new case files. The first was a slam-dunk murder fraud case. A husband supposedly shot in a botched burglary with a year-old million-dollar policy on his head. Whoever she hired left so much evidence at the scene that, when the cops tracked down the shooter, he sang like a canary. All the case needed was my signature.

"These people are so stupid," I said out loud.

Janice came in with a huff and stood with her fist against her boney hip.

"Don't you ever knock?" I barked at her.

"Who were you talking to? I heard you whispering."

"I was on the phone with my bookie. I placed a bet on the third horse in the fifth at Aqueduct."

Janice dropped a thick file on my desk. "Season doesn't open 'til spring."

"What's this?"

"My letter of resignation."

"Seems excessive," I said, "even for you."

"I have a lot to bitch about," Janice snapped. "Give me any more shit, and I'll cut off your other hand."

"Let's see you try."

Janice gave me an evil smile. "Don't think I could?"

I held up my hook. "I'd manage. There's plenty I could do with two of these."

"I'd like to see you try and jerk off."

"I'd just have to be careful."

"Yeah, right. These are two new cases. Carl said you wanted the hard copies."

"So?"

"It's all on the computer. You're killing trees asking for these." She pointed at my desk. "You're still going over the Franklin case? You think something new just magically appeared?"

"I just have a hunch."

"You and your hunches. Carl says he's coming in later and wants to know your final thoughts. So if you're going to go through it again, you better be quick about it."

She was not the quintessential detective's secretary. Janice was more like that girl's homely sister. Nothing about Janice was attractive. She was virtually flat-chested, but her ample nipples pressed through her shirtfront like .45 caliber bullets. I once asked her why she didn't wear a bra, and she snapped back, "Those are for women with tits. I don't have any, so I don't wear one."

Hard to argue with that kind of logic.

"Anything else?" I asked.

"Want to have me for lunch?"

"I'm a vegetarian," I said.

"You're no fun," she said and left.

"Gina would kill you if she heard you were hitting on me like that," I yelled after her.

"Don't flatter yourself. Besides, she doesn't scare me."

"Funny, she scares the hell out of me."

I watched Janice's narrow hips sway with pathetic allure down the hall to reception. I eyed the new files and looked at the clock. Twelve thirty. I knew if I opened one, I'd lose myself in work and forget to eat. I'm an angry bear when I don't keep my stomach happy. Corned beef on rye with hot mustard sounded great, and my stomach growled like that bear. I collected the folders, grabbed my jacket, and left the office.

San Francisco is a city of extremes, whether you want to talk about the weather, the districts, or the philosophy. The soft sun reflected off chrome and glass while I walked the four blocks to Murphy's Tavern. Built back when San Fran was a shipping town, a rusted three-foot-high cleat jutted from the sidewalk like a lost remnant from a maritime museum. A plaque announced that ships used to dock outside the building. Apparently, sailors wound thick, salt-encrusted ropes around the sturdy stud while they went into the tavern for drinks, food, and the company of a woman. Not much had changed in a hundred years.

Clive, the bartender, gave me a hearty hello when I bellied up to the bar. He placed a tall glass of diet coke in front of me. Everyone knows I'm sober and glad of it. During the bad times of resurrection and restitution, many of these same folks watched me brawl my ¬way into forgiven trouble, only to have my former cop brothers take me home.

Clive placed silverware rolled in a paper napkin in front of me. His round Irish face, freckled and happy, always made me smile. "What'll it be?" he said.

"Beef and cheese."

"Slaw or fries?"

"Both."

"Coming right up."

People came and went. Several slapped my shoulder or said hello. I sipped my soda, opened the folder, and kept the papers clamped between the curves of my hook. As cumbersome as the hook was in so many ways, the simple things made up for the inconvenience. I scanned the summary of a new case and carefully read the police report. My mind, though, kept returning to Franklin. I shook my head and tried to focus, but my mind demanded that I review it again. So I did.

David Randall Franklin went to work at the Asbury & Associates advertising agency on a Friday morning. He put in his time, ate lunch at his desk, and then drove to the station. He was supposed to park his Hyundai in the Park N' Ride and take the train home to his family in San Mateo.

He didn't get off the six-fifteen commuter, so his wife Claire assumed he missed his train. When she couldn't reach for hours afterward, though, she became desperate. Her repeated calls to David's phone attracted a jogger who found David's car in a parking lot behind a closed appliance store. The keys were still in the ignition, and blood splattered inside the vehicle. The police reported two bullet holes – one in the dashboard and one in the windshield. There were signs of a struggle and more blood on the asphalt. The content of David's wallet scattered across the parking lot. That's how the police knew who was missing.

At first, the authorities thought David might have gone looking for help. Every hospital and doctor's office was contacted but with no results. By law, gunshot wounds must be reported to the police. They expected a call about a man who staggered in seeking medical attention. He never surfaced.

Three weeks later, there was still no body, no clues, and no motive. David's wife waited for a ransom note, but none arrived. She desperately pestered the SFPD with relentless grief and anger. Mrs. Franklin haunted the hallways of city hall and begged for help. She went on the radio and local TV, pleading for whoever knew anything about her husband to come forward. Either nobody cared or knew anything because the poor guy was just gone.

Then the experts began their talking head routine, speculating that David could be already dead. If his alleged attackers hadn't done the deed, he was at significant risk from cancer itself. It seems this particular form could sneak up and snuff you while you still felt okay. But – and there is always a 'but' – he could live a year or more with the disease. The story became a regional media phenomenon. Everybody wanted to know what the hell happened to David Franklin. And therein lay the problem; there were still too many unanswered questions to settle a claim.

In the event of a missing body, especially under questionable circumstances, life insurance firms tend to hold on to the cash as long as they can. Death in absentia, or presumption of death, is the legal declaration that a person is deceased in the absence of remains. In some cases, this requires a court order. The process can take seven years if there is no evidence of foul play. We had evidence of foul play, but it could still be construed as a kidnapping on the surface. Hence, David Franklin could still be alive. Despite his health issues, he could be tied up in a basement with a blindfold over his eyes, living on canned beans and tap water.

"If David were kidnapped, there would be a ransom demand," his wife kept insisting to anybody who would listen. "If you believe he could be dead, then please consider our claim. For the wellbeing of his children, for Christ's sake!"

She was right on both counts. I had read the report from his oncologist, and David had indeed been diagnosed with late-stage pancreatic cancer. He had no chance of survival without radical treatment. Before I could get completely wrapped up in my speculation, Clive slid my sandwich in front of me, and I absently took a bite. When the savory corned beef and smooth provolone hit my tongue, I forgot David Franklin long enough to chew, sigh, and appreciate life. That was more than I could say for this poor bastard.

My phone rang. Janice.

"I'm eating."

"Oh, excuse me, Mr. Jacobi," she said, sounding snide. "Carl decided that since you're still agitating over the Franklin case, he wants you to interview Franklin's wife. I called, and she'll see you tomorrow morning at ten."

"In San Mateo?"

"Yes, in San Mateo."

"I'm sure she'll get a kick out of me."

"But you're so handsome," Janice teased.

"And you look like a pageant winner."

"Go fuck yourself."

"I already did. I was great."

I hung up and went back to concentrating on the crisp fries and how the slaw tickled my tongue with a bit of sweetness and a touch of sour. I let the flavors take over my senses, and I forgot about David Franklin for the remainder of my lunch.

Outside, the city worked and played while the tourists thronged. The bay glimmered, and the Golden Gate stood majestically against an ice blue sky. Around me, people drank and laughed, came and went, and participated in life like we all sometimes take for granted. In San Mateo, a wife and mother wrestled with sadness while her children suffered from their loss.

As I pushed back my plate, I knew that somebody somewhere was faced with the end of life at that very moment. A doctor stood over a patient and gave a diagnosis. A car lost control. A junkie overdosed, or a child ran into a street. Husbands and wives wept, bystanders screamed, paramedics frantically worked on heart attack victims and car accident traumas. Yes, somewhere, people were dying, either by age, accident, or foul play.

You see, that's inevitable for all of us. And behind the tragedy and the weeping, the bean counters catch the insurance claims as they roll in. They look at the numbers, categorize the claims, and treat death as a business. While they make their decisions and stamp the forms, they do so under the shadow of one undeniable truth; the premiums will always outweigh the payouts. That's life. Or death, I suppose.

CHAPTER THREE

My boss Carl Hardman is a bit of a conundrum because he isn't a hard man, not by any definition. He stands five feet nine inches tall and what I call middle-aged portly. With a pasty face and thinning blond hair, his hands are like gel-filled gloves. But – and here's the odd part – he has a black belt in Brazilian jujitsu. I watched him spar once, and he was a complete badass. By his own admission, though, he would be too afraid to use his fighting prowess in the real world.

"I'd probably forget all my training and cry like a baby," he said.

I still gave him credit and often offered my macho support to encourage the warrior within him. Carl owns a boat, a twenty-three-foot sports beast with a wakeboard tower, and all the fishing gear. In the three years, I've known him, he's never had it out of dry dock. He's a bachelor and seems to like it that way. He's inept around women and a poor dresser, but he knows insurance. After lunch, he knocked at my office door.

"Got a minute?"

"For you, Carl, I have five."

He took my chair, his way of reminding me he had a higher rank. I denied him his symbolic power play by sitting on the edge of the desk, my bulk looming over him like a punishing demigod. He seemed to miss the point and thought I was friendly, so he patted my leg.

"So we've had this claim for, what, six weeks?" Carl dipped his fingers into the jar of M&Ms I kept for visitors.

"Just shy of that."

"Still no body."

"Nope. And nothing new from the Oakland PD."

"You know his wife is pestering us to settle."

"That bothers me," I said. "She sounds too eager."

"But she also sounds pretty tore up," Carl offered.

"It's more than that. We're dealing with an unresolved balance of probability here. The evidence still doesn't work for me. I'm convinced there's a possibility he could still be alive."

"That's the cop in you talking."

"But you have to think like a cop. You have to examine all the possibilities. I'm just being thorough, so we don't pay out on a bum case."

"All the evidence points to him being dead."

"No," I said. "It's still wide open."

"Explain."

"Okay, both Franklin and his wife were given full screenings when they purchased the policies. We ran the standard cancer test, and they both came back clear."

"Lab work mistake?"

"No. There was enough to go back and retest, and he was fine when the sample was taken. They had no medical insurance when he got sick, and he now had the mother of pre-existing, so they couldn't get shit to cover any expenses. His diagnosis and the follow-ups alone came to over twenty thousand."

"How much does the treatment for pancreatic cancer cost without insurance?"

"Around three hundred grand. Not to mention aftercare, medication, and additional costs if there are complications. Generally, pancreatic cancer doesn't become symptomatic until it's too late."

"Then what's the treatment for?" Carl asked.

"To prolong life. But the mortality rate is almost a hundred percent."

Carl raised his eyebrows. "So you spend a fortune just to fight the good fight? Sounds like Custer's last stand. That's an expensive proposition for end of life. So what's your gut say?"

"What my gut thinks is irrelevant. We have to find out what happened to this guy." I stood up because my ass was falling asleep from sitting on the corner of my desk.

"Then give me your rhetorical theory of deception."

"Faked death goes off someplace to die," I said. "The wife collects the cash, and he doesn't burden his family with medical debt and prolonged grief."

Carl put his index finger to his chin. "And we don't pay out for suicide for at least three years."

"But if he were murdered, we'd have to pay," I said.

"So when you see her tomorrow, you'll get a better idea?"

"Yes. When I leave there, I'll know if she knows anything. Are they pushing to settle upstairs?"

"No. If it were up to them, they'd never pay out. We have a little more time on this one. You know our policy if there's a way to keep the dough, let us know."

"That's fucked up."

Carl nodded and pulled himself from my chair like an old dog climbing up the front house steps. "Good luck. Call me after and let me know what you think of her state of mind. You going to the meeting later?"

"Yeah." I settled back into my seat. Carl's conservative smell of aftershave and Preparation H hung around like a sad and odorous ghost.

I dialed the Franklin home and left a message, reminding Mrs. Franklin I had an appointment for ten in the morning. I spent the rest of the afternoon researching the symptoms and pathology of Pancreatic death. It was grim.

At five, I called Gina, but she was busy. I grabbed a bite and went home, where my one-bedroom apartment welcomed me.

I'm a simple guy with simple tastes. No doodads or knick-knacks sit on my shelves. No bad paintings of ships at sea adorned my walls. I don't even have pictures of the family. Mom died when I was a kid, and dad passed away five years ago. Maybe it's a cop thing, but there was little sentimentality in the Jacobi home. I like things that fit me and are reliable. A 2003 Dodge crew cab gets me around, and my only luxury is a seventy-two inch flat screen TV that fills the only windowless wall in my apartment.

Then there's Butch.

He showed up at my back door one night, yowling for help. Bigger than any cat I'd ever seen, his face was lacerated, and his back was slashed with fighting wounds. He must have come to the closest place for refuge and found me. We were two maimed creatures brought together by fate. With eyes like yellow marbles and one fang that dropped below his lip like a mono saber tooth, he looked like a throwback of some kind. I cleaned him up, fed him, and he never left. Before long, Butch was mine, even that only means I leave water in a bowl and the window open. Not that he's devoid of connection. Occasionally he comes and plops beside me, rolls on his back, and wants me to rub his stomach with my hook. When he's had enough, he bites the metal and runs off.

Tonight Butch slept in a ball while I pondered my upcoming meeting with Mrs. Franklin. The muted TV silently displayed an action movie that roiled out mindless violence without a laugh track while the Franklin crime report replayed itself in my head.

I guessed that the first shot punched the hole in the windshield. The second went through what I assumed was Mr. Franklin's body at nearly point-blank range. There were powder burns on the flesh fragments found in the splattered blood. The bloody handprints on the side of the seat and the driver's side window indicated a body in movement.

But why was the wallet left at the scene? So we'd know for sure it was Franklin? It seemed ham-handed, even staged. Or did the perps drag him into a van and speed away to finish him off and drop the wallet? What about the wound? Even with a single shot in him, Franklin would have bled like a stuck pig and left their vehicle looking like a slaughterhouse.

"What do you think?" I asked Butch, who answered with a yawn. "Did he pass out? Did he fight back? Did anyone hear anything? Why was he behind the empty store in the first place? Was he forced there? How?"

Butch closed his eyes.

"You're worthless."

In the life insurance game, there is one primary question – who would profit from death? While the beneficiary is always suspect number one, I've come across conspiracies that made my head spin. I had to entertain that Franklin's wife might be responsible. Not that I suspected she laid in wait and shot him while he drove home from work. If she were involved, she would have hired somebody to do that for her. From what I had seen in the press, she didn't seem the type, but she and David were facing financial ruin and his certain, impending death.

I rubbed my eyes. "Shit if I know."

A car silently exploded on the television. Butch got up, arched his back, and jumped down from the couch.

He gave me a look over his shoulder and hopped out the open window for a night of carousing. The clock said it was after eleven, so I stretched my back and switched off the set. After rinsing my coffee cup, I pushed the auto timer for the percolator and dragged myself to the bedroom.

Taking off my prosthetic is no easy task, and the tension strap around my shoulders always rubs me the wrong way. Despite the muslin liner, the cup over my stumped forearm always leaves me sore. I put the contraption on my side table and rubbed lotion into my stump. When the soreness calmed down, I slipped a cotton sleeve over my arm and went to the bathroom. I brushed my teeth, gargled with Listerine then and crawled into my king-size bed. Typically I was asleep in five minutes, but tonight the cop in me sat in the bedside chair and wouldn't shut up.

Hey, Bobby, he whispered, what about the car being pulled over? Maybe the murderer said he had a low tire. There could have been a confrontation, and the gun came out, and there was a scuffle. The shots got fired, and the rough handling started. Think that's how it went down?

"How should I know?"

Hey Bobby, maybe he cut the wrong people off. Perhaps that's how it started. Maybe he was in the wrong place at the wrong time. Think that's how it happened?

"Shut the fuck up."

Hey, Bobby…

"Bullshit." I got out of bed and went to the living room to lie down on the couch. I finally fell asleep and dreamed of gunshots, quiet explosions, and splattered blood. At five in the morning, Butch woke me with a yowl. I was sleeping on his spot. He curled up where I'd warmed the cushion, and I went to clear my muddled mind with a hot shower.

Outside, the fog swallowed the world. I found momentary peace beneath the beating streams of water. While I soaped up, I rehearsed my questions, practiced my compassionate expression, and prepared myself for my face-to-face with Mrs. Franklin.

*   *   *   *

Between my police pension and my salary, I do pretty well. I better; San Francisco is one of the most expensive cities in California. My ex collected a bit of my retirement but soon found herself another tough cop and fell in love. She was married within six months of our divorce. She forgave me for being maimed and weak – her actual words – and then walked down the aisle with the new guy. He was nobody I knew, of course. She was desperate but not stupid. The break was clean with no kids, and I was left with nobody needing, wanting, or demanding anything of me. That's a good place for a broken, alcoholic cripple. But life goes on, and with the Job and sobriety, life became easy and predictable.

"No dating for your first year," Carl said. "I don't want you stumbling into potential relapse because some woman breaks your heart.

"He's right," Paul stressed. "I set myself back six months because I wouldn't listen to that same warning."

The day I took my one year token, I had coffee with Gina. I'd seen her in meetings and talked to her once or twice. Before then, I had kept my eyes down and the showers cold. I'd never seen a more beautiful and sexy woman in my life. So with Carl's blessing, I asked her out. She said yes. I asked why, and she laughed.

"Hey. When you're almost six feet tall and look like I do, most men are either too overwhelmed or too intimidated even to try. Besides, I love how honest you are with your shares."

We saw a movie, walked along the wharf, ate ice cream, and talked about her. She'd heard my story, and now I knew hers. When she took my hand, it was the hook, and we both laughed.

"Wanna' change sides?" I asked.

"No, this is fun, and it makes the tourists gawk."

I fell in love that night. Neither of us was looking for marriage, and certainly not kids, so we took it slow. We waited a whole week before having sex, and when we did, she fell in love with me too. After a year of celibacy, I was making up for lost time. That memory helped pass the time while I drove along the bay. Just before San Mateo, she called. "Hello, baby."

"How're things in the bakery?"

"Two parties today. When I started this cupcake thing, I thought I'd get an order or two once in a while. If I'd known this was going to turn into a job, I would have run screaming."

"You know you love it."

"I just wanted to wish you luck today. I've seen this woman on TV, and she's genuinely broken up."

"I'll be easy."

"Okay. Call me after and let me know how it goes."

"Will do. I love you."

I turned the radio on and was accosted by a generic country crossover bimbo screeching like a cat with its tail caught in the door. I hate modern rock. It's as manufactured as fast food and just as lacking in musical nutrition. Give me The Stones, David Bowie, The Who, The Guess Who, or any of the storytellers and musical geniuses. James Taylor, Jackson Browne, and The Kinks. I see Neil Young every time he comes to town. Call me a dinosaur, and you're right, but my tastes are simple and set in stone. After a few more songs, I rolled into the town where David Franklin used to live.

San Mateo is classic new California. Native Americans once lived there because of its freshwater creeks and accessibility to the ocean. Unfortunately for them, the Europeans found it just as appealing. Driven by a sense of entitlement, they drove the natives out and killed those who wouldn't leave. Once they had the property, they cut paradise up into huge land tracts. They brought in stage stations, connected themselves to the outside world, and built Ranchos. Then San Mateo became a real town with the addition of the railroad in 1894. As is the way of invaders, they kept the old world feel with Indian motifs and pseudo early California architecture. I suspect this is how marauders soothe their guilt. In the end, the only Indians left were made of wood and standing in front of cigar stores.

The old town is upscale and quaint. The outskirts peppered with pre-recession communities full of wandering streets lined with expensive housing. They are not quite McMansions, more the younger siblings. My GPS device seductively told me I had arrived. I pulled up to a faux Mediterranean, three-car garage, two-story home that must have cost eight hundred thousand before the economic crash cut that figure by a third. The street was smattered with real estate signs, some of which sported bank-owned caps like scarlet letters. I called the office, and Janice assured me Mrs. Franklin was expecting me.

"She never confirmed."

"Just go knock on the door, you pussy."

"Yes, dear," I said with a snide laugh.

An older man on the opposite side of the street was hosing down his driveway despite the ongoing California water shortage. He gave me a look of suspicion. He was bald, thin, in his seventies, and he wore brown sandals with black socks. With his Bermuda shorts pulled to his armpits, he reminded me of the kind of man who volunteered to be the homeowner's association watchdog. I could see him with his binoculars and making notes for the next meeting.

I waved at him with my hook. "Good morning."

He raised his free hand. "Morning." His voice was like a shovel on brick.

Five flagstone steps led to a stamped concrete stoop and a heavy wooden front door. I knocked, and I heard a low scuttle when the small-hinged window in the door opened. A tired yet attractive face looked through the crossed iron bars that gave the door its rustic charm.

"Yes?"

"Mrs. Franklin, I'm Robert Jacobi from Bayside Consolidated Insurance. I believe you're expecting me?"

"Yes, I'm sorry," she said. "I was resting and lost track of time. May I see some identification, please?"

I fished my wallet out of my pocket with my right hand. I kept the hook hidden in my coat pocket. She was careful, and I applauded her for that.

"Can you take it out of the wallet?" she said.

I obliged her and waited until I heard the deadbolt slide back. She peeked through the gap.

"Thank you." She unhooked the caution chain and opened the door. Claire Franklin was typical of upper-middle-class wives with her yoga body and well-manicured nails. French nails, I think they call them, with the white tips. Her snug pants and loose shirt exhibited what I like to call presentable causal. She looked me over. It became awkward.

"May I come in?" I said.

She waved her hand and headed for the kitchen. I closed the door and followed. I smelled the wine in the air before I smelled it on her. Ten in the morning and she was probably into her second glass. It smelled like a decent California cabernet. At least it wasn't whiskey. Many people in grief turn to the bottle. I took a seat at her table and snapped open my briefcase while hiding my hook in my pocket.

"Thank you for seeing me," I said.

"Is there anything I can get you?" she asked. "Water, soda, wine?"

I shook my head and managed to take out the case folder and my notebook with one hand.

"Mind if I do?" she asked.

"Not at all."

She poured another glass of pungent grape. "Are you here to give me more insurance company run around bullshit?"

"I just need to ask some questions about your husband's disappearance. It should only take a few minutes to clarify some things."

"The kids are at school," Mrs. Franklin said. "We won't be disturbed. They are still traumatized, and they cry a lot, but I thought school would help them get back to normal."

"I understand," I said, though I hadn't asked about her children. "I know you've already told this story many times, but I'd like you to go through the events of the day your husband didn't come home.

I know it's painful, but we may find something that may have been missed."

She leaned against the kitchen counter. "I've already told the police this story a hundred times. Then I told the papers and the news. I told everybody that would listen. Don't you read or watch the news?"

I smiled at her. "I may have a different perspective. So if we could start from the beginning?"

Claire held her glass and her eyes had an angry fear in them. Her slouched shoulders and tangled hair contrasted with her beauty as she stared at me with defiant grief.

"Jesus, this is so stupid," she said with a sneer. "My husband is dead!"

"Mrs. Franklin, if this is too painful, we can do this another time."

"What's in your other hand?" She asked.

"Pardon?"

"You're keeping your hand in your pocket. Are you hiding something?" She took a sip of her wine. "Are you recording this? Do you think I had something to do with David's death? Is that it? You want to trick me into to saying something that makes me look guilty so you can deny my claim?"

"No. Just a habit. That's all, just something I do."

"I don't believe you. I think you're trying to trick me." It was the wine talking.

"I promise Mrs. Franklin; I have nothing in my pocket."

"Show me," she said, her voice edgy.

"I have to ask you to calm down."

She nearly hissed at me. "Let me see your hand."

"Yes, ma'am." I pulled my hook from my pocket and set it on the table.

"Jesus." She broke into an odd smile. "I just didn't expect that. I thought you had a tape recorder or a gun or something. I wasn't expecting that."

"Most people don't," I said. "Can we refocus on my questions, please?"

"How did you lose that?" Claire asked.

I realized she was drunker than I first suspected. It takes one to see one.

"Farm accident when I was a kid," I said.

"You don't look like you grew up on a farm. You look like a city guy."

"Mrs. Franklin, can we please get back to this?"

"You don't look like an investigator for an insurance company, either." She took another sip. "You look like the kind of person who probably killed my husband. You look like a thug. Like the kind of guy who'd work for the mob."

I gave her a blank stare and realized I had probably underestimated the number of glasses she'd had before I arrived. The air was almost buzzing with her repressed emotion. I could feel the hairs on the back of my neck stand up as if in anticipation of an attack. I knew the situation was potentially explosive. It was pointless to try and have a rational discussion with an irrational person. But I tried once more.

"Mrs. Franklin, can we focus on the reason for my visit?"

"You have scars on your cheek, little pink nubs like acne scars. But the rest of your face is not like that. It makes you look dangerous. I'd think your boss would send somebody out here that looked compassionate and would help me feel better. You look like a hitman."

Her face was now red, and her words slurred.

"Mrs. Franklin?"

"Why would a man like you – what are you, six foot three?"

I nodded. "Yes."

"David was six feet. He tried to build more muscle, but he was always thin." Her eyes misted, and her lower lip began to tremble. She was about to lose it.

"Mrs. Franklin."

"I can't believe you're here," she growled. "Why are we having this conversation?"

"I'm sorry."

I knew what was coming. I made a great target, and her tipsy, heartbroken emotions were about to come at me like a pit bull. I closed my folder, zipped it into my leather case, and stood up from the table. Her eyes flashed, and her lips curled back from her perfectly white teeth.

"Why are you asking me questions when I've already told every fucking person in the police and your office exactly what happened?"

"I'll show myself out."

I backed out of the kitchen, and she followed me. Her head swiveled like an exotic dancer, her movements gracefully sloppy. Her words came out laced with pure venom. "Who are you?"

"I'll call another day." I worked my way down the hallway.

"What the fuck are you doing here?" she screamed.

"You have my sympathy. I'm sorry to have intruded."

"Tell me! What do you want?"

"I'll leave my card right here."

I put it on the small table by the door.

A tall vase held three long-stemmed silk red roses. The falseness of the flowers was suddenly evident in the very core of the home. The only genuine thing here was her furious sadness. I got what I came for; Claire Franklin was hiding nothing. Her words came from a deep and dark place where her love used to live.

"He's dead. Do you hear me? David's dead! Can you help me understand that? Can you help my children understand that? Can you explain that to Kelly and Brenda? That's their names so that you know."

"Good day."

I slipped out the door.

She followed me outside. Her angry shouts pushed me out of the neighborhood like a tsunami.

There was no need to speak with her again. But more than that, her intense emotion embedded David Franklin's plight like a tattoo on my psyche. Her emotions somehow made me care, even if I didn't know it yet.

My phone rang, and I answered with a gruff hello.

"Hello to you too, sunshine," Janice said.

"What's up?"

"You done with the wife already?"

"I am," I said.

"How'd it go?"

"It was ugly. She's lost in grief and decided to take it out on the big, scary investigator."

Janice laughed. "Did the little middle-class housewife beat you up?"

"Not physically. I can tell you she's for real."

"Boss wants a debriefing," Janice said.

I called Carl.

"How did it go?"

"Brutal, drunk, sad, lost, and hurting."

"So, you fell in love with her ?" Carl said. "Gina will be pissed."

"Hey, I'm not that codependent."

"You think she's legit, no complicity?" Carl asked.

"Claire Franklin chased me out of her house by throwing her heart at me. I barely escaped with my life. Nobody is that good an actress."

"Okay, one more thing to scratch off the list. What's next?"

"Tomorrow, I'm going to go talk to the people where he worked."

My drive back was a struggle between my rational thoughts and my internal voice screaming we had to solve this case – the same voice that had driven me in the old days – the voice of a cop.

Then another voice joined in. She's so broken-hearted, the voice pleaded. We have to ease her pain.

"That's not my job," I said out loud.

We have to find him. Something is wrong here, my cop voice ranted.

"Not my job!" I said again.

Help her, the other voice said.

"No," I nearly yelled.

Then listen to me, the cop said. We know how to solve this.

"I'm not a cop anymore."

So when did that ever stop you?

I had no argument for that.

After I got back to the office, I filed my report and had coffee with Carl – as my sponsor, not my boss. Then I called Gina and gave her the details of what went down.

"Baby, that sounds intense," she said. "Are you okay?"

"Yeah, but what I need is a night out with you and some time in your loving arms."

"I can accommodate you on both those things. Besides, I'll be out of town this weekend, so I need a good dose of you to hold me over at the women's retreat."

"Otherwise, you'd come back a changed woman?"

"Been there, tried that. I'll save myself for you."

We ate pasta at a little place near her apartment. Afterward, we went back, and she urged me to lose myself in her. That was the easy part. The wonderful thing about loving a woman with a past that matches my own is that we understand each other. That night I slept like the dead.

CHAPTER THREE

After his design business nose-dived, David Franklin took a contract job with Asbury & Associates Advertising in North Beach. Not a huge company but with stable, recession-proof clients. They specialized in liquor, pharmaceuticals, and economy cars. Things people still need when the extra cash for vacations and big nights out dried up.

North Beach is an odd place that caters to business, tourism, and titty bars. This strange balance offers excellent Italian food sandwiched between strip clubs. On the weekend, nightclub barkers call out while folks go to dinner, offering invitations to families as well as single men. It's a fun and obscene experience that drives the tourists to distraction and sends them home with stories to shock the heartland.

I located Asbury and Associates in a mid-century, three-story commercial building hidden in a stand of windswept pines. Spectacular ocean views completed the picture. I pushed four quarters into the meter and walked a winding pathway to etched glass double doors. I approached a low reception desk and a gorgeous blonde receptionist with features as sharp as chipped ice. Her neckline plunged, and I tried not to stare at the swell of her breasts while I presented my card.

"I have an appointment with Herbert Baxter."

"Your name?"

Her smile did not warm her one bit.

"Robert Jacobi."

"I'll announce you. Please take a seat."

A glance at the registry board showed the building housed high priced accountants, psychiatrists, and lawyers who likely charged three hundred an hour. The ice blonde wasn't just a receptionist - she was the gatekeeper. Her desk plate said her name was Helen. Like Helen of Troy, a woman so beautiful men went to war over her. She looked like a supermodel.

I settled into an overstuffed upholstered chair and took in the lobby. The modern decor sported floor to ceiling windows that looked out over the rough Pacific with sea birds coasting on updrafts. Local art adorned the walls, and a tall copper sculpture of sea kelp wound its way up the wall beside the elevator. Helen hung up the phone and gave me a Miss America smile.

"Mister Jacobi. Mr. Baxter will be right down."

A few minutes later, a stout, graying gentleman in an expensive suit approached me with his hand out. I kept my left hand in my pocket and gave his right a vigorous shake.

"Welcome to Asbury. I'm Herb Baxter, managing director."

"Robert Jacobi."

His hair looked artificial, and I realized he recently had transplant plugs. It reminded me of the hair from those creepy baby dolls when I was a kid. Funny how men equate hair with virility, but women often consider bald men incredibly sexy. I once read Yul Brynner was voted the sexiest man alive in 1957.

"We were so sorry to hear about David," Baxter said as we started to drift toward the elevator. "He was a hard worker, and we were considering hiring him on as an employee."

"I appreciate your giving me access to his computer," I said. "Do you practice Internet tracking to see what your people are up to when you're not looking?"

"We do. But we're pretty lenient when it comes to what they do on their lunch break. We knew David was recently diagnosed with a serious illness and gave him plenty of support."

"I'm sure you did."

The elevator carried us to the second floor, where the doors opened directly into a busy office. The same floor to ceiling windows opened the back wall to the ocean. The view was even more impressive.

"Great place to work," I said.

"The view keeps us inspired, and in advertising, that's important. David worked right down here." Baxter gestured like a woman on a game show.

David's desk sat in a cubicle surrounded by a high tech print station but no view of the inspiring ocean. The screen on his Mac swirled with deep blues like the electronic brain dreamed of cyber heaven.

"Here is the access code to get into his history. He has some protected files on the hard drive, and we got permission from his wife to open them up. Let me know if you have any questions. We have a protection block on anything not connected to his personal activity, including all the files he worked on regarding our client's campaigns. For our own protection, you understand."

"Of course."

I tapped the keyboard, and my jaw twitched at the sight of his desktop picture. He and his family sat on a bench at Fisherman's Wharf in San Francisco. They looked happy.

The password took me to his desktop. His Internet connection gave me a history of websites David visited on his own time. It was all alternative cancer treatment sites involving everything from bee sting therapy to coffee enemas. I highlighted the entire list, over three hundred sites, and emailed them to myself.

After searching his files and folders, I found two short cell phone movies of the day the family spent at the wharf. Both were of the kids frolicking along the boardwalk.

"Kids," David's voice said off-camera. "Kids, look over here."

Now I had a voice to go with the face and a name for the voice in my head. David Franklin.

"Mr. Baxter," I called down the hall.

"Yes," he chirped.

"I've got what I need. Thank you for your cooperation."

"By all means. I hope this helps. David had become like a member of our family here. We miss him and his creative energy. We were entertaining the idea of hiring him full time."

"Yes," I said, "you told me that."

Baxter flushed. "Right."

"Until you heard he had cancer?" I gave Baxter my most malicious smile.

"Excuse me?"

"You considered hiring him full time until you found out he had cancer?"

Baxter's face went red. "What exactly are you implying?"

I imagined his blood pressure jumping higher, his arteries contracting, and his sweat glands seeping like a swollen earthen dam. I could almost hear his suit soaking up his sweat.

"Nothing, just a job habit. Sorry." I extended my hand.

Baxter shook it tentatively and then looked at his palm as though I left something sticky there.

"If there's nothing else," he said, "I have work to do."

"No, that's it. Thanks again. I'll let you know what I find out. I'm sure you'd want to hear about it since he was so close to you. Have a nice weekend."

Baxter watched me leave wearing an expression of anger and embarrassment. It was a cheap shot, I know, but I despise false emotion, and I tend to call things as I see them. As a result, I've been slapped, punched, and chastised more than once. It's worth it to make sure things stay black and white.

Back at the office, I downloaded the list of websites I'd retrieved from Franklin's computer and began clicking and reading. I gave special attention to the sites he visited often. Almost every site offered a possible cure for desperate people searching for some miracle.

Janice barged into my office. "What'd you find out?"

"Not much. Jesus Jan," I said with an angry laugh. "What if I'd been doing something private in here? Knock next time."

"You're too obsessed with work to be doing anything private."

"Then do it as an act of common courtesy."

She sneered at me. "There is nothing courteous about you, and I have no tact. It's a perfect fucking marriage. Deal with it."

"I'll start locking my door."

"I'll just break the fucking window," she said. "I'm relentless."

"And try not to say fuck so much."

"Why the fuck not?" Janice's voice held ironic humor. "Oh. Mrs. Franklin called and said she was coming in to see you Monday. She's bringing her cell records and her husband's phone."

"Oh, goody. Franklin's drunken wife is coming in to give me more shit. I can't wait."

"Then she's having a meeting with Carl."

"Sounds like a great day. Now get out. I have to work."

Janice paused. "What are you looking at?"

"Pure human desperation."

She walked out with a huff. I returned to the website list and made notes on what Franklin found most interesting. The topics ran from hypnosis, meditation, acupuncture, aromatherapy, biofeedback, massage, and music therapy. Everything seemed to make the list, including Tai Chi and yoga. There were carrot juice infusions, Native American medicine men, high alkali water, mushroom juice, electric shock, and Vitamin C overloads. My favorite was bee sting therapy. The theory was that the reaction to hundreds of bee stings would send the body's immune defenses into overload and wipe out cancer.

I kept reading and shook my head. Each treatment had a picture of a robustly healthy person claiming to have been cured. They even presented before and after photos, though I suspected they had the images reversed. One site suggested laugh therapy, claiming that cancer cells couldn't survive in a happy body.

My thoughts returned to the prospect of having to face Franklin's wife again. I hoped she arrived sober.

"Bobby." Carl's voice cracked through the COM.

I picked up. "Yeah?"

"I just got off the phone with Herb Baxter at the ad agency. He said you suggested they were heartless assholes who decided not to hire Franklin because he had cancer."

"They were."

"And?" Carl said.

"And nothing. I pointed out that they chose not to hire David because he was diagnosed with cancer. Did I lie?"

"I'm sure the answer is no, but—"

"But nothing. Baxter said Franklin was like family and—"

"Yeah, okay. I'm speaking as your sponsor right now, okay?"

"Shoot," I said.

"If you can't say anything nice, don't say anything at all."

"I'll try and remember that. Are you ready to face the grief-stricken wife?"

"I hope she's not going to tell me you insulted her too."

I laughed. "We can only hope."

CHAPTER FOUR

Gina left for her retreat and I took in a meeting. Then I joined the guys for coffee and went home. I read a Patterson novel with nothing but crap on TV, ate some ice cream, and watched the clock. When you don't party, and your girl is gone, there ain't much to do.

I dropped in a DVD and watched the original Terminator, got bored of Arnold killing folks, and went to bed, but the Franklin case decided to keep me up. Around midnight I figured a shower might help me wind down. I held my head under the stream of hot water until the sound of the torrent drowned out the small voice in my head. Then I soaped up and slowly ran my right hand over the smooth knob where my left arm used to be. I felt the scar like a blind man, tracing the pellet scars up my left bicep to the rise of my shoulder and finally my neck and cheek.

I still remember the doctor's ghost-like voice as I slipped into oblivion; He's one lucky son of a bitch no buckshot hit his carotid artery.

I honestly was lucky, and I thank God I didn't die that day. The pellet in my elbow caused a twinge of pain and reminded me that my handicap was a matter of courage, not fear. I got out of the shower, stood naked in front of the mirror, and stared at the stump. A missing appendage is hard to grasp, even when it's yours. The rest of me still looked fit and strong, more than enough to cause fear in the hearts of mortal men.

After getting dressed, I plopped on the couch. Butch was out doing what he did, and the night was quiet by city standards. Some distant sirens and car alarms twittered like night birds. An occasional dog bark broke the stillness, and my head finally mirrored the night. I dozed off and woke up an hour later with a stiff neck. Butch was home, and he gave me a questioning look.

"Hey, buddy, done chasing pussy?"

I got to my feet with a groan. The soft cushions had left me feeling bent. Butch took my place and gave me a stare.

"What are you looking at?" I said.

Butch half-closed his eyes and gave me a soft cry. Then he looked at the floor where a dead bird lay stiff and molting beneath the window. It was headless and lay with its feet sticking up, looking like something out of a Hitchcock movie.

"Is that for me?"

Butch stretched, yawned, and curled up. I went to the bathroom, returned with a wad of toilet paper, and scooped up the corpse. It felt artificial, like those fake feathered crows they sell in the party stores at Halloween. I wrapped it in an old vegetable bag from the grocery store and tied off the bag with my right hand and teeth.

My heart skipped a beat. Had this happened to David Franklin? Did thugs roll him in plastic and weigh him down, haul his body out to the deep channel beneath the Golden gate and drop him to sink to the depths? The bird suddenly felt heavy, and I put it in the freezer where it would keep until I left for my Saturday 7:00 AM men's meeting. Then I slept.

I woke before my alarm and slapped it before it screamed. Then I filled Butch's water bowl, downed some coffee, and remembered the bird in the freezer. On my way out, I dropped it in the dumpster behind the building and had another feeling of dread. Was David Franklin rotting in some dumpster somewhere? He had better be, or I would kill him for causing all this trouble.

On my drive downtown, I imagined Franklin's last desperate days searching for some magic cure through the Internet. The photo on his computer popped into my head, and I imagined the tourist they must have stopped on the wharf. I imagined his voice; hey, could you take a picture of us? Thanks, thanks so much. I hoped the meeting would distract me. I found the club full, so I took a seat in the back until I saw Carl waving to me. He patted the empty chair next to him.

"Morning sunshine," he said. "You look like you've been wrestling demons all night."

"Yeah, tough night."

"The meeting will do you good."

Afterward, Carl and I had breakfast, and I didn't say much.

"What do you have to be so mopey about?" he asked.

I shrugged. "Just the usual."

"Well, the guys and I are going to a movie tonight. Why don't you come along and watch Bruce Willis protect the world from Russian scum? C'mon, it'll keep your mind off whatever is ailing you."

I said I would, and we parted ways. The gym offered some physical relief, and food pacified my anxious heart, but nothing stopped the voice in my head. It was the longest day of my life. When Gina called, I was in the theater. When I called back, she didn't answer.

"I miss you, babe. Call me in the morning."

When I was getting into bed, she called.

"Hey there, sexy."

"Ooh, I like the sound of that. So you miss me, huh?"

"Just a little bit. How's the retreat going?"

"Great, lots of good stuff. I picked up a new sponsee, and we talked all afternoon. She's like me, so we connected right away."

"You mean she's tall, beautiful, and sexy as hell?"

"No," she barked in false anger. "You know what I mean. How was your day?"

"Lonely. You back tomorrow?"

"Not until late. I'll see you Monday."

We said our goodnights.

The next day I killed my Sunday with football and food. I couldn't wait for Monday.

*   *   *   *

Monday morning, Janice met me at my office door.

"Mrs. Franklin is already waiting. You didn't tell me she was so pretty. I'll tell Gina if you do anything stupid."

"Jan, do you sleep with every good looking guy you meet?"

"Of course I do. Good luck."

"Stall her," I said. "I got to have a cup of coffee before I face anything."

"She's drinking tea in the lounge. She seems very nice. Nothing like you described. Sure you didn't just make that up?"

"Don't let her fool you. She probably has a pint of whiskey in her purse."

I poured my coffee, splashed it with half and half, then went to my desk. I tried to straighten out the mess of papers but was only pushing piles around. An empty drawer in my file cabinet hid the catastrophe. I told Janice to bring her in.

Janice knocked softly and opened the door. In her nicest voice, she said, "Mrs. Franklin's here."

I was ready for anything, but Claire Franklin was a different woman than the one I had met before. She dressed in tight but tasteful jeans and a peach-colored shirt that hugged her at the waist. She wore her hair in a ponytail. Her green eyes were bright with emotion. She gave me a gracious smile when I offered her the chair in front of my desk.

"Can I get you some more tea?"

"No, thank you, but I do want to apologize for my behavior the other day." Her voice sounded small and soft, hardly the brash and lashing tongue I had met before. "I'd had a very bad morning, and I should have called and canceled. I truly am sorry."

"I understand," I said.

"Thank you." A flush came to her cheeks.

"Janice said you were bringing me something?"

She suddenly dug in her purse, and for a split second, I imagined her pulling a gun and shooting at me across the desk. I shook it off and blinked.

"I brought you my husband's phone records and his phone."

"Thank you. I won't need the phone. The records are fine. I want you to know that—"

She interrupted me. "I need you to know how terrible I feel about how I treated you. It was unforgivable. I've been so angry with myself."

"No apology is necessary. In my line of work, I've been accosted by the best of them. At least you didn't threaten to kill me."

Her face went red. "Still, that wasn't me. David would have laughed. I'm usually such a calm person, but when something sets me off, I lose it. Especially if I've been drinking a bit."

"I understand."

"No, I don't think you can." Claire cocked her head with her hands frozen in front of her. She looked as though she were searching for the right words.

"Are you okay?" I asked quietly.

She put her hands in her lap. "It has been weeks since David went missing, and I know he's dead. Not because of the car or the bullet holes and blood, but because I can't find him in my heart. He's gone from here."

She clutched her hands to her breast and grimaced.

"Take your time," I said.

"Can you understand what it feels like to have something so precious to you taken away and just know in your heart it will never come back?"

I held up my left hand. "I do."

"Oh, of course," she whispered.

I knew exactly what she meant. After losing my hand, I remember the sadness I felt each time I looked at my bandaged stump. For days and weeks, I tried to adapt to life with one hand. It was fucking miserable. From washing my hair to taking a piss, buttoning a shirt, tying my shoes, and eating a meal. I imagined her emotional pain when she stared at the empty bed, his empty chair, and her empty life. My plight suddenly seemed trivial. She looked pale.

"Can I get you some water?" I asked.

Claire regained herself. "I'll be fine. Did you really lose that in a farm accident? I think you said that when you were at the house."

"I lost it in the line of duty."

"Oh, I just keep putting my foot in my mouth."

"Not at all."

She gave me a smile of gratitude. "You must know what I mean. My heart knows David is gone, but my head still thinks he's just on a trip or working late. I'm afraid the two will never reconcile themselves."

I gave her a supportive nod.

"David said something so odd the week before he went missing." Claire fought her emotions. Her green eyes looked like oiled emeralds.

"Mrs. Franklin. Please don't feel you need to share anything that may affect the parameters of the case."

"I'm sorry?"

"I mean, your husband's disappearance is still under investigation."

"Oh." She looked confused. "I thought we were here to discuss the case so I could tell you what I knew."

"Sure, we can do that."

Claire dabbed at her nose with a tissue she pulled from her purse. "Anyway, when David was diagnosed, the Oncologist suggested a course of treatment. He counseled us on the emotional and financial costs. Later in bed, David said he was sorry there wasn't a way to make sure I would benefit from his death."

"It sounds like he was looking at the situation pragmatically," I said.

"No, it was more than that. He was acting detached, almost clinical. It wasn't like him, and I was afraid he would – I don't know."

"I appreciate your sharing that with me," I said in a calm tone. "I'll go through his phone records to see if we can find a connection between his activities before his disappearance and what happened."

"You think he's still alive, don't you?"

"That's what we're trying to find out."

"Okay then. I guess that's it. Thank you for listening, and, again, I'm sorry for the other day."

"I do have a question for you if you feel up to it."

"Of course."

"Did he discuss the idea of alternative treatment with you?"

She nearly smiled. "Oh, that. We talked about it, and he even looked at some websites. It all seemed so silly and out there, you know? We agreed it was wishful thinking and left it at that."

"Thanks for your honesty."

She looked smaller than when she had first come in. Her shoulders drooped with the weight of the world. To think a woman could love a man that much. Or was it an act? No, this woman is devastated. Not all women are like your ex.

"Thank you for coming in. Do you need me to call somebody for you?"

"No, I still have an appointment with Carl Hardman." She walked to the door, where she stood with her hand on the knob. Without turning around, she said, "He's dead, I know it. So do the kids."

"Kelly and Brenda," I said with a smile.

She looked at me in surprise. "Yes." Then she left my office and carefully closed the door. While I listened to her unsteady footsteps fading down the hall, Janice charged in, dropped in the chair, and chased away the specter of Claire's sadness.

"You think she did it?"

"What the hell? What did I tell you about knocking?"

"I told you, it would never happen. Think she did it?"

"Did what?" I asked with a dramatic expression.

"Killed her husband for the insurance money?"

"No." I meant it.

"Oh please," Janice nearly screamed. "She killed her husband so she could avoid the medical bills and collect on the insurance and not have to pay any of it out. It's perfect. They probably planned it together."

"Murder-suicide pact for the payout? Genius, why didn't I think of that? Now can you get out of my office? I have work to do."

Janice gave me a suspicious glare as her thin chest heaved. "You falling for her?"

"What? C'mon Jan. This is not a pulp paperback."

She waved her hand like she had a sore wrist. "But she was hot."

"And devastated by loss," I pointed out. "Real fertile ground for a romantic interlude. That only happens in the movies. Get out. I have to go through all this shit and see if he was calling crack dealers."

"So she's not your type," Janice said playfully. "And just what is your type?"

"Mean, nasty, callused, heartless, selfish, and in no way concerned about my well-being. Claire Franklin has none of these wonderful qualities."

"But I do." Janice headed down the hall, refusing to close my door. "I have them all."

I studied the web searches until Carl called me down to his office. I dropped in one of the two overstuffed chairs facing his desk.

"How'd it go with Mrs. Franklin?" I asked.

"Well, you were right. She's either a heartbroken, devastated woman or the best fucking actress on the planet. So if she's not complicit in any way, do we have a real case of foul play?"

"Seems that way," I said.

"So what do you think?" Cal said softly.

I laughed. "Why are you whispering?"

"Sorry, just caught up in the drama. What do you think?"

"I think I need to know exactly what David Franklin was up to, who he was talking to, and if he was the kind of man who could orchestrate this level of deception. All I know is she's sure he's dead."

"She has half a million reasons to feel that way."

"We'll find out," I assured him and stood up. "Anything else?"

"Mrs. Franklin agreed to let us have their phone records."

"That'll help. I can compare them to his cell and web surfing into alternative treatment facilities. I'll follow up on these places and see if he visited any of them. It's a long shot, but it could help pinpoint his intentions."

"Or maybe," Carl said, "you'll find one that heard from him after he disappeared."

"Now why didn't I think of that," I asked sarcastically.

After I spent an afternoon listing the sites Franklin visited the most, Gina called.

"How was the retreat?" I asked.

"Great, but I want to see you."

We met for a night out of fish and chips, darts, and club soda. That's what I love about her; she's one of the guys until she's ready to be the only girl in my life. We had fun sitting in a pub watching the yuppies come in and get sloppy drunk as the night went on. One especially obnoxious guy stumbled and knocked over a table of craft beers.

"Well, blokes," I said in my best Cockney accent. "Gotta' go. G'night and have a pleasant tomorrow."

"I've seen enough," Gina said. "Let's go home and get reacquainted."

*   *   *   *

The morning opened with crisp light. The fog was gone, and the city gleamed. Gina kissed me goodbye and went back to bed.

"Don't you have to bake today?" I teased.

"I have two evening parties, so I don't have to get in until later."

"Must be nice."

I arrived at the office and was accosted by Janice. She looked excited.

"We got a call from Oakland PD about Franklin."

"Don't tell me they found him hiding in a drain pipe."

"Well, kind of. Call your Oakland PD buddy Joe Santos. He's on it."

"What's this about?"

She followed me down to my office. "Well, you know how most people leave their hearts in San Francisco? It seems Franklin left something of himself on the other side of the bay."

"What did they find?"

"They got a thumbprint that matched Franklin through DMV records."

"Where did they find the print?"

Janice gave me a playful smile. "From the thumb."

I gave her an unbelieving look. "Don't fuck with me."

"I swear."

Joe answered on the first ring. "When can you get here?"

"On my way. Tell me about it."

"It's a grisly scene in a small warehouse not far from where your arm left an impressionistic splatter on the wall."

"Be there as soon as I can." Before I left, I called Carl. "I assume you heard about Franklin's thumb?"

"I did. Fucked up shit, huh? Get out there and see what this is all about. If this pans out, we may have grounds to settle."

"I'm off," I said to Janice.

"Watch your fingers," she yelled back.

The best way to describe Oakland is as San Francisco's redheaded stepsister. Less majestic and a bit more tattered than her sister city. Not that they don't try. In recent years the old neighborhoods have seen a renaissance with trendy restaurants and boutiques popping up in once bad neighborhoods. But try as they might, some areas are just pure trash, and no amount of good intention will reclaim those places from the derelicts. Oakland is to San Francisco what New Jersey is to New York. Both have their flair and beauty. They're just competing in different pageants.

Traffic was rough, especially in morning rush hour in a truck as big as mine. I'm always amazed at the drivers in pissant cars that cut me off. Once over the bay, I changed lanes off the Bay Bridge and dropped down into the harbor district. Two Oakland PD blue suits waited with Joe at the warehouse. I experienced a shiver; this was the first time I'd come back here since the shootout. Joe waved me down, and I greeted him with a handshake.

He looked harassed. "How's it hangin' Bobby?"

"Down around my knees."

"Got it to my ankles."

"But you're shorter than me."

Which was true. I always imagined Joe like a pissed off Jack Russell Terrier. When I was a cop, I'd seen him take down men twice his size. He was the only one to make good out of a family of nine Mexican hell raisers. Joe worked out hard and played harder. His musculature was that of a small marble statue.

We walked toward the open warehouse.

"This is one for the books," he said. "If we'd found a head, we'd have the whole department down here. For a thumb? The brass only gave us these two greenhorns."

The patrolmen had the look of pure rookie in their starched uniforms. Their faces like high school seniors, they seemed to be proudly conscious of their badges. One was black and the other white. They looked me over like a dangerous dog wandering up their street.

"Kids, this is Robert Jacobi, the baddest ass that used to be a cop. Now he works insurance and could still kick both your butts. Bobby, that's Johnson and Farrell."

They both looked at the hook hanging from my shirt sleeve, so I opened and closed it for added emphasis.

One of them whispered, "You see that?"

I raised my claw and tipped an imaginary hat. "Lost it gator rasslin' in the Florida Keys. I don't recommend it."

Joe shook his head. "Still tellin' lies about that horror?"

"Too much fun to stop."

"Here we are," Joe said when we got to the small warehouse no bigger than ten by twenty. It stood empty and open.

"This is where we found the thumb," Joe said, "right near the base of that wall."

The scene was already bagged and tagged. Only the bloodstain on the floor remained. I gave the space a once over and let my mind do its trick—broken window, debris in the corners, fast food wrappers, and footprints in the dust. There was the unmistakable smell of urine and rat droppings alongside the walls. This place may not have been rented, but it was far from empty most nights.

"Tell me what it looked like," I said.

Joe waved his hand toward the wall. "Old straight back chair on its side. A dirty coil of yellow nylon rope splattered with blood, and some spatter on the wall. The management company stooge opened the place for a prospective renter, and they found the chair and the rope. It was the guy looking to rent the place who noticed the thumb, and the agent called 911."

I pointed to the baseboard where a pool of blood had dried to rust. "Did they take blood samples?"

"They did, but the scene is pretty old. We're hoping for a match."

"No sign of a break-in?"

Joe shook his head. "Just the window. There's no alarm. I guess the management company figured there was nothing to steal in here anyway. There's evidence of some homeless squatting, but the place was locked. For somebody to stage what we found, they would have to have access."

"That means somebody had a key or picked the lock."

"Wouldn't be hard. I could've done it with a paper clip."

"Tell me about the thumb."

"It looked like it had been here a while. It was severed at the hand. It looked like a clean cut. We'll have to wait for the pathology boys on the details."

"So the scene says he was tied up, tortured, and they cut his thumb to make a point. Then they untied him, dragged him out, and left the thumb, even though they tossed the body in the bay?"

"You don't buy it." It was not a question.

"The only reason to leave the thumb and the other evidence is so his captors could send the message that he's alive. Normally that would mean a ransom demand."

"Which never showed up."

"Or maybe they're sending a message that this guy did something stupid and nobody else should do the same. But I've been climbing up this guy's ass, and I haven't found a smidge of scandal. No gambling, drugs, smut, other women, or anything else. I saw the wife yesterday, and she's convinced he's dead."

"I'd say a lot of other people would agree with her now," Joe said. "Whatever the scenario, with cancer and this blood and the thumb, it looks like this one is sewn up. We'll probably find the rest of him wrapped around a bridge piling in a month."

"Thanks, Joe. I'll let you get back to saving the world."

"And you can go back to that desk job of yours."

The boys in blue stood by the roll-up door like security guards. Joe and I walked out, and I gave each of them a nod. They returned the gesture. Joe patted my shoulder, and I headed back to my truck.

"Call me later," Joe said. "Maybe I'll have something new."

"Thanks."

A light wind came off the bay and carried a promise of some rain with it. I stood by the truck and looked back across the water. Clouds wrapped around the city like ghosts. The glinting towers lost their luster as the weather rolled in. Another gust tightened my cheeks, and I climbed into my truck out of the weather. I waited for Joe and the blues to pull away, keyed my ignition, and followed.

Did I die in this warehouse? Franklin's voice asked.

Did David Franklin sit gagged and tied to an old chair while goons beat and questioned him? Did they bother with a gag? In this part of town, a man could scream until his lungs burst and not draw the attention of a single caring soul. Had his captors cut off his thumb, strangled him, and now his corpse was weighed down in the cold waters of the bay?

Wait. My cop voice interrupted. Could a man cut off his thumb to make sure his family was taken care of?

Could I, especially if I knew I already had a death sentence? I looked at my own missing appendage. As tough as I think I am, I don't think I could. I took my time driving back to the city while I fought the urge to go to Oakland, P.D., and demand to see the evidence. Instead, I went back to the office.

My day dragged on, and I was unable to focus on anything. Gina called to say she'd be home tonight after nine. That was good. Her good sense always calmed me down, but first, I had to attend our monthly case status meeting with the suits. I met Carl at the elevators and rode up in silence.

The conference room table for Bayside Consolidated Insurance is embarrassingly opulent. Fifteen feet of teak and oak inlaid with glass and polished to a brilliant shine. Twenty leather and chrome chairs surround the table, and floor to ceiling windows look out on the sprawling city and the bay beyond. I call it the billion-dollar view. But that's insurance. I call it legal extortion.

The mafia has this scam where they come into your business and make you pay protection money to protect yourself from them! Bayside Consolidated is similar in scope. Insurance in its simplest form is good money paid out by somebody hoping they never have to use it. The company shares your sentiment. Each year insurance companies raise their rates and complain about operating costs, but there is no other industry more profitable in reality.

The for-profit insurance moguls tend to earn in the range of thirty-five million to three and a half billion in profit per year. It boggles the mind. So the gold leaf and walnut paneling and crystal glasses are but a drop in the bucket for a company like Consolidated. I once saw the CEO's yacht.

I sat with my case reports and stared out the window while the suits bantered about figures and speculated on risk, futures, and returns. Carl nudged me so I would pay better attention. I did my best to seem less bored.

At the head of the table sat Jacob Caleb Henderson, the founding partner's COO, and grandson. He was richer than God and only came into the office to boss people around. Henderson is in his mid-sixties with the quintessential silver hair, tennis tan, and perfect nails. He's the antithesis of me.

"So Carl," Henderson said with a practiced smile. "Where do we stand on life claims under investigation?"

Carl opened his folder. "Healey settled, the lawyers are pushing for Deeds to withdraw their claim, and we won the civil claim against us from Loury."

"Very good. And what about this Franklin case? Where do we stand on that?"

I cleared my throat. "I have that one. We have probable evidence Franklin is most likely dead, but we have no body, so we're examining evidence of potential fraud. The case is in limbo until we get some forensic evidence on tissue found that may belong to the insured."

"Tissue?"

"A thumb." I enjoyed the suit's expressions of mild shock. "Oakland PD is examining it, but we're pretty sure it belongs to Franklin."

"When will we know for sure?"

"About a week," I said.

The meeting broke up, and the suits took the elevator up while Carl and I took it down.

"I hate those meetings," I said.

"You could make a better showing of giving a shit."

"Why am I even in there?"

"Henderson likes having you there."

"Why?"

"Because of who you are. The cop hero is working for him. He can act like you guys are buddies."

"But I hardly know him," I said.

"The picture he has of you shaking hands says otherwise. He and the Councilman whose daughter you rescued are friends," Carl said. "I can imagine he loves to talk that up when they get drunk together."

"That's fucked up in so many ways."

Carl nodded. "Yes. Henderson's an asshole."

The elevators opened, and Janice handed me a sheet of paper when I walked by her desk. "Franklin's home phone records came in."

"Thanks."

I plopped in my chair and read through the numbers. What stood out was the number of times he called a place called Dr. Whitley's Health Farm in San Diego and the bee sting immune therapy place in Ranchita, California. East of that, I found a place called The Native America Alternative Cancer Treatment Center located in the desert region near The Salton Sea. I imagined that it must be an interesting place. Then there was a call to Halberson Publishing in New York and one to The Valley Center for Alternative Health in Mill Valley, right across the bay in wine country.

I spent the next two hours cross-referencing the cell and house lines. Most of the calls he made after his diagnosis were to mainstream clinics. As time when by, the calls were to more questionable places. His consistent calls were to a Gary Colbert in Carlsbad, California, and Carlson Consultations in Walnut Creek.

Five o'clock came blessedly fast, so I put off the follow-up calls until the next morning. I packed my shit, locked my door, and walked the long hall to the elevator. The weather turned to rain, and the steady drizzle drove worms of water down the hallway windows. Janice was already gone, so I left the building without having to go through any verbal sparring.

Night fell on the city, and the wet weather chilled me. In my truck, I waited until the heater washed me down with warm comfort. My drive home was stop and go. I swear nobody in California knows how to drive in the rain. My phone twittered, and I punched the speaker button and dropped the phone in my lap.

"Hello lover," Gina said.

"And back at you."

"You driving?"

"I am."

"Don't go home. I'm back from the great outdoors, and I'm a very dirty girl. Come over, and I'll wash your back if you wash mine. Then we'll order pizza delivery."

"On my way," I said

CHAPTER FIVE

Gina asked me to sleep over. She also washed my clothes, so I didn't have to leave early to change for work. Janice struck the moment I came through the door.

"Same clothes. House burn down?"

"In a manner of speaking," I said.

"Oh, you dirty boy," she teased. "Did you come up for air at all?"

"You're sick." I walked down the hall.

"Oh, you noticed," she yelled at my back.

I poured coffee, took my seat, and looked over my list of calls to make regarding Franklin. First was the woman in Walnut Creek. Karen Carlson Consultations. I assumed she was some kind of alternative health provider like the rest. But twenty calls? It was by far the most active of his outreaches. I was about to dial the number when Janice called through.

"Joe's on line one."

I punched the button and said, "Hey, buddy."

"I got some info on that thumb."

I opened my folder on Franklin. "Hit me."

"It had been frozen."

"Say again?"

"I shit you not. Forensics said the thumb was frozen before it was left at the scene. Like somebody brought it along in a cooler and dropped it for us to find."

"They're sure of that?"

"Yeah. They said it showed crystallization in the tissues and freezer burn and probably kept that way for quite a while. Figure that?"

"Can you send me the info?"

"It's already on the way."

"Thanks," I said. "You're the best."

Then I stared out my window and scratched my cheek with my hook. Frozen? That put a whole new spin on this deal. A courier arrived an hour later, and I signed for copies of the forensic report. I looked it over, went online, and looked up some unfamiliar terms before calling Carl.

His disbelief was evident through the phone. "Frozen?"

"I'm looking at the report right here."

"What do you make of that?" Carl asked.

"Well, the perps that killed or took Franklin may have cut his thumb off and then planted it at the warehouse to throw the cops off."

"Or?"

"Or they could have had his whole body frozen and then cut and dropped the thumb as a message," I said thoughtfully.

"Message to who?"

"I have no fucking idea. Maybe Franklin had gambling debts or owed a loan shark."

"But you don't buy it?"

"I don't know. If I were torturing some guy because I thought he jacked my crack, I wouldn't freeze him after I killed him. I'd take him out to the country and put his ass through a wood chipper."

"But that's you, Robert," Carl said. "Who knows how some goons think?"

"No idea."

I finally got to the task of following up on Franklin's call list. The health clinics listened until I mentioned that a potential client had disappeared, and then they referred me to their legal counsel. Dr. Whitley's Health Ranch was different. A woman named January looked through her files for me. She almost sounded disappointed that David Franklin was not on her list.

"What if he had used a fake name?" I asked.

"That would be impossible. We would not approve treatments without a name, ID, and a number for next of kin. And we follow up with that information. We'd lose our license if we broke protocol."

"What if he claimed he had no family and no ID?"

"Oh, we get a lot of drifters here, but that is a separate area. The treatment facility and the visitor's commune are segregated and watched very carefully."

"Commune?"

"Yes, the general visitor center. We never turn anybody away unless they are dangerous or too sick to participate in the collective work schedule."

"If I emailed you a picture would you be able to recognize him?"

"I'd love to try," January chirped.

"I'm sending it now." I pushed David's face through cyberspace.

"Got it," she said through the phone. "No, he doesn't look familiar, but if we turned him away, it would be harder to remember. Let me recheck my records, and I'll email you back if I find anything."

"Thanks, January."

I doubted she would. Not because she was protecting anybody, but if the Health Department scrutinized them, I figured they'd turn away a drifter with no ID with an apparent bullet wound and missing a thumb.

Next was the publishing house. It took some lying and some schmoozing to get through to Jerry Shapiro, but he finally took my call.

"Shapiro." His voice sounded like a man pissed off most of his life.

"Thank you for taking my call," I offered with mock appreciation.

"Forget the pleasantries. Who are you, and how did you get through to me?"

I explained who I was and why I was calling.

"Former cop?" he asked.

"Yeah."

"You sound the type."

"Can you tell me what you and David Franklin talked about?"

"He wanted me to advance him some money on a book about him dying of pancreatic cancer. I told him it had already been done. Besides, he would have been dead before he could finish the book."

That made me laugh. "I can see that as a problem."

"Let me tell you a little story," Shapiro said. "I once made a serious bet on a horse running at Aqueduct. According to my connections, it was supposed to be a fixed race. He had a 5-length lead coming to the wire. Ten yards short of the finish line, it dropped dead as a fucking doornail. That race took less than 90 seconds, start to finish. A book takes a lot longer, and it's even less a sure thing."

I liked Shapiro; he was my kind of guy. "Okay."

"What's really going on here?" he said.

I told him what I knew and what I suspected might be true.

Shapiro's voice changed, so he sounded intrigued. "Now that would make a great book. The last words of a desperate dying man are crap. What you said is a fucking great idea for a mystery novel. Want to write it?"

"Sorry, I can't. I'd get fired and sued by the wife."

"Well, let some time go by and then change the names. Call me when you're ready."

"I'll do that."

The number in Carlsbad was David's lifelong friend Gary. He told me he consoled David as he struggled with his disease.

"Did he confide in you about any crazy ideas he might have had regarding his situation or his family?" I asked.

"Oh yeah. David was very creative. Each conversation was a new idea on how to cheat death. I just listened and let him get it out. I knew he was just talking. That's how he got out of his own head. He often thanked me for listening."

"Can I ask a brutal question?"

"Sure."

"Do you think he was kidnapped, tortured, and killed?"

Gary took a deep breath. "Well, David was a very dynamic guy, and strange shit was always happening to him. I swear, more odd things happened to him than anybody I knew. Every day was some new adventure or strange coincidence."

"Was he a bullshitter?" I asked.

"Every time I thought he was full of shit, something or somebody collaborated his story. If what you suggested was going to happen to anybody, it would be David."

"So, do you think he's dead?"

Gary's voice was suddenly rough with emotion. "Let me put it this way. I've already mourned him."

"Thank you."

I hung up and then dialed a former cop friend, Buddy Hood, now working as a private investigator. In the three years I worked insurance Buddy begged me to join his firm. But taking pictures through keyholes and serving warrants was not my style.

"You ready to quit that desk job and come have fun with me?" Buddy asked.

"Hell no. I was hoping you could look into something for me. It's a claim case, but this is outside the lines for my usual job. I have a guy that may or may not be dead. See what you can do for me, and I need some hard info overnight."

"Down and dirty, straight general info?" Buddy asked.

"Exactly. If I did it myself, I'd lose my job."

"Then you'd have to come work with me."

"Yeah, right. How much for the snoop job?"

"I'll do it as a favor. Gimme' the name and social security number. I'll have something in a day or two."

It was risky sharing confidential info with a freelancer, but I needed to know what Franklin was up to and what was in his head before his disappearance.

Thank you, David whispered in my head.

"Fuck you," I said and went back to work.

*   *   *   *

Gina was busy comforting a struggling alcoholic mother of two, so I sat home thinking about mutated cells.

88

Cancer is something we all know about and knows somebody who had it or died from it. I believe anybody would be hard-pressed to find a soul who had not heard of pancreatic cancer, but few know how it kills you. I didn't. In fact, I'd only known one person to die from any kind of cancer. My old captain wasted away from lung cancer, but he smoked two packs a day for thirty years.

While I pondered David Franklin's plight, I found myself needing to know what a pancreas was, why it was so important and why it's so good at killing. Thankfully the Internet is more than happy to dispense the ugly details.

The pancreas is a six-inch gland behind the stomach that helps digestion and controls blood sugar levels. I learned that a shit diet with lots of fat, exposure to toxic chemicals, and stress are the main reasons people get this thing. That was unsettling because every American I know lives with that combination every day. No wonder it's an epidemic. The bitch of is, by the time you feel sick, you're already history. And it's a motherfucker.

The survival rate is so small it's barely worth mentioning. If you have a few million in the bank, there are some extreme treatments where they re-pipe your system. But even most of those people still don't make it.

No wonder Franklin was so desperate. Chemotherapy can slow it down, but pancreatic cancer metastasizes to the liver, lungs, diaphragm, and adrenal glands, making sure you die.

Gina called and snapped me out of my horror.

"Hey there," I said.

"Uh, oh, you sound down. Tell momma what's wrong."

"Just work. How'd it go with the newbie?"

"She's willing and wants to keep her suburban life, so I think she'll do okay. Did you eat?"

"Just leftovers," I said. "Why?"

"I'm suddenly craving an In-and-Out Double-Double and some greasy cheese fries. I'm just off Bayside, wanna meet?"

Grease and salt, and fat make cancer. Oh well, I thought. "I'll be there in ten."

I paid for it later. The junk food rotting my guts kept me awake, so I read more about cancer online. It's unsettling to learn just how many things can go wrong and cause the human body to start killing itself. I took some solace in recent studies that claimed coffee was beneficial in staving off certain cancers.

I came in Tuesday morning suffering from sleep deprivation. Before I had much of a chance to get settled in, Buddy called.

"I've got some shit on Franklin," he said. "Can you talk?"

"I'll call you back in five." I took the elevator to the lobby, walked to the street, and pulled out my phone. "What's up?" I said once I got Buddy back on the line.

"He was in debt up to his eyeballs. Even after the bankruptcy was charged off, there wasn't enough money to go around. He got caught in the payday loan shop merry go round."

"How bad?"

"He had payday loans out with four different shops and was juggling ten running chainsaws. He was behind with his taxes, and the I.R.S. was threatening some serious shit. The only things he made sure he paid were his mortgage and his life insurance. Everything else was going to hell."

"Sign of the times," I said.

"I don't think his wife knew what he was up to. After he disappeared, those payday places called his cell number and got no answer. It must have come as a shock to the wife when those checks got deposited."

"I can imagine," I said.

"Here's a thought. Franklin's thumb was found in Oakland. Maybe he got desperate enough that he went to some nasty characters for some help with cash flow," Buddy said. "Maybe he borrowed and didn't pay back one of those scumbags."

"It's possible. Anything else?"

"Just that his credit was shot. Let's see, no health insurance, no outstanding warrants, and nothing criminal. No register of ownership for guns. He was not a registered sex offender. First glance shows no girlfriends. Basically, Franklin was a regular guy with some irregular problems."

"Okay. I owe you lunch. Call me if you find out anything else."

"What you owe me is to quit that shit job and come be a real private dick."

"In your dreams." I hung up.

I called Joe and asked if he knew of any strong-arm lenders that a guy like Franklin could find easily enough.

"A few. Why?"

"Turns out Franklin was in deep shit money troubles and was borrowing from Peter to pay Paul, then robbing Paul to pay Judas."

"Okay," Joe said. "A question."

"Shoot."

"Is this official business? Bayside Consolidated Insurance sanctioned and necessary work for the sake of payout and book balance?"

I paused for a moment. "No."

"Why are you asking?"

"I'm looking for a body," I said. "Maybe they whacked him because he didn't pay."

"That's a stretch," Joe said.

"That may be, but it's all I have at this point. I'm reaching and praying. Besides, I have to come to the table with something for the suits."

"Okay, I'll ask around."

"Thanks."

My chair groaned as I settled back and put my right hand behind my head. The terms of payout on life insurance are tougher with no corpse, but not impossible. The first thing I learned in this business is that insurance has a sliding scale regarding when and how the cash is paid out. If an airplane explodes on take-off and your name is on the passenger boarding list, it doesn't matter if they can't find a body – we pay. The classic case was the 911 attacks. So many were just gone, no evidence of their physical bodies, but the checks got mailed.

In a case like this, the suits look at what they call the profit from the loss. What is the loss or the gain, the terms of the tragedy? If there is a hundred grand on the line and no body, pay it off and close the book. If there's a million at stake, put a man on it. The suits require some investigation to justify handing over half a million. Had I gone past that in my work? Yeah, I had. The cop in me had made this personal.

My phone buzzed. It was Carl.

"Yeah?" I said.

"You got a minute?"

"Be right there."

I found him eating pistachio nuts from a one-pound bag and tossing the shells in a soda can. Fat and salt, the stuff cancer feeds on. But then, everything gives you cancer.

"What's up, boss?"

"I got authorization for you to follow up on those crackpot medical leads on Franklin. I got you a traveling allowance and another week. If we don't find a smoking gun, the suits want to figure a way to close the book on this."

"Somebody must have got a call from the Mayor."

"Maybe. Will that shit box truck of yours make it to where you need to go, or do you need a rental?"

"The Dodge is fine. I'll keep my gas receipts. They'll make accounting shit themselves."

"Give me an itinerary. I want you to start tomorrow."

The funny thing was I'd been fighting the urge to go on the quest myself. That pesky cop voice and David's whispers had me thinking of calling in sick and going on a lunatic mission. Now I was free to look into the lurid life David lived behind the veil – a life of desperate lies by omission and impending doom.

Janice was in my visitor's chair when I got back to the office.

"On a coffee break?" I said.

"I don't drink coffee. You know that." She was acting like a schoolgirl with a secret. She gave me an ironic smile and giggled.

Whenever Janice got like this, she wanted me to play the game. I'd ask, and she'd shake her head and giggle until I finally guessed right. I hated it and decided this time not to play along. It was usually gossip that I couldn't give a rat's ass about.

"Unless you have something to tell me, I have work to do."

She put her thumbnail between her teeth and sniggered. I ignored her.

"Guess," she said.

"No."

"C'mon, guess."

I put my elbows on the desk and brought my hand to my hook. "No."

"Then I won't tell," she said and jumped up from the seat. "Last chance."

"I don't care."

"Yes you do," she whispered and took a step toward the door.

I gave her a steely stare. "No, I don't."

"Wanna' bet?"

She hurried down the hall.

Carl called through. I snatched up the phone. "Hey boss. What's going on?"

"David Franklin's wife just tried to kill herself," he said gravely.

"What the fuck?"

"She didn't pick the kids up after school, and they grabbed a ride with another mom. There was no answer at the house, and the kids let themselves in. They found her on the couch with an empty bottle of pills and half a bottle of wine on the coffee table."

"Holy shit. But she's alive?"

"Yes, and under observation from what I heard. I know it's a bit outside of our realm, but could you look into this and see what's up?"

"What is the usual protocol on this?" I asked.

"Well, it would be a whole new ballgame. If she had succeeded, we would have a mess with two policies under investigation to pay out to minor children. If she's really trying to kill herself, we may want to intervene somehow. Personally, I hope to avoid that, so look into it and get a feel for what's up and let me know."

"Happy to. What about the medical stuff I've been looking into?"

"This is lead number one."

I grabbed my case, stuffed what papers I needed, pulled my coat from the hook, and locked my office behind me. The hall was quiet, and my footfalls sounded like a heartbeat.

"I'm gone," I said to Janice. "Good chance I won't be in tomorrow."

"Don't leave until you hear what I know," she sang.

I walked up to her desk and leaned over her. "What is so Goddamn important?"

"Paula from billing knows Rita that runs the front office over at Asbury Advertising."

"And?"

"Rita told Paula she was banging David Franklin."

I gave her my full attention. "Okay."

"Swear to God. Rita at Asbury was fucking Franklin. He said he was going to leave his wife for her, and then the cancer ended it."

"So Rita dropped him because he was sick?" I asked.

96

"No," she dropped her voice. "He dumped her because he wanted to be with his wife when he died. That's what she said."

"How credible is this?"

"Paula and Rita do yoga together," Janice said as though yoga was some sanctified bond of sisterhood.

"I'll follow up with Paula," I said. "Then I'll talk with Rita."

"Now you're talking." Janice spun in her office chair.

Jesus, I thought, it just gets better and better.

CHAPTER SIX

When my marriage ended, I swore I would never get married again. But when I met Gina, there was an instant attraction. Once we were dating, we finally got around to the discussion of our pasts. I thought when she heard my story she'd run screaming, but she only smiled.

Then she told me hers.

Gina's husband grabbed the kids and ran when her addictions took her down the rabbit hole. She ended up homeless, soulless, and lost. Jail, institutions, and halfway houses were her life until one day. She found herself standing on the Golden Gate Bridge, imagining how cold the water was at the bottom of that two hundred foot drop. That was her moment of clarity, and she was in a meeting that night.

She started her cupcake business to keep herself busy and discovered she loved it. She became a woman who needed nobody but loved everyone. Even me. Now she has a relationship with her kids, is on speaking terms with her ex, and sponsors about fifty women.

We keep our real lives pretty separate but date only each other. The best way to describe it, our hearts and today belong to each other, while our futures and our 'out there' life is none of the other's business. Not that we don't talk. She tells me about everything, but it's not a discussion, more information exchange – usually followed by two hours of sex that would kill most people. Gina is blonde and heavy breasted, fit and hardworking. I find it funny that she owns a cupcake shop. A tough, hard-drinking, and hard using former lost cause finds her serenity behind a counter baking gourmet sweets. To each his, or her, own.

Tonight we met for dinner at the Bay View Bistro, owned and operated by another sober friend. No matter how busy they are, Wally makes sure we get a table. Always window side, city view, and elbow to elbow with the other diners all talking over one another. The food's great, and the banter all about San Francisco. Tonight the city councilman whose kid I rescued dined with his family, and he gave me a respectful smile.

Wally greeted us. "How the hell are you guys?"

"Good sweetie," Gina said. "Business good as usual?"

"I'm blessed for an old drunk. By the way, and don't look now, but Councilman Hennessey insists on picking up your tab. He said if you say no, he'll make a scene and blow both your anonymities."

"No problem." I returned Hennessey's smile.

"The usual?" Wally asked.

Gina put down the menu. "Perfect."

Wally smiled wide. "Seafood stew, calamari appetizer, small house salad with bleu cheese, and whole wheat rolls. I have something else I want you to try. Our soup tonight is Lobster bisque, and you'll love it."

"Thanks," I said. He patted my shoulder.

The woman at the table to our left took a furtive glance at my left hand. Her face remained placid, but her eyes flared for a moment with – what? Disgust? Surprise? I never knew. Gina took notice, and when the woman stole another look, she smiled at her.

"He lost it lobster fishing. He supplies all the lobster to this restaurant."

The woman suddenly became very focused on her meal.

I whispered. "That was mean."

"Learned it from you. By the way, what's up with you? You seem a thousand miles away."

"Just work."

"You said you didn't have to go into the office tomorrow."

"I still have to work. I don't want to mess up tonight with talk about the office."

"Later then," she said. "I want you to come clean."

Wally put a bowl of steaming soup and a basket of rolls between us. Two spoons.

"You'll die when you eat this," Wally said. I cringed with a quick thought of David Franklin.

"What was that?" Gina asked.

"Just got a chill."

"This delicious soup will warm you up."

It was excellent, and I was glad when Gina began talking about the bakery and what was up with her latest sponsee. Her words kept me distracted from my thoughts. Wally finished us off with a single piece of chocolate silk pie and coffee.

"So I told her she had to stop going back to the asshole or her life would never change," Gina said and licked the last smear of chocolate from her fork.

"Good advice," I said. "So, my place or yours."

"Yours. Does Butch have a date, or is he going to sit and watch us like before?"

"I'll call him and make sure he's out."

We thanked Wally, and he dramatically put his hands over his heart. Gina followed me back to my apartment, and we fell onto the bed. When we both had enough of one another, we spooned while I kissed her neck.

"I love you," I whispered.

"Okay, what's with you? You going to tell me?"

"That's out there stuff," I reminded her.

"But you brought it in here." She wasn't scolding, just pointing it out.

"Did I?"

"You just said I love you first."

"Just this case," I said.

Gina rolled on top of me. "Why are you owning it?"

"I'm not owning it," I said. "It's got me thinking like a cop again. There's too much gray in this one. Too much what if and why I guess."

"It must be for you to be distracted when we're in bed."

"That obvious?"

"As much as that mechanical hand of yours."

"Sorry. I've never had a case like this as a civilian. It's got me wanting to know the truth. Tomorrow I go out on the road to wrap up loose ends before the company sends it to the final review."

"On the road? Where?"

"Walnut Creek and San Diego. And the Salton Sea if the suits think it's necessary."

"Why there?"

"Another hit on the clue list," I said.

"You know, I heard that place had become a toxic shit hole, and all the fish died. Then the town died too."

"I know, I looked it up. I'm trying to forget the whole thing. I promise."

Butch began yowling at the window, but we drowned him out with our own song.

*　　*　　*　　*

It was good to be out of the office. Gina had a party to cater, so I went to the gym early, took a steam, and showered. Back home, I petted the cat, cracked open a diet soda, and sat down at my laptop. With my notebooks open on my left and my five fingers dancing on the keyboard, my first task was to look into this gossip Janice had shared.

I jumped on the Asbury website and clicked the 'about us' link. Halfway down the staff listings, I found Rita Wagner. I switched to Facebook and searched by name, and there she was. A glance at her profile told me she was married, lived in North Beach, and had worked for Asbury for three years as an executive manager. She probably had a pay grade to match. What, I asked myself, was a high priced office manager with a husband doing running around with a has-been, contract designer with a wife, kids, and a mortgage? People are strange creatures when it comes to indiscretion.

I logged on to my office network, opened our call transcripts, and searched for Paula Danforth's activity records for both phone and email. I isolated the thousands of entries by typing in 'Rita'. A long list of emails dropped down my monitor, and the phone trace showed seventy calls to and from Rita's cell in the last three months. It wasn't horrible, small-time in regards to the use of company resources but more than enough to collaborate Janice's rumor.

I called Paula's office.

"Paula Danforth."

"Hello, Paula. This is Robert Jacobi in security."

"Oh, uh, yes," she said. "What can I do for you?"

"In the course of following up on a claim investigation, I came across a connection between one of our pending investigations. In looking into his place of work, I found correspondence between you and their office manager."

"Okay."

"David Franklin, our client under investigation, worked for Asbury Advertising as a contract designer.

Our records show many emails and some phone calls between you and Rita Wagner."

"Yes. Rita and I went to school together, and we are friends."

"I see," I said seriously. "Since Mr. Franklin worked there and we are trying to follow his course of action leading up to his disappearance, could you tell me if Rita happened to share anything with you that might shed some light on Mr. Franklin's fate?"

"I don't think she said anything to me about him specifically. We just talked, like girl talk."

"No gossip, no discussion about him having cancer, anything like that?"

"Oh, she said something about that. Yeah, I think we talked about what a shame that was. Stuff like that."

"I see," I said. "You can see where this relationship and any discussion regarding Franklin could be construed as a potential conflict of interest, inappropriate sharing of confidential information and could affect our investigation and our case?"

"I hadn't thought of that." Her voice was shaking.

"We have come into information about Mr. Franklin and Mrs. Wagner. If collaborated, it could be pertinent into the mindset of Mr. Franklin in the face of his diagnosis. His policy was not mature enough to pay off in the event of suicide. If you know anything?"

I left that hanging.

"I…" she began.

"I don't need anything this minute. Just contact me if anything comes to you. Thank you for your time. Have a good day."

Paula would probably fret all day and, most likely, come to me and privately to confess she knew of the affair. That would keep it between us.

Gina called to say her party would end around six and asked me to meet her at the wharf.

"Got it. See you there."

After an hour of hurting my brain with what-if and who-knew-what, I turned my attention to Mrs. Franklin. What single piece of her husband's disappearance pushed her to the brink? I imagined her at that moment, like Gina staring over the railing of the bridge. But Claire Franklin let herself fall. Luckily she was caught before she hit the concrete hard sea.

My cell called out to me. It was Joe.

"Got something for you," he said.

"Shoot."

"I did some asking around and found out there's a new crew working the street in Oakland. They loan money at sky-high rates to troubled former yuppies with shit credit who can't get the cash anywhere else."

I leaned forward. "Who are they?"

"Russians. Old Eastern Bloc guys with no necks and deep pockets."

"And strong-arm tactics," I added.

"Oh yeah. If you can't pay, they hurt you a little and give you more time. If you don't ever pay, they make you disappear. That shallow grave found last month north of the city? The former highbrow gone broke with the recession? We think that was their handiwork."

"Sounds charming."

"These thugs are taking over the rackets. The word is they're using neighborhood businesses as fronts for the lending. Local bars, stuff like that. If you want, I can send a man out to meet with these guys, give them a fake story of want and woe."

"Live bait," I said.

"Always works best to catch the big fish. You want me to drop in and see if I can get a nibble on the line?"

"No, I think I got what I needed. Thanks, man."

"Anytime, brother."

Russians. In the last few years, the old guard of organized crime has been pushed aside by this new breed of gangsters. The Italian mob had nothing on these guys. I guess the years under the old regime created angry and tough men who came to America and found a cozy and lucrative field filled with scared sheep. Even the cops were intimidated. Joe was right. To get anywhere fishing to connect to Franklin's possible fate, I would have to stake out the field with fresh meat. And that meant me.

What? I asked myself. Really? You'd really take that chance?

When I went back to my list, David's voice hissed in my head.

Did you hear what happened to me? I borrowed money from the Russians and couldn't pay them back.

"Stay focused. There's plenty to do on this list."

Find me, David whispered.

"Fuck you, Franklin."

Gina asked it perfectly – why am I owning this? Because I think I know the truth. I dialed Carl's number, and he answered happily. "Hey big guy, how's it hanging?"

"Not good," I said.

"Talk to me."

Now here was my conundrum. As my boss, the last thing I should do is let Carl know I was considering a lunatic, hunch-driven extracurricular snoop session into the realm of Russian loan sharks. As my A.A. sponsor, he deserved to know I was up on two wheels and about to roll my career over and into a ditch because my compulsive personality was running amuck. I had to do this carefully because I knew full well I was off the beaten path.

"I'm obsessing about Franklin," I said.

"That's your job."

"No, this is different. Normally I can leave work at the office and live my life. But since the news about the wife, I've been consumed by this case. I'm thinking and doing things that are above and beyond my normal protocol. I need you to talk me down off the ledge."

Carl got serious. "Okay, this is triggering the old cop in you. You're an alkie, so you obsess more than the average guy. You need to get quiet, clear your mind, and get centered. Regain your serenity. I know you know this, but you called me."

"Yeah, got it."

"And if it gets too bad, go to a meeting. I mean a hard-ass men's meeting where you can say shit that would shock the ladies. That'll help."

"Thanks." I meant it.

Carl cleared his throat. "Now, as your boss. Though the brass gave us the green light to look into these possible clues, we're not talking about a huge sum here. We just need acceptable proof the guy is dead. We got a week before we have to show cause for stalling. By then, a guy sick as him without treatment would be dead anyway. Right?"

"Gotcha' boss. Thanks."

"By the way, I got you an appointment with the Doc who treated Mrs. Franklin. Normally he couldn't tell us anything, but her actions fell into a special category regarding the policy. They agreed to give us cursory information about her diagnosis, but you have to sign a declaration of confidentiality as a representative of the company."

"When do they want to see me?"

"In an hour."

"I'm on it."

While I was looking up the hospital address, Butch arrived home with an ear that looked like he stuck it in a food processor. He had an air of accomplishment in his swagger, which meant the other guy was much worse off.

"Been kicking ass?" I asked. "Let's see if you need treatment."

The wound was starting to scab over, so I left him alone. I had just enough time to change and drive to the meeting. I'm not too fond of hospitals. The time I spent there with my hand, the surgeries, and the prosthetic fitting left an indelible mark on my psyche. Luckily I was treated in a reputable place, unlike where I was heading.

San Francisco City Hospital has a less than stellar reputation. It's located in old town and services people with no insurance. Illegals, homeless, and the downtrodden flock there for medical attention ranging from the sniffles to gunshot wounds. For years it has been on the brink of bankruptcy with a higher than average mortality rate. As sad as that may sound, the medical field's plight has become as segregationist as diners in the 1950s, Georgia. Not by race – but by the ability to pay.

A single day in the hospital costs around seven hundred dollars these days, so until the new national insurance debacle is sorted out, those with no card get shuttled to SFCH. Claire Franklin was taken there. I parked in the only lot, hung my disabled placard from the mirror, and checked in at reception.

"I have an appointment with Dr. Sarin."

Most of the doctors who passed me while I waited were East Indian or Asian of some sort. Most of the nurses appeared to be Filipino. Five minutes later, a five-foot-seven, dark-skinned man in a traditional doctor's dress approached me with bright eyes and a wide smile.

"Hello, I am Dr. Samir Sarin." He looked up at me and laughed.

"Robert Jacobi," I said. He laughed again. "What's funny?"

"I am sorry," he said. "You are so big. Most insurance people I have met are much shorter. I mean no disrespect."

"None taken."

"Come."

I followed the small doctor to the elevators, and we rode to the tenth floor while he spoke on his phone in his native tongue. Many others quietly conversed in the crowded lift, and I understood nothing. I was a head and a half taller than anyone else there. When we exited, Sarin took me into a small conference room off the hallway.

He opened a manila folder. "Claire Franklin was brought in on a suspected overdose of barbiturate and alcohol. She was unresponsive, and pumped her stomach but found the narcotic levels in her blood were not life-threatening."

"Meaning what exactly?"

"It means she was, most likely, not trying to kill herself. I suspect the grief of her husband's death and the subsequent financial difficulties became overwhelming, and she used the pills and wine to escape, but not die."

"I see." And I did. More than once during my post-injury depression, I used my prescribed Vicodin and a bottle of booze to kill the world for a few hours.

Sarin continued. "The report said she was unresponsive, and nobody knew how many pills were in the bottle, so the neighbor called 911. She was stabilized, and a social worker spoke with her, and she was released the next morning. It says she was ordered to see a family counselor. That is all I can tell you."

"Thanks. Oh Doc, I was hoping I could ask a question."

"Certainly," Sarin said.

"Would it be possible to cut off your own thumb and not go into shock?"

He stole a glance at my hook. "Yes. Shock is caused by the body producing a natural opiate that fights pain and lowers blood pressure. Anything that elevates the blood pressure would work to fight shock. Why?"

"I'm just curious. How could a person stay still enough and have the courage to cut off something? Wouldn't the natural desire to avoid injury stop them?"

"An animal will bite off its limb to escape a trap. A movie was made about a man who cut off his hand to free himself from a rock. Maybe the question is what type of self-preservation would help a man cut off his thumb. Do you know such a person?"

"How bad would it bleed?"

"What part of the thumb?" Sarin seemed intrigued.

"The whole thing, down to the hand."

"Oh, it would bleed an incredible amount. Not to mention it would require cutting through the joint and severing the tendons." Sarin nodded as though seeing the operation in his head. "The open wound would bleed very much, the pain would be terrible, especially if the person were on narcotics to elevate the blood pressure."

"Not an easy task," I said.

"Very difficult. If done with a heavy knife or cleaver, a fast hack to remove the thumb instantly. Even then, the pain would be excruciating, and the removal would be imperfect."

"I understand," I said. "Thank you."

He looked at my missing hand. "I apologize for my inappropriate question, but as a doctor and from the topic of our conversation, I can't help but be curious how you lost your hand."

"A brown recluse spider bit me, and they had to cut it off."

"Oh my," Dr. Sarin said, his voice almost a squeak. "Why did they not give you a better prosthetic?"

"No insurance."

He gave me a sympathetic smile.

When I got back to the office, I found a thin and somewhat effeminate young man sitting at Janice's desk. He looked up as I approached, and his eyes widened just a bit. I'm sure he'd been warned about me, but I doubted that would be enough to prepare him fully.

"Hello, I'm Robert Jacobi. We'll be working together, I guess."

"John Fitzgerald. I'm getting familiar with the system. I have worked for many insurance companies, and they all used similar programs."

"Sounds good. What's up with Janice, or do you know?"

"Called in sick," he said.

"I'm in the office at the end of the hall."

"Okay." I left him, and I heard him exhale loudly. "Wow."

I laughed under my breath. On the desk blotter was a piece of paper folded in half with a heart drawn on it. I thumbed it open. Janice had left me a note in her child-like scrawl.

I feel sick. You probably gave me aids. Will try and find a cure and be back ASAP. It was punctuated with a sad face.

I dropped it in the trash and called Carl. "I'm back."

"And?"

I gave him the rehash on what the doctor told me about David's wife. He made a grunt of acknowledgment.

"So she wasn't trying to kill herself. She must have needed some serious downtime," he said.

"Or maybe she got some more bad news."

"Like what?" Carl said.

"I don't know, I.R.S. or some such crap. Want me to ask her?"

"No," Carl said. "If she's that upset, the last thing she needs is your scary face back in her life. Let it go. What's next on your list?"

"I'm going to make an appointment with the consultant Franklin was talking to in Walnut Creek and get by there tomorrow."

"Take the rest of the day off," Carl said. "Go home, see Gina, go to a meeting, and shake this whole Franklin thing off."

"Is that an order from my boss or my sponsor?" I asked.

"Both." He killed the line.

Before I left, I Googled Carlson Consultations and found the number. After three rings, a message center picked up, and a sultry voice asked me to leave a message.

"I'm calling to make an appointment for tomorrow afternoon. Please call me back and let me know if that works for you. If I don't hear from you, I will be in your area and will drop by. Hopefully, you have time to see me."

I left my number.

I left the building under Carl's orders, but I did none of the things he suggested. Instead, I headed home and changed into jeans, a t-shirt, and a baseball cap. Then I headed back over the bay bridge and cruised the tough back streets of Oakland. I knew this was stupid, but Joe's words kept running through my head.

Was I here? David's voice asked. Did I borrow money from a loan shark?

"Probably not," I said out loud. "Just want to scratch something else off my list.

On the rough side of town, I wandered into a few pawnshops and did my best to look desperate. I asked around about anybody looking to loan money. Most people gave me a look of suspicion and said no. I pushed further into the bad neighborhoods and decided to take Joe's suggestion about potential front businesses. A few local bars looked too ordinary for this kind of thing, but when I entered the Bull's Eye Saloon, I felt I might have hit pay dirt. The place was old and weathered like the neighborhood. Not a single person looked local.

A man with my height and build stood behind the bar. He gave me a once over as I dropped my weight onto a stool. I let out a dramatic sigh. Back in the dark reaches beyond the bar area's dull lights, a man sat and smoked. California law prohibits smoking in bars and restaurants, so this felt promising.

"Help you?" The bartender asked without coming my way. His accent was Eastern European, most likely Ukrainian.

I dropped a ten-dollar bill on the bar. "Shot of Jack and a draft."

He poured the whiskey, pulled a glass of beer, and put both drinks in front of me.

"Thanks." I stared at the booze sitting under my nose. My mouth suddenly tasted like metal, and I swallowed hard. For the first time in three years, I sat at a bar and was this close to the poison. It made me shiver.

"There a problem?" The bartender asked.

"Oh yeah," I said with a sad laugh. "With the I.R.S., the credit card companies, and everybody else I owe. I have money problems as bad as you can have 'em."

"Sorry to hear that. Take a drink and take the edge off."

"Oh I will," I said. "But what I need is a loan. Since I lost this hand, life has gone to shit. I got a job, but the money is crap, and I need a lump sum to get some assholes off my back."

"Can't help you there," the big Russian said. "Good luck."

"Sure about that?" I asked and looked him in the eye. "What I mean is, I heard there are some people who can."

"Drink up and get the fuck out," he said.

I picked up the shot glass. My nose took in the heady richness of the liquor, and my eyes watered. My throat closed off, and I took advantage of the reaction to feign emotion. I let tears run from my eyes, put down the drink, and dropped my head.

"That's enough," the bartender hissed. "Stop this."

"Please," I said with a choke in my voice. "I just – oh God."

With a heave of my shoulders and a sob from my voice, I got up off the stool and headed for the door. The entire bar watched me make my way to the exit. Just as I reached for the door handle, I heard a voice from the back of the bar. "Wait." The same accent as the bartender but higher in tone, almost effeminate.

I held my breath and waited for him to speak again.

"Come here, my friend. Let's talk about your problem."

I squinted into the darkness. "I'm sorry?"

"I said come join me."

"I'm not looking for any trouble," I said in my meekest voice. Not easy for me, but it sounded pretty convincing. "I didn't mean to cause any trouble."

"Forget it. Come join me for a drink."

I carefully walked to the back of the tavern and took a seat across from a guy about five foot six. His pockmarked face looked intense, and his thousand-dollar suit fit him like a wetsuit. Ghetto gold covered his hands, and his wrist looked too thin under the weight of a huge Rolex watch.

Rizzo the Rat, I thought – Dustin Hoffman in Midnight Cowboy. The bartender put my shot and my beer back in front of me, and I had a sudden thought, was it a slip if I drank to save my life?

"You say you need money," Rizzo said, and I nodded. "Please, don't be nervous. Take a drink. We have money to lend." His we sounding like vee. Pure old world.

"I need quite a bit."

"How much are you looking to borrow?"

"Ten thousand dollars." Enough to show I was serious.

"We can lend that much," Rizzo said. "But the interest will be quite a bit. These are short term loans and must be paid back in three months, plus interest."

"How does it work?"

"You give us your address, and we make an appointment. I come by your house, and we give you the money. You agree to pay us three payments and cover the entire amount, and then you are in good standing with us. If you need another loan, we're there for you."

"What if I can't pay back the entire loan in that amount of time?" I asked.

"Then we would have to take action to collect. How did you come to find us?"

"My friend David. He suggested I come to see you."

"What is his last name?" Rizzo's voice shifted slightly. I had struck a chord.

I ignored the question. "If I can't pay it back, will you hurt me?"

"I'm sorry, Mister...?" Rizzo asked, his voice now suspicious.

"Roosevelt." It was the first name that popped into my head.

"I see," he said slowly. "I don't think I can help you."

"Why? I really need the money."

"The police department doesn't pay well?" Rizzo asked.

"I'm not a cop. I'm just a guy that needs some money."

"Please," Rizzo said and waved me off. "This is over."

"I swear I am not a cop," I said. "Please, I'm desperate."

"Well, Mr. Roosevelt, what is it that you do?"

"I'm a bouncer. I work nights in North Beach at one of the strip clubs. It pays next to nothing. I just need to get caught up, and I'll be okay. The I.R.S. is garnishing my pay."

"Before that?" Rizzo asked. "What did you do before you lost your hand?"

"I was an auto mechanic," I said.

"How did you lose the hand?"

"Car accident. I was drunk and crashed my wife's Honda. I lost the hand, and she left me. I got medical bills and other problems. She's marrying somebody else."

It was almost true, I thought.

"What club do you bounce at?" Rizzo said.

"Danny's," I said. "Near the business district."

"I know it," he said. "I know the manager. Who was this person you said told you about us?"

"His name is David," I said.

Rizzo was pushing for a flaw in my story, and I could tell by his tone and body language he suspected I was full of shit. My heart went cold, and I got ready for anything.

"And your family," Rizzo said. "They will suffer if you do not get this money?"

"I have no family. Like I said, I'm divorced and no kids."

"That's good to know." In other words, nobody would miss me.

When he moved, I knew he was going for a gun, so I surged across the table. Rizzo screamed in his high-pitched voice when my hook caught him at the elbow as his hand came up. His gun went off, and the ceiling rained plaster. Time slowed down, and when I drew back, Rizzo lost his balance. I threw a sharp left jab, and my hook curve struck his left jaw with a stomach-churning crunch.

"I'll kill you," the bartender bellowed and scrambled over the bar. His lunge sent glassware and booze flying to the floor. Rizzo was out cold, so I turned to bolt for the door when the big Russian rushed me with a small baseball bat. I skirted the brute and ran around him. I had my keys out and was nearly free when he threw the bat. A beer mirror exploded next to me, and I covered my face.

With my head down, I spun away, lost my footing, and nearly fell. The bartender was on me like a freight train, so I dropped, tucked my hook into my abdomen, and threw myself at his legs. He rolled over me, and I jumped to my feet and used his broad back like a trampoline to propel myself at the door. I broke out into the daylight and was in the truck before I heard his roar.

By the time he was out the door, I floored the accelerator and left him behind.

I gulped air. "Son of a bitch!"

My face felt sticky, and I looked in the rearview mirror. Blood ran from my hairline and down my left cheek. I hoped I didn't need stitches. My heart slowed, and I carefully drove north out of the shit side of town and found a gas station, pulled around back, and used the restroom to examine my injuries.

"That was insane," I told myself in the mirror. "That was fucking stupid."

One thing was for damn sure; if David Franklin had borrowed cash from these animals, they very well could have done terrible things to him for not paying them back.

While I drove across the bay bridge and returned to my own fair city, I realized I was lucky to be alive. For a moment, I wondered how badly I might have hurt Rizzo and then remembered I didn't give a fuck. I headed for home to clean myself up. Butch was sleeping on the couch as I came in. He lifted his head, gave me a cursory glance, and went back to sleep.

"When you come home beat up, I take care of you. Earn your keep you lazy cat."

My clothes smelled like fear and sweat, so I stripped and tossed them in the hamper. I could see the cut to my scalp in the mirror was no more than a small nick. I took a shower and washed away the sweat and grime of the altercation. Once the initial adrenaline surge left me, I was stiff from the scuffle, so I took two Advil and drank a giant glass of water. Clean and relieved, I was suddenly ravenous. I made a sloppy sandwich from sliced turkey and Swiss cheese on a croissant. I ate it standing by the kitchen sink while I relived the incident in the bar.

It wasn't until I mentioned the name David that Rizzo went hard ass on me. That bastard was willing to kill me once he was sure I wasn't a cop and had no family. Did he think Franklin sent me? No, too obvious. Then again, how many desperate Davids were there in the city? What had Joe said – even the cops didn't intimidate these guys? I decided to contact Claire Franklin and ask if anybody had come calling. But my first call was to Joe. I told him everything.

"Holy shit. And you think you busted his jaw?"

"Had no choice. He was about to kill me right there."

"I warned you. Did they get a picture of you?"

"No, I'm not that stupid," I said. "Besides, it was dark as shit in there."

"You're lucky, but how many giant, bald one-armed men come looking for a loan? They'll figure this out soon enough. They may be foreign, but they ain't dumb."

"Well, I'll keep this one between you and me."

Joe laughed. "You are one crazy, lucky sum-bitch. I'd stay out of Oakland for a while. So, what's your theory, if your hunch is even close to right?"

I exhaled dramatically. "Best guess? David Franklin took a loan, couldn't pay, so they killed him. Old Rizzo didn't blink when I mentioned ten grand, so maybe he took more. Either way, my guess is they froze him for some strange reason and then dropped the thumb and set up the scene to give you guys something to stew over."

"Probably a warning," Joe said.

"Come again?"

"Franklin got some press. His wife went to the city, and he was all over the news for a few days. The Russians might have dropped the thumb because they knew it would be identified. That sent a message to their other customers they were not kidding when they said bad shit would happen if they didn't pay up. Free advertising."

"Sounds right."

I was shocked I hadn't thought of it.

"So, maybe we have a solved mystery. You'll have a case closed and a big check to mail, and we all move on with our happy horseshit lives, right?"

Happy horseshit was right. It all made sense, and the plot felt right. All the players played their parts, and this time the bad guys won. Claire would get her money, and – I stopped right there.

If she knew about the loan and was scared to tell from fear of reprisals, then she was a scared housewife with a pissed off Russian loan shark on her back. If Rizzo thought I was there because of her, he could have already threatened her. If that were true, then the pills and wine made sense. I rifled through my papers, found her number, and called the house. The machine picked up, and I controlled my tone. I left a message asking her to call me, and I hung up feeling helpless.

David Franklin may well be dead and weighted down in the bay, but now I had his wife's wellbeing on my mind and in my hands. I paced my apartment. My phone rang.

Claire's voice was calm. "Hello, Mr. Jacobi. I'm returning your call."

"Yes, thank you," I controlled my tone. "We're finalizing our investigation, and I had a few more questions."

"Do you need me to come into your office?"

No, I thought, have any scary men demanding money been knocking at her door? Instead, I said, "How about tomorrow around two?"

"That's fine. See you then."

That gave me the morning to follow up with Walnut Grove and get out to see one of the first health clinics on my list. It was across the Golden Gate, deep in the wine country, and advertised as exclusive.

I knew I had to let this go, so I headed to the gym, where a brisk run on the treadmill and a long stew in the steam room melted away the soreness from my dance with the bartender. I laughed at how far off the path I'd gone on this case. If Carl knew half of what I'd done, he would fire my ass, then make me go to lots of meetings.

It was almost over, I decided. After tomorrow we'd all accept that David Franklin was dead and gone. After recovering from her grief, Claire could smile all the way to the bank. Life insurance benefits are tax-exempt, so she could sit back and think about what to do with the rest of her life. Yes indeed, after tomorrow, all would be right with the world.

You're full of shit, the cop voice said.

Please, David begged.

I decided to go to a meeting and shake off the ghosts.

CHAPTER SEVEN

Mill valley is an interesting place. Tucked back in the rolling hills and redwood forests of Marin County, it is an enclave of wealthy people pretending to be hippies. They pass laws outlawing perfume as odor pollution. Traffic is frowned upon, and political and environmental opinions are worn proudly on the residence's sleeves.

I arrived in the town square and parked in the roundabout separating vehicles from the plaza. Small groups of people sat at tables and sipped coffee from the small shop and bookstore. The line curved out the door, and I had to laugh. Nobody worked in this town except the shop help that commuted in from outside. The small information center sat tucked under the canopy of trees, and an older woman smiled at me when I walked up.

"Good morning," she said. "How can I help you?"

"I'm a bit lost. How do I get to The Valley Center for Alternative Health? My phone has no signal, and my map is of no use at all."

"That's Mary Phillip's place. Go back out of the village and take the first right. Keep driving until you see a sign with the lotus flower, then turn left up the hill. It's way back in the hills. Just when you're sure you're lost, you'll come to it."

"Thank you so much."

She was right. Once I turned off the highway and began my drive into the hills, I felt like I was off the map. The single-lane cracked asphalt road wound through redwoods high into the foothills. Signs announcing people's homes disappeared, and fifteen minutes later, I broke out onto a grassy plateau with breathtaking views of San Francisco gleaming like Emerald City. In the distance, I saw what looked like an old homestead, now refurbished to rustic splendor. The only sign was a Lotus flower carved into a redwood plank.

Slowly I drove up the gravel driveway through the rolling grass to a simple gate, guarded by a uniformed attendant. I rolled to a stop, and the guard smiled at me.

"Hello. Are you here for a visit, or do you have an appointment?"

"I have an appointment to see Mary Phillips. Robert Jacobi."

"Hmm, you're not on my list. What is the nature of the visit?"

"I represent Bayside Consolidated Insurance. We're investigating the activity of one of our claimants. I called and told I could drop by." I extended my card with my hook.

"I see. Please wait a second."

For five minutes, the young man whispered into the phone, then came back. "Our General Manager will speak with you. Please pull up to the main lodge and wait for him."

"How will I know him?"

"You can't miss him."

The guard was right. The man waiting was taller than me, broad as a barn, and dressed in an expensive suit. With skin so black it didn't reflect the morning light, he waited for me by the door.

"Mr. Jacobi." He shook my hand. "I'm Roger Fellows, general manager of the resort. Follow me."

I suddenly recognized him. "Excuse me for saying so, but I followed your career with the 49ers. I always thought you carried the team."

"Nice of you to say," Fellows said. "In here, please."

We sat facing each other in a modern conference room. I felt a sense of deja vu, minus the billion-dollar view. Fellows folded his hands that looked as big as baseball gloves, and his bull neck bulged against his shirt collar.

His voice rumbled like a volcano. "How can I help you?"

I produced the picture of David Franklin. "I'm trying to find out if this man came here for treatment?"

"You know better than to ask me that."

"It's just a formality."

"The only reason I'm talking with you is that I recognized you too. We met at the party when you were decorated for heroism in a kidnapping case. Let me put it this way. Unless this man could afford ten thousand dollars a week, he would not be here. And if he could afford that, we would be sworn to secrecy, and anybody coming to this door would be immediately turned away."

"I see."

"And no, I never saw this man. But I never said that."

"I understand."

"The councilman's family is a benefactor. I'll tell them you said hello."

He dismissed me with another intimidating handshake and then had me escorted off the grounds by a uniformed man in a golf cart. Once I was back in the truck, I imagined the rich and famous languishing in herbal baths and taking Omega 3 enemas in spiritually balanced environments. Such people were no different than David, except they had more money. I was reminded of the classic rock tune that explained that 'all our money won't another minute buy.' That was for damn sure.

One place down and three to go. I traversed the rural highway and left Mill Valley, and headed for Walnut Creek. I called the office to follow up with Carl.

"What'd you find out?" he asked.

"Nothing. This place was out of his league. Now I'm headed for the consulting company in Walnut Creek."

"We found out he designed their website and handled the logistics for them. Prepare yourself."

"For what?"

"She's a psychic."

My phone beeped and announced Janice calling. I let it go to voicemail. "Like a palm reader?"

"Something like that. Just thought you should know. Have fun."

"Have we heard anything from Mrs. Franklin?"

"She hired a lawyer. He called and said if we didn't settle the case, he was prepared to sue us."

"Wonderful. Thanks."

Janice had left an irreverent message telling me she was getting seaweed enemas and having sex with the UPS delivery guy as part of her recovery. I tapped my chin and wondered if I could construe that as sexual harassment and sue the company.

Janice's replacement called.

"Hey John," I said.

"Yes, Mr. Jacobi. I–"

"Call me Bobby."

"Bobby. A woman named January called from Dr. Whitley's Health Ranch. Wants you to call back."

I pulled over and wrote down the number John gave me. She answered on the second ring.

"Mister Jacobi, I'm sorry to bother you, but you asked me to call if I found anything about David Franklin."

"I appreciate your call, but it may no longer matter."

"So he died?"

"It seems that way."

"I'm so sorry," she said, as though apologizing for us having to shell out half a million dollars. "It's just that I found something that I was unaware of before. But if it's already too late, I guess it's not important."

"I should probably document it anyway," I said. "Go ahead."

"Well, I was having my treatments, two days of colonics, so I wasn't working the office. My assistant was. I was behind on my paperwork, and it took me a few days to sort through all the backups. We document all our visitors through logs because we sometimes have to show these to the health department."

"January," I interrupted. "I apologize for being abrupt, but I'm pretty busy, and I just need the details for my records."

"Yes, of course." Her voice cooled. "When we have visitors, we take a Polaroid picture and write down a name if the visitor has no I.D. That way, we can keep track of who is who. I was logging the visitors who had left us, as a matter of record for our own insurance needs, and one of the pictures caught my attention. I compared it to the photo you sent me, and it looks to me like a possible match. He gave his name as Bill Johnson."

"Any way of sending me a copy?" I asked nicely, and she warmed up a bit.

"Just scanned it for our records, and I'll send it along if you give me your email." I gave it to her. "I'm sending it now."

"Thank you so much, January. I wish I had one person on my staff half as efficient as you are."

"I try," she said.

My Wi-Fi was a bit iffy on my phone, but I finally got to my server and clicked the attachment. A picture of a thinner, hollow-eyed David Franklin-ish man popped up on my screen. I stared at it for a full minute. His expression was grim, and his eyes had dark circles beneath them. I pulled out the other photo and compared them side-by-side. If it wasn't David, it was his very sick brother.

"Jesus H Christ," I whispered.

She also sent me the accompanying information sheet and the arrival date of this no I.D. drifter's visit to the health ranch. Three days after his supposed abduction. Three days?

I called January back. "I'm sorry to bother you this time. On any of the information regarding Mr. Johnson's info, did it mention any distinguishing characteristics?"

"Such as?"

"Was he bandaged or hurt in any way?"

"It doesn't say anything here," she said thoughtfully. "We generally don't ask questions or document anything like that unless they have special needs. If he had no special needs, he would have been assigned a cot and put to work. If he were unable to work, they would have confirmed why."

"Work?"

"For the commune, in the gardens. We grow all our own food organically here."

"Okay, thanks very much."

Damn! Three days after his kidnapping, somebody that could have been David was flopping on a cot and tending the herbs at the health ranch in San Diego. He still had all his digits, I suppose, or somebody probably would have tended to his wound and wondered how he lost a thumb.

I called John at the office. "Can you go into my computer?"

"Give me a minute. Okay, I'm at your desk."

"Look on my desktop and click the jpg marked Franklin."

"Got it."

"Now go to my email and download the attachment January just sent."

"Okay, done."

"Does that look the same person to you?"

"They are similar. The one on the right looks older and thinner."

"If you had to testify in court, would you say these men were the same person?"

"No," he said. "Not in court. I'd say they could be brothers, related, yeah. But positively the same person – I couldn't swear it."

"Think of them as pictures taken a few months apart after he was diagnosed with cancer," I suggested.

"Well, I guess that would make the difference, but I still wouldn't swear they were the same person."

"Okay, that's all."

"Was I right?" he asked.

"That's the half-million dollar question. Thanks." I killed the line. "Fuck, fuck, fuck, and more fuck," I barked.

I got back on the road and realized I was running out of time. Walnut Creek welcomed me into old world charm and wine stores. Antique shops invited me into the past while my phone gave me directions to a rural road bordered by old Victorian houses and newer vineyards. Finally, a driveway led to a craftsman style house tucked under a stand of giant Oaks. I searched for Karen's website and found it easily. I clicked a testimonial:

Karen is amazing. I went in for a reading, and she nailed my problem. She explained what was up with me and made a very sensible suggestion to address my situation.

Her photo was alluring with wild hair and heavily made-up eyes. Her mouth was full and seductive. They'd done an excellent job of making the picture look old, like a poster from a traveling carnival. I suspected she would turn out to be short, ordinary, and far from exotic. I dialed the number to announce my arrival.

"Hello?" She sounded like a heavy smoker.

"Karen Carlson, please."

"Madam Carlson isn't here right now," the voice rasped.

"I'm here for an appointment."

"Please come in."

That confused me. Was she there or not? I kept my hook hidden in my pocket and stepped up on the porch. A woman answered the door before I knocked. This had to be the woman I was after. Looking to be in her sixties, she oozed the quintessential psychic persona complete with long hair, clothes right out of the sixties, and more costume jewelry than a street fair. I smelled no smoke but noticed a thick scar on her neck. My guess was throat cancer.

"Karen?" I asked.

"No, she should be with us in a moment. Please follow me."

We entered a living room decorated with more icons, candles, and spiritual statues than I'd ever seen. Leaded glass windows high in the wall cast prisms of light, and the dark wood of the walls evoked a sense of eerie expectation. It was a great shtick. The true believers probably ate it up.

"Please sit down. Can I ask what your questions pertain to? It helps if she knows what you are looking for."

"I need help finding someone."

"Can I have a name?"

"David Franklin. When will Karen be here?"

Suddenly the haggard woman before me changed. Her face softened, and her eyes brightened.

"Hello Mr. Jacobi," she said. Her gentle voice caught me off guard. "You ask about David Franklin. David as the world knew him is dead."

"Karen?" I asked.

"Of course. Again, the person I knew as David is dead. He has moved into another realm."

I fought to hide my cynical doubt. I nearly laughed, but it was a great bit.

"Well, yes. But before David disappeared, he had given me your number and said if anybody could help me, it was you."

"You are a terrible liar."

"You're right," I said. "I am a horrible liar."

"You are looking for David, that is true. You know he was in contact with me, and you are hoping I may have information regarding where he went and where he transitioned."

"And you got all that just looking at me?"

"You don't hide your judgment very well," she said, "but I also sense you hope I can help. It must be awkward to be that divided in your faith."

"My shrink says the same thing."

"Your sarcasm is sharp, but I see you have come to a crossroads in your search. Not just for David, but many things in your life. I feel you are conflicted by who you used to be and what you've become."

I chuckled at that. "You're good."

"And you're so guarded. Do you have problems in your personal relationships because of your shielded nature?"

"More than you'll ever know. I'd love to keep this going, but I really need to ask about your relationship with David. His phone records showed that he called you many times. Was he calling you for guidance of some sort?"

Karen's face wavered like I saw her through vapor. "Ours was a business relationship. But you know that. I knew he was very ill, very frightened and desperate for a miracle – but our relationship was strictly professional."

"I see. Well, thanks for the therapy session, and I'm sorry to have bothered you. Have a nice day."

"Please wait," Karen said. "Don't run out of fear."

"Oh trust me, I'm not doing that."

"You have a missing appendage, don't you?" Karen asked.

"Uh, what?"

"May I see your left hand?"

"Sure." I pulled the hook free and felt my ears get hot.

"Violence, pain, shame, and defeat," she said. "Loss of people and career."

"Something like that."

"Like David," she said softly. "I feel his pain, his loss, his sadness – through you."

"Very good trick."

"So sad," she said. "You want so badly to know the truth, but you're afraid of what it might be. People are telling you to deny your heart, and you are feeling frustration and worry. But you still search for answers though it could cost you everything. David's flesh is on your mind, and David's life weighs on your heart. I feel your anger."

"Okay." I laughed again because this was beginning to spook me. "Can we keep this about David?"

"Your search is so desperate," she said. Her voice projected what seemed like genuine concern. "Long miles and strange places. Part of David is dead. Some of him has transformed. He is no longer David Franklin. He is new, changed, saved."

"Uh," I managed. "And what does that mean exactly?"

"Follow the flesh."

"Can we bring this whole deal back down to earth, and can you answer me just a few questions?" I blinked, and the disheveled woman was back in front of me.

"Hello. Your time is up. Do you want to make another appointment?"

"Uh, you're kidding."

"I am afraid Karen is finished with the reading," she said.

"I was asking questions about David Franklin."

"He designed our website."

"Yes, I know. I have some questions regarding when Karen last spoke to him and when she saw him last."

"He's dead," the gravelly voice said.

I became impatient. "Yes, well, may I speak with Karen again?"

"She is not here."

"I just spoke to her."

"She is no longer here. She will only return if you have an appointment for a reading. Would you like to make an appointment for her to do that?"

"Can you please just have her come back and answer one more question?"

"Karen Carlson is only available for readings."

"Where is she now?"

"She left the realm," gravel voice said.

"Thank you for your time." I turned to leave.

"Mr. Jacobi?" Karen was back.

"Yes?" I asked indignantly.

"Your desperation is heartbreaking. We'll speak again."

"Wait."

"She is gone," the odd voice said.

"Where?"

"Back to her realm."

"Meaning what?"

"Her spirit has fled. She died in 1937."

I had no answer for that. David designed a website for a ghost? My scalp crawled. I felt as though a goose just walked over my grave, to coin a phrase. Bizarre.

"Thank you for your time."

On the drive back, I vacillated between humorous dismissiveness and spooky shivers. Traffic was light, so I made good time getting back. I'd have a full hour before Claire arrived. Five minutes from the office, my phone rang and snapped me back to reality.

"Yeah?"

"Bobby?" It was John. "Paula Danforth is here to see you. She says she has an appointment."

"Stall her, I'll be there in a minute." I had forgotten about her. I parked and went up the fire stairs. I was in my office in minutes and called John. "Send her in."

Paula was not unattractive, but she tried too hard. Her makeup was heavy, and she wore an outfit that deemphasized her flat chest and wide bottom. Yeah, I'm mean, but I know people.

"Hello Mr. Jacobi," she said.

I folded my hands by laying my right in the curve of the hook. Paula gave it a terrified look.

"Thank you for coming," I said softly. "I appreciate you talking with me. We're close to closing our investigation, and I want to make sure there are no snags."

She looked like she would cry. "I understand."

"Nobody is in trouble here. We just need to clarify what Rita said to you about David Franklin. Some rumors are flying around."

"This is just between us, right?" She asked.

"Absolutely."

"Rita had the hots for David. She started talking about him as soon as he started working there. Rita's not happily married, and I know she cheated on her husband before. She and David worked together one night, and she put the moves on him, and he shut her down. Guess she did some talking, and I did some whispering, and a different story started circulating."

"You said he told her he had cancer."

"He told the company he had cancer," she corrected me. "Rita said how sad it was, and I mentioned that to somebody."

"And they told somebody and so on," I said with a nod. "You can see how dangerous that is, especially when we covered him. Did Rita say how David was handling the news?"

"She said he came to work, did his job, and kept to himself. He had a meeting with the bosses and then he disappeared. Rita thought he killed himself."

"Which would have canceled his life insurance coverage," I explained. "That's where the danger lies in gossip."

"Yes, I understand."

"Thank you for coming in. I don't see how this is relevant to what's going on, so this is just between us."

"Thank you."

I excused her and decided I wanted to talk to Rita, the home wrecker. My report went unwritten, and I stared again at the photos side by side on my desk. The phone rang. It was Carl.

"Hey."

"What do we know that we didn't know before? What about the wife?"

"It wasn't a suicide attempt. The doctor said she took a bit too many happy pills and drank a half bottle of wine."

Hiding from the Russians, I thought.

"Sounds like my ordinary Wednesday night back in the bad old days."

"Mine too," I said. "I'm not sure exactly where we stand on all this. Mill Valley got us nothing, and Walnut Creek was a nutcase washout. The lady psychic there seemed to think he was dead. I got a call from the health ranch in San Diego, and we have a possible hit there."

"Meaning what?"

"The woman who runs the place thinks she remembers Franklin showing up three days after his disappearance. I'll send you the photo she sent me right now. Other than that, I have the wife coming in today in about an hour."

"Send me the pic."

I dragged and clicked until Carl said my email showed up in his inbox.

"Okay, yeah," he said. "I see the resemblance. Man, that's spooky. Let me see if I can get you a flight voucher and have you go see these folks in person."

"Sounds like fun."

"What does your gut tell you? Not your cop gut, your insurance gut."

"Honestly? I think he's dead. I don't think he was when the claim was originally filed, but I've done my research, and, yeah, he'd be dead by now."

But a death would have left a body, which would have been reported. An I.D. would have been made. Unless the Russian loan sharks killed him, then we'd never see his corpse. But if he set something up and jumped off a pier with bricks tied to his feet? Well, that's another story. Either way. Other than his voice in my head, David Franklin was gone.

"Okay, let me see what the suits say and get back to you. Good job. Meantime, good luck with the widow." Carl hung up.

John called through and told me Claire had canceled our meeting. "Did she say why?"

"No, just canceled and hung up."

The rest of my day was cups of coffee, killing time online, and talking with John. I finally put him at ease. I even had him laughing at some of my stories. While we chatted, Janice called. I took the call at John's desk.

"You dead?" I said.

"You wish. I wanted to let you know I'll be back to work in the morning. I know you've been going crazy not having me there to give you shit."

"Trust me, I've been wallowing in the peace and quiet."

"Liar," she said. "Did you scare the hell outta' the temp?"

"We're buddies. Can't wait to meet his friends."

I left at four and met Gina for an early dinner. She had a cupcake party at six. We talked, but I secretly grappled with the idea of Franklin's confusing journey.

"Okay, where are you, Bobby?" Gina asked.

"What?"

"I've been talking about my lesbian love affair for two minutes, and you've had a blank stare. I am not having a lesbian love affair, and you are not paying attention. What the hell is wrong with you?"

"Work," I said.

"The same case?"

"Yes, as a matter of fact."

"Can you tell me?"

After a minute of frantic thought, I took a deep breath, and I told her the whole story.

"Jesus," she said. "I remember that being in the paper with the car and then the thumb. Why didn't you tell me you've been working on this?"

"That's not all I didn't tell you," I confessed and told the tale of my trip to Oakland.

"Baby, that is fucked up," she hissed. "You could have died, and I would have had no idea what happened to you. Not cool."

"I know, and I'm sorry. Don't be pissed at me. I'm struggling with what's the right thing to do. My cop head is off the charts, but my insurance head is fast asleep."

Gina looked at her cell. "Well, I gotta' go. Promise me you'll talk with Carl and sort this shit out. Forget he's your boss and tell him as your sponsor. Promise me."

"Okay."

She kissed me, playfully slapped the back of my head, and walked away, shaking her head.

I called Carl, and he asked me to come to his place. He lives in a third-story walk-up just south of China

Town. Most of the surrounding buildings have an Asian influence, and I always laugh at that. Most people don't know that after the big quake that leveled the city in 1906, the restoration of the area was intentionally done to make the heavy Chinese population feel at home. The funny part was that the architect got it wrong and built a mostly Japanese-influenced neighborhood.

I climbed the stairs, which took three flights at three angles to reach the top. Before I knocked, I gave the city a quick look and gazed at the lights that illuminated San Francisco. Carl must have heard me on the stairs because he opened the door with a flourish.

Dressed in a sweatsuit and slippers, Carl invited me in. We sat at his dining room table. The first time I came here, I was eight days sober and wondered if this guy was gay. Today the overly decorated and purely masculine decor was like coming home.

"So, what's so important you came all the way from the wharf to talk?"

"Business and program."

He popped open a flavored water. "Sounds serious."

"Let me say what I have to say, and don't say anything until I'm done, okay?"

"Did you drink?"

"There you go," I chastised. "Let me tell the story."

He sipped his water. "Fine."

I told him almost everything; I left Paula out of it. I'd promised. He shook his head and rubbed his neck, and finally drew the most profound sigh I'd ever seen.

"Jesus." Carl took another sip from his water.

"I've been so far off in left field it's had me losing sleep. I swear David Franklin has been whispering in my ear every step of the way."

"Not to mention no regard for protocol," Carl said. "Endangering yourself by wrestling with Russian criminals and putting the company at risk for lawsuits and bad publicity. Bobby, this is out of control. You said it yourself. You now think this guy is dead, right?"

"Yes, but—"

"But nothing." He stopped me with his palms up. "It's over. I sound like the captain on one of those cop shows, but you're off the case. Oh, wait, after you go to San Diego. The suits want you to follow up on this health farm lead. You'll go tomorrow. When you get back, we'll walk into that suits meeting and say you believe Franklin to be dead. I'll share the same opinion and nature will take its course. Mrs. Franklin will get her money."

"I don't know," I heard myself say and instantly regretted it.

Carl surprised me by slamming his hand down on the table.

"Robert, there is no gray area here, understand? David Franklin is either dead, or he isn't. If you have hard evidence he's alive and hiding in a drainpipe somewhere, then you better have the pictures and the affidavits to prove it. If not, you can't offer theories based on hunches and suspicion."

"They're not hunches," I said, my temper rising. "What about his picture showing up down south three days after he was supposedly killed?"

"We'll know if that washes tomorrow. If you come back with him in tow, missing a thumb, then we'll reopen this thing, and he'll be charged with fraud. If not, we're done."

"Okay."

"Seriously?"

"Yes, Jesus H. Christ."

"Otherwise, you better have blood, tissue, or have him locked in the trunk of your car. Even then, I'd want DNA and a signed confession."

"I hear you." I got up and paced the floor as he watched me wave my arms and grumble.

Carl sat back. "Besides Bobby, with his wife hiring a lawyer? It's time to put this one to bed."

"I know that."

"I know how you are, and you'll only feel better if you give me your theory. So what do you think happened?"

I exhaled dramatically. "I think he took the cash from the Russians, so he had a travel purse, and I think he visited every possible miracle worker, didn't find shit that would actually help him, and eventually died somewhere along the way." I waved my hand at oblivion. "Probably in some flophouse, shit box treatment center in Mexico."

"Like Steve McQueen," Carl said.

I suddenly felt spent. "Yeah, just like old Steve. So it's down to San Diego, come back, and it's over."

"Why don't I believe you?"

"The insurance man in me agrees even if the cop is pissed."

"This is all between us," Carl said. "Everything you told me is in the strictest confidence of the sponsor-sponsee relationship. If the Russians come calling, I'll swear you were out of town. Neither of us will ever speak of this again."

"Thanks."

He stood on tiptoes to hug me, and then I descended his Asian steps and went back to my car. The drive home was solemn. I imagined David beside me, as silent and sullen as I was.

Sorry buddy, I thought the suits have this one.

Gina called. I assured her that I told Carl everything and I was letting it all go.

"Good," she said. "Now maybe I'll have my old grumpy hardass back."

"We can only hope. I have to fly south tomorrow and wrap up one official loose end."

"Need a ride to the airport?"

"Company is dropping me."

"Call me from the road."

Butch was home, and this time, his hind leg was a mess, and he'd bled on the couch.

"We're both beat to shit, aren't we, buddy?"

Butch yowled at me, and I knew he was in pain. He let me look him over and gave me a sad expression while I dressed his wound.

"He must have been as big and bad as you."

That put me in mind of the Russian bartender as he hurled headlong my way.

"We're quite a pair."

Butch grabbed my hand and bit me. Then he hobbled away.

"I love you too," I said and turned on the television.

The movie was shit. The cat came to apologize, and we drifted off into a twitchy doze together. Images darted through me, almost sleeping head, and nothing made sense. David was there, and so was Carl. Both of them seemed upset with me.

I was suddenly in the water, and my parents were watching me from a lifeguard tower. I jerked awake. Butch wanted his spot, and the sun was coming up. My back stiff, but my head clear, I showered, dressed, and took myself out to breakfast. Two cups of coffee and some eggs helped me feel more human. I was almost whistling when I arrived at the office. Janice met me with a smile.

"Hey boss."

"Done playing hooky?"

"I went to Vegas and got a tattoo and danced naked on a blackjack table."

"You know, I just about believe you did."

"So what did I miss while I was gone?"

"Oh, not much." I leaned back in my chair. "Same old thing."

She leaned over my desk. "Bullshit, you're in too good a mood. Who died?"

"Were done with Franklin as soon as I write up my report when I get back from San Diego. So go get caught up on your stuff and fix what John messed up."

"Already did." She left and didn't close the door. "Your car is here."

CHAPTER EIGHT

The drive to San Francisco International Airport is always an adventure, as is the check-in process. After a thorough pat-down, my body and appearance set off all alarms, so I waited for my flight. I'd land at 10:45 in the morning and return at 9:45 at night. I'd have plenty of time to kill.

The small plane was half full, so I had no neighbors to scare. Out the window, I watched the state roll under me. Central California rolled along like an eternal landscape of golden hills spotted with oak tree clusters, ranches, and small towns tucked into fertile valleys. Earthquake faults run through there, and seismic activity grumbles beneath the ground, releasing plumes of hot vapor from some of the foothills.

Then we began the pass over Los Angeles. Unlike the obnoxious song and ad campaign from the eighties, I hate L.A. There may be lots of oddballs, strange characters, and total whack jobs in San Francisco, but they come by it honestly. I've sometimes suspected that even the homeless and hookers in LA are from central casting, or at least carrying their headshots in case they proposition a director.

Orange County and the blue Pacific passed beneath us, and soon they announced our descent. With seatbelts and tray tables in proper order, we came in low over the city and dropped onto the tarmac. I had no luggage, so I was out of the terminal and at the car rental counter in no time.

"Here's your rental agreement, wait outside for the shuttle, and we'll have you to the pickup lot in a jiffy," the attendant said.

"And that's a premium?"

"Dodge Durango, yes."

A Dodge. I was right at home.

In an hour, I was cruising along the harbor and heading for Interstate 5. Running from the Mexican border to the top of Washington State, the 5 Freeway is the West Coast Route 66. A driver passes through three states on its path, coastal stretches, inland forests, small towns, and big cities. The onboard GPS instructed me to turn left to merge onto the 5 in less than a mile.

One thing I can say about Southern California, they've done a great job whitewashing over the fact that it's a coastal desert. With borrowed water and clever disguises, they make it look green. The water is scarce, and the window dressing drops, the sandstone, and yellow clay expose the truth. The further the navigation took me east, the harder it became to sustain the illusion. Unlike up north, down south, the air is fucking dry. I drank water constantly.

More than once, I thought the navigation made a crucial mistake and was taking me on a wild goose chase. But just as I was feeling lost, civilization showed up tucked in valleys. And these inland cities were low, ugly old places where illegals that crawled across the border put down roots. The town of Escondido looked lost in the seventies, and the distant foothills were barely visible through the haze of shit in the air. Like a bowl, this valley held the pollution for all to share. I had a headache within an hour.

When I left town and began the drive to the scrubby foothills, I was sure I would find a bald kid with white eyes playing the banjo on a rooftop. I followed directions and turned up a road named after a lake that was supposed to be up there. I climbed a winding two-lane road that eventually ran along with a sweeping drop to a hundred feet below. I breathed easier when I reached the summit and ran into, sure enough, a lake created by an ancient concrete dam that blocked a gorge. It was a puddle by Northern California standards, but to these water-challenged yokels, it must have seemed like a veritable ocean.

Across the two lanes from the lake was a classic, old school' resort' – only by name. It was a shit hole if I ever saw one. I took a picture out of the pure need to prove I visited it. A cinderblock building housed a restaurant advertising the best fried catfish in the county. Terraces climbed the small hill behind the resort, crowded with ancient mobile homes. Some were funky fun, some rustic, but most looked like cheap rentals for crack addicts. I could only imagine what the inside of the resort building looked like, so I parked and went to take a look.

"My God," I whispered under my breath.

To the left were the fishing tackle shop and convenience store backed with dark paneling and dusty mounted fish. Glass cases displayed lures and weights and hooks while nets and fishing rods hung from the walls. A Hamm's beer sign hanging behind the register looked circa 1952, complete with the bear struggling to hold his balance while he caught a cartoon fish.

The restaurant offered a counter and half a dozen Formica top tables. I nodded to the waitress, a pretty young thing with a pierced nose, and grabbed a cold soda from the cooler. I paid at the register.

"Anything else?" An ancient Mexican man asked as he handed back my change.

"Am I close to the health ranch?"

"Few miles more. Follow the signs."

I thanked him and got back on the highway. The road forked, a carved wooden sign pointing into the hills that read Dr. Whitley's Health Ranch.

My GPS didn't seem to have any data for this tiny road. It kept telling me to return to the main highway, so I turned it off. A mile ahead, another sign pointed down a dirt road that wound back into a valley. The high valley offered more trees, and I made my way over the gravel road. After a dip into a sycamore-filled hollow, I splashed through a small stream, and the health ranch came to view. And it was a ranch – complete with a giant red barn, running white fences, and scattered outbuildings. I motored through the main gate and parked in the gravel lot. The only way in was through the door of what must have been the main farmhouse fifty years ago. Beyond the fences, people worked gardens, livestock roamed in fields, and small cottages gave the place the look of a summer camp. Opaque fencing and warnings that only medical personnel was allowed sequestered on the opposite side.

Yeah, I was here! David's voice said. I fingered his photo in my jacket pocket.

"Hello, can I help you?" A woman asked when I walked inside. She stood behind a counter, and the whole layout reminded me of a dentist's office.

"You must be January," I said.

"I am."

"Robert Jacobi." I offered my right hand while keeping my left in my pocket. "We spoke about a man I was trying to track down. You sent me his picture."

"Yes, well, hello. Did you get that sorted out? I was sorry to hear that he passed away."

"Well, I'm still trying to wrap up some loose ends. We're trying to track his movements for the family."

"Was the photo I sent of him after all?"

"We're still not sure. That's why I'm here. I was hoping there might be somebody else that may have seen him who could give me some insight."

"That was what, two months ago?" January looked in her files. "Yes, about two months ago. Here he is."

She handed me the Polaroid, and I placed my picture next to it. I found they didn't look as similar as I first thought.

"Is there anybody else who might remember?"

"Maybe the other staff members. We can't bother the visitors."

"Can we ask the staff?"

"Just a moment." January disappeared behind the opaque glass walls and returned with a thin man with hollow eyes and curly red hair.

"Henry, this is Mr. Jacobi. He's a private investigator."

I could understand why she thought I was a P.I., so I left it at that. "I was hoping you could tell me if you remember this man."

Henry looked at both photos. "He does look familiar. He would have had no I.D. Without a name, it's hard to tell. We get so many through here."

"What about the doctor? Would he remember?"

"No," Henry said. "Dr. W. only sees the people who are here for treatment. This man was a pilgrim, so the doctor would never have met him."

"He may have had a bandaged hand or a wound on his arm," I said. "If that helps."

"Oh, that wouldn't help," Henry said and handed back the photos. "So many who come here show up wounded and bloody. It's the nature of many who come to us. We offer care and shelter. They mend and get well. I'm sorry, he could be anybody."

"Thanks anyway." I handed the Polaroid back and slipped David into my pocket. I sensed no deception in Henry. They were all the same to him, lost sheep that needed shelter.

"I'm sorry we weren't more help," January said.

"Thanks for your time."

Back in the truck, I sat and watched the activity around the farm. People Lush tilled lush gardens while others carried whatever burden they were assigned. Everything went on behind a six-foot-high chain link topped with razor wire.

Maybe it wasn't me, David said. Perhaps I went someplace else.

The drive back took less time than the drive in, or so it seemed. The long winding road went by in a few minutes, and I stopped to take more pictures of the lake. In no time, I was back in the smoggy flats. My phone showed a missed call from Gina.

I called back. "Hey, babe."

"Well, hello, traveling man. How is everything?"

"It's been an adventure," I told her about exploring the San Diego County backwoods. I described the resort and the surrounding country.

"Are you taking pictures?" Gina asked.

"Just with my phone."

"Can't wait to see them. Please be careful. I miss you."

"We sound like a couple of teenagers," I said. "Let's talk about sex, so I feel like myself."

"Just wait until you get home," she said. "I'll fuck you silly."

"Thanks, baby," I said. "Now go make some cupcakes."

"And you come home soon."

"Tomorrow," I promised. "Gotta' go, I have Carl calling through."

I clicked a button.

"Hey Bobby," he said. "Any luck?"

"None at all."

"Well, we got a hit. Records show he called that bee sting guy in Ranchita seven times. Bank records show a one-time charge to their joint account for a hundred dollars one month before he disappeared. I Googled the address, and it's not too far. You could easily get there and back and still have time to catch your flight home."

"Ranchita? It sounds like someplace the Manson family would've holed up."

"It ain't much. Are you being good? That's your sponsor asking."

"Dry and honest." So far, it was true. "Call you later."

"Here's the address. We're not sure about the Salton Sea connection. I'll call you if that's a go."

"I'll wait in desperate anticipation."

I tapped it into the GPS, and the woman's voice started leading me down through a series of roads. I went past a local high school, the turnoff to the San

Diego Safari Park, back onto Interstate 15, and headed north away from Escondido.

The now mildly irritating navigation voice drew me off the freeway and out a winding highway that passed abandoned nurseries and towering Indian casinos that sat like hulking stone cathedrals. I took a picture of one for posterity. Then I was on a lonely desert highway toward the small town of Ranchita where a reclusive bee sting therapist guy called home.

I kept myself occupied by singing along with a local classic rock station. I ate crap, drank one diet soda after another, and began to feel disconnected from my real life. I imagined this state of funk is what long haul truckers must endure, only worse. No wonder they drank and used pills to jack themselves up to cover as many empty miles as they could.

The high desert is a clusterfuck of rolling scrubby hills, piles of rocks, and deep ravines where the little water in the region settles and blossoms with oak and sycamore trees. Driving through the ridgelines and squinting into the sun, I gawked at small farms and odd lone homes nestled back into groves of sad palm trees. There was nothing here that even remotely attracted me; a yearning for the bayside splendor gripped my heart. Oh, so poetic, but if my prose is the only thing between this desolate shit hole and me, then I'd wax poetic.

I drove through corner burgs that looked like lost old women and climbed into the scraggly foothills. Finally, I came to the small burg of Ranchita. It was barely a town, more like a smattering of buildings that included a feed store, a couple of Mexican restaurants with questionable fare, and a sight that made me pull over and stop. In front of a small market, I stared at a twelve-foot tall, snow white Yeti. The thing was as bold and tall and static as, well, a statue. Its head was slightly bent down, and its enormous hands hung at its side. The beast's face and fingers were as pink as a shaved pig. The expression was one of near contempt. I imagined the monster to be shocked that it was standing on a block of fake ice in the middle of triple-digit heat.

"Jesus," I said. I took a picture and shook my head. A soda and some beef jerky sounded good, so I locked the truck and entered the small market. I was met with a maze of freestanding racks that offered just about anything a soul could want. Everything from nail clippers to condoms was presented on pegboard.

"Hello," a voice said.

I found the cashier back in a corner. She looked like a wrinkled leather bag with eyes, but her voice sounded like she was fifteen.

"Hi."

I pulled a diet Coke from the cooler then looked around.

"Excuse me," I said, "where's the beef jerky?"

"Ah, don't have any."

"You don't carry beef jerky?" I was as shocked at that as when I had found the snow monster in the parking lot.

"Owner's a vegan, won't sell anything with meat in it."

"But you sell soup," I pointed out.

"All vegetable. We sell milk 'cause kids need it, but nothing with meat."

"Just the soda then."

She rang me up, took my two bucks, and counted back my change.

"Thanks," I said. "I have a question. What's with the Yeti?"

"Come again?"

"The snow monster outside. What's that all about?"

"I don't have a clue. I just moved here and got the job. I know about the vegan thing 'cause the owner told me when she hired me. I didn't think to ask about the statue."

I thought this whole scenario was a bit surreal when she adjusted her glasses and said. "You know, you look a lot like my second husband. He was a big bastard like you, mean as a snake and drunk as a skunk most the time."

"I'm flattered," I said with a chuckle and headed for the door.

"Come again."

"I certainly hope not," I shot back.

She cackled like an old witch.

Ranchita was a strange place. I passed more buildings and more small farms until my navigation told me to take a right. A long row of rusted mailboxes barely clung to a weathered four-by-six rail, held up by three metal pipes set in concrete. I turned onto the dirt road and carefully descended into a valley of sagging homes, distressed single-wide trailers, and cars on blocks.

The GPS became confused again, and I switched her off. At the very bottom of the winding, rutted dirt road, I found the address. To say it was a shack was being generous. Two broken down cars languished in the front yard. A chained Pit Bull raised its head and eyeballed me from the porch. The flight of wooden steps looked too rotten to support me, and bed sheets were stretched over the windows. The dog barked, and I squinted at the house. Nobody looked home. I could see the square white hives and bees circling the boxes like lazy helicopters behind the house. A small hand-painted sign advertised honey and medicinals.

The dog barked louder, and I gave him a wide path. His teeth were the color of old mustard, and his muzzle was as gray as Santa's beard. He might be old, but I got the feeling he would be happy to take my throat out for the sake of protecting his farm. Flyers jutted from an old box nailed to the porch railing. I pulled one out. It was a price list for the treatments and jarred honey. The dog snarled at me.

"Easy boy," I said, and that pissed him off more.

"Help you?"

I spun around to face a tall, gaunt man dressed in dusty white clothes with a netted hat over his head. He wore thick gloves. "You scared the shit out of me," I said.

"Didn't mean to. I was tending the hives across the road. Can I help you?"

"God, I hope so."

He pulled off his gloves, and I could see his fingers were scarred and scabbed. He and his hands looked like they had lived a hard life. The dog whimpered, and he stroked its back.

"What can I do for you?"

"The medicinals?"

He removed his netted hat. He could have been the scarecrow from the Wizard of Oz with a weak chin and giant nose. But his eyes had a simple wisdom in them. "You're not from the authorities? You don't have that look."

"Robert Jacobi, insurance." I extended my hand, and he gave me a firm shake. His palms felt like rough cowhide.

"Henry Reed. Insurance doesn't cover my medicinals, I'm afraid."

"I know. I'm here because I'm trying to find out if one of our clients might have come to see you. Could you look at his picture and tell me if you treated this man?"

"When about would he have come here?" Reed asked with the same deliberateness as if he was defusing a bomb.

"Sometime in the last three months. He had cancer."

"Lemme' take a look."

Reed stared at the photo, his eyes steady while the light wind stirred his gray-blonde hair. This exaggerated the scarecrow image. I imagined him on a wooden cross in a cornfield, like the crucified savior of the frightened and dying.

"Couldn't say," Reed said.

"You don't recognize him?"

"If it was more than three months ago, I'd have to say no."

"Why three months?"

"Desert Storm," he said cryptically.

"Meaning?"

"Operation Desert Storm. I remember the war, but I don't remember what happened there. There's a whole lot of black after that. The doctors say I have Post Traumatic Stress Syndrome. My mind's way of keeping me sane is to not remember anything after about three months. I keep journals, but I don't keep records on my clients. If he was here three months ago, he's in the blackness."

"I've never heard of anything like that."

"Neither have the doctors." Reed rubbed the dog and stared at the photo. "No, sorry." He handed it back.

"How do you keep bees and do what you do?"

"I do that every day," he said. "If I don't do something for three months, then I don't know anymore."

"Well, this man paid you a hundred dollars about two and half months ago. Is that within your memory?"

"That's what I charge for a session with the bees. Lemme' see that picture again." He stared for a full minute, never blinking. "Could be. That's close to when I lose things. Maybe, but don't hold me to it." He nodded at my hook. "Lose that in the war?"

"No. A dog bit it off."

"They can do things like that." Reed reached behind his head, pulled a struggling bee from his tangled hair, and then crushed the dying bee under his thumb on the porch decking.

"Good thing you're not allergic," I said.

"Maybe I am. I wouldn't know if I haven't been stung in three months."

"So I guess you wouldn't know anything about the Yeti at the market."

He smiled wide. "I made it. Cast it in fiberglass up there in the barn."

"Sure about that?"

"I see it twice a week when I go to town. I still have the mold in the barn."

"Why a Yeti?"

He shook his head. "That I can't remember."

"Like David Franklin."

"Who?"

"Thanks for your time."

I drove the rutted dirt road back to the main highway and was happy when I had smooth asphalt beneath my tires again. I felt itchy from the heat while I drove back toward San Diego. So bee sting was a bust. My mind drove me crazy with the image of the abominable snowman and the scarecrow from Oz wandering through the desert together.

I looked at Reed's flyer sitting on my passenger seat and suspected I'd been duped. A quick search on my phone brought up nothing on PTSS amnesia. I suspected it was Reed's way of establishing plausible nondisclosure. No insurance company will continue coverage of any patient that breaks treatment protocol and pursues alternative medical attention. If he was full of shit, he was brilliant and played it well. I pulled off and called the number on the flyer.

"This is Reed."

"Hello Henry," I said with mock elation. "This is—"

"I know who this is."

"You sure?" I chided. "Maybe I've been gone for three months."

"You sound sarcastic. Careful there, I have trouble telling shit from Shinola."

"Then this is the Shinola," I said. "David Franklin was not under the care of a doctor, and he had not filed any claim because he had no insurance. I'm investigating a life insurance claim, not a health claim. I have to say, it's a great bit."

"I really have PTSS," he said. "The bees help keep me calm and focused."

"So did you see him?"

166

"Who?"

"David Franklin," I said, losing my patience. "The man in the photo I showed you."

"I think I might have. We might have talked. I don't think I could help him."

"Henry, did David come to see you or not?"

"Was he really sick? Like going to die soon sick?"

"When was he here? We can stop with the games."

"If he did and if that's the guy that came by it would have been a couple of months ago," Reed said.

"But you're not sure if it was him?"

"Who?"

"David Franklin," I said very slowly.

"I don't think I know him."

I thought I heard a tone of playful irony in his voice. "It's a great gag, Henry. Fools them all, doesn't it?"

"Never can tell." He hung up.

I had nothing. My phone rang. Carl.

"Yeah?"

"You heading back yet?"

"Just left Ranchita. Now am heading back."

"Well, turn around. They want you to see the guy at the Native American Center."

I pulled over to the side of the rural highway.

"The toxic lake?"

"Hey, that place used to be a popular vacation spot for lots of people."

"On purpose?" I asked.

"Hey, my dad took us when I was a kid. It used to be a very cool spot. Here's the address."

I jotted it down and then typed it into the GPS. The woman's voice said I had 104 miles and two hours to drive.

"There's no way I'll get there and make it back for my return flight."

"We changed it to tomorrow night," Carl said. "You just have to be back by 3:00 tomorrow afternoon."

"Lucky me. Okay, gotta' go."

I texted Gina and broke the news. Then I checked the time, and I realized I wouldn't make it to the Salton Sea before dark. The next big town was Borrego Springs. If there were a decent place to stay, I'd stop there. From what I'd heard about the toxic sea, there would be nothing but shit holes renting rooms.

I took the slowly rising highway back through Ranchita. I waved goodbye to the Yeti and chuckled when I passed an odd roadside house faced with what looked like dollhouses. After the Yeti and the bee string man, nothing would surprise me about this place. Once out of the small town, I climbed a series of scrubby foothills sided by rock outcroppings that resembled monsters and cathedrals. When the road reached a summit, I held my breath when I broke over the rise and stared across the vast horizon, stretching out to the Eastern horizon. Beneath a haze hanging over the great desert basin, the enormous salty inland lake's dull blue blot looked like a mirage.

Around a tight turn, I could see the road switchback down the mountains to the desert floor. Up ahead, a guardrail was the only protection from the sheer drop to the rocks hundreds of feet below. A quick movement caught my eye, and suddenly a large deer jumped from a shelf on the low cliff to my right. With no time to react, I could only watch as the animal gracefully hit the pavement, took a short step, then bounded across the highway. Then it disappeared into the brush.

"Holy shit," I said out loud.

I looked in my rearview mirror, but the road was empty. Had that just happened? My heart beat in my chest like a drum, and I was in a sweat. If I'd been going 5 miles per hour faster, that majestic animal would have landed directly in front of me or even on my hood. I imagined the twisted wreck of the Durango plummeting down the side of the mountain as a fiery ball of twisted metal. The shock caught up with me, and I pulled over at a turnout and parked until I calmed down.

"Holy shit."

I nearly screamed when my phone rang. Gina.

"Hey," I said.

"Hey back. I just got your text. Are you jogging? Why are you out of breath?"

I gave her the rundown. "So I'm just a little freaked out."

"More than that," she almost scolded me, "people die from hitting deer. You're lucky to be alive."

"I guess. Before this, the worst I'd endured was slowing down for a raccoon on the road. This little excursion of mine has been wrought with peril and mystery of all sorts."

Gina laughed. "Now you sound like a Sam Spade novel. All you have to do is call me' dame,' and you'll be Mike Hammer."

"It kind of feels like that."

"Well, I'm glad you're okay. Now please be careful driving down your mountain and get home as soon as you can."

"I promise."

After declarations of love, I hung up, took another deep breath. I made it down the twisting highway without another incident and rolled into Borrego Springs twenty minutes later. The sun threatened to disappear behind the blanched mountains, and the desert had taken on the hues and view of a Discovery Channel documentary. I had to admit it was beautiful. To the right of the stop sign, a gas station sat empty but opened, so I decided to gas up and ask about accommodations. Here in the great outdoors, gas prices were fifty cents a gallon more than in the city. I imagined the residents of this place didn't travel much. On the pump, a small handwritten card said to pay inside.

"Evening," the guy behind the counter said. His shirt was embroidered with the name 'Lester.'

"Hey, Lester. Give me twenty on #3." I handed him my card.

"Anything else?"

"Yeah. What're my hotel options in town?"

"Well, there are several motels to choose from. All about the same." Lester rocked his hand, indicating they were all a bit questionable. "Then there's the Lodge, but that's expensive. There's the old western town hotel and R.V Park, but that's like staying at Disneyland and kind of pricy."

"I wouldn't have thought there to be so many choices."

"Yeah. Oh, then there's 'The Palms.'"

"And?"

"It's a retro, historic place that a lot of people like. Great restaurant, lots of the town folk eat there when they want something nice. Built in the fifties, lots of Hollywood types used to vacation there."

"And that's not expensive?"

"Cheaper than the western town."

"How do I find this place?"

"Easy. Back through the intersection and take the road down about a mile and a half. It's on the left. You can't miss it. Great pool, too."

"Thanks," I said and went to pump my gas.

The sun was behind the hill, and the distant mountains glowed nearly purple. I could only think of how much Gina would love this place. I imagined there must be a raucous biker bar in town with a live band and cheap draft beer. For the sake of my emotional and physical sobriety, I decided not to find out.

Gas pumped, I pulled around and followed Lester's instructions. He was right. I couldn't miss it. A near billboard sign announced, 'The Palms,' and towering palm trees swayed in the darkening sky. Lighted from the ground, the trees looked almost ethereal, like an oasis with soft lights and what looked like an illuminated gallery. The second story rooms looked over a lighted Olympic sized pool. Gina would love it.

I locked the Durango and walked the cracked concrete steps to a pathway that meandered through desert plants and fenced gardens. The lighted gallery was just that, an art gallery displaying what looked like local artists. Canvases depicting desert sunsets and rock-strewn washes covered the walls. Most of it was quite good.

Double glass doors invited me into the rustic lobby, where a flight of stairs met me with walls displaying black and white photos of long-dead movie stars. The check-in desk was empty, but an old-fashioned desk bell waited. I happily tapped it, and the chime echoed through the high ceiling room. I half expected a little man with a pencil-thin mustache to welcome me in an old-fashioned suit.

"Hello," a voice called from the back. "Be right there."

"Not a problem."

The pretty woman dressed in jeans and an Indian print blouse smiled at me. "Welcome to The Palms. I'm Shelly. Checking in?"

I kept my hook hidden in my jacket pocket so as not to make her nervous. A guy like me, checking in with no luggage and a missing hand, could raise some eyebrows. "I need a room for the night. Any openings?"

"Several to choose from. We have our upstairs King rooms or poolside cabanas with wood-burning fireplaces."

After hearing the prices, I agreed on one of the King rooms. Lester was right; the midweek rates were very reasonable. I chose room 4 with a view of the pool. Shelly swiped my credit card and handed me a pool towel and a manila folder with my room key and a breakfast coupon.

"We serve dinner in our restaurant. Our sister restaurant is in town, and you can use the coupon there. Directions are on the back."

"Bed and breakfast, that's great," I said.

"Do you need help with your luggage?"

"No thanks," I said.

"Take the stairs and turn left down the balcony. You'll find number 4 halfway down."

"Thanks. Is it okay if I look around first?"

"Please," she said with a beaming smile.

Off the lobby was what I could best describe as a living room complete with overstuffed couches, a fireplace, and a baby grand piano. The décor could best be described as rustic desert, with a hint of old Hollywood. Expansive windows gave me a full view of the impressive pool and outdoor dining area. A pretty

hostess smiled at me from the entry of the restaurant –
The Crazy Coyote.

All I could think was I wished Gina were here.

"Good evening," she said.

"Evening. Busy tonight?"

"Not really. But the kitchen is open."

"Can I see a menu?"

The special jumped out at me. Charbroiled New
York steak. "I'll be down in twenty minutes."

My room was cozy with a traditional peeler log four-
post bed and wall-to-wall glass walls looking out over
the pool, the hotel grounds, and the desert beyond. From
there, I could make out the small community by the
lights. What looked like a business park paralleled the
main road, and homes peppered the surrounding areas.
Borrego Springs was bigger than I first thought.

Tied off drapes could be pulled to create privacy. An
old fashioned television sat on a small table in a corner,
and a basket filled with books sat in a curious posture by
the two overstuffed chairs. After dinner, I decided that
I'd go into town and buy some basics, like deodorant
and a cheap bathing suit for the pool. In the meantime, I
scrubbed myself and splashed water on my face. Then I
called Gina. I got her voicemail.

"Hey. I gotta' tell you; I'm in the coolest place.
Imagine Morocco meets Palm Springs. I wish you were
here. Call me when you get in."

Then I went down to dinner. Tracy, the hostess, lead
me to a nearly empty dining room. I kept my hook

hidden in my lap when I took my seat at the table by the window. I half expected a less than subdued theme with a name like The Crazy Coyote, but the eatery's décor was pure class. When my waitress approached, I smiled at her.

"Good evening," she said. "Welcome to the Coyote. I'm Jenny and will be your server tonight. Anything to drink?"

"Hello, Jenny. Diet Coke with a lot of ice. And I know what I want."

"Very good," she said with a genuine smile.

"The special, medium rare with a wedge salad and the baked potato."

"That was easy."

She swished away, and my phone rang. Gina.

"Hey there."

"Hey back," she said. "Morocco and Palm Springs? That sounds great. Tell me more."

"I'm in the restaurant and about to eat what is sure to be a great steak."

"So this place is pretty special."

"Oh babe, this place is over the top. The rooms are funky, with lodgepole poster beds and Native American prints on the walls. The views are spectacular, and the whole vibe is very cool. Movie stars used to stay here in the fifties. You should see the pool."

"I'm jealous."

"We'll come back together, I promise."

"Take some pictures and send them to me."

"Okay, but you know my old phone takes shitty pictures. But I'll do my best."

"When you get back, we're getting you a new phone."

Jenny came back with a basket of rolls and a wine carafe filled with Diet Coke. She balanced an ice-filled glass in her other hand and put it in front of me. Then she poured expertly and gave me a wink. I nodded and got back to Gina.

"Okay, I'll call you back in an hour."

"Oh, so it's like that," Gina joked.

"No. These rolls smell so fucking good, and I'm starving, and I only have one hand."

"Okay, I get it. Eat big boy, call me later?" Gina teased.

"I promise." I hung up and reached for a roll.

I had to use both hands, and the hook came out just as Jenny came back with my salad. Her eyebrows went up. I stopped with a yeasty roll in my hook and a knife full of butter in the other.

"Surprise," I said.

"It is, but not in a bad way," she said.

"Well, I guess now we know each other a little better."

"Okay, now I have a question. It's a bit awkward, and please don't take offense."

I smiled wide. "Lay it on me."

"Do you want me to cut the steak up for you? Or can you manage."

"That depends on how tender your steak is."

"Like butter."

"Then, no."

When the plate came, I only needed one hand, and the flavor was equal to the tenderness.

CHAPTER NINE

I woke in time for the sunrise over the desert and lay in bed as the horizon bloomed like a rose. Clouds streaked the sky like paint strokes and the dusty gray of the failing night sky drew back like a veil. Man, I was feeling good, and waxing so poetic surprised even me. But there I was. When the sun climbed above the hills, the desert floor looked like a watercolor painting. The soft sheets and deep mattress seduced me to stay in bed for another hour, but the idea of a dip in the Jacuzzi before breakfast was too inviting.

My prosthetic lay in a discarded attitude on the chair by the bed. There was only one problem; I had no trunks. After a quick look, I decided to get by with my boxers as long as nobody else came down. So I wrapped a towel around my waist and headed for the pool deck. It was deserted, but for me, so I relaxed about the boxers.

No steam rose from the pool surface, so I dipped a foot and drew back with a shock. The water felt like ice. I could imagine heating a pool of this size, twelve-foot deep in the deep end, must cost a fortune. But if it felt this frozen in the dead of summer, I could only imagine diving in during the winter. It made me shiver.

I prayed the Jacuzzi was a different matter. The vapor rising from the water gave me hope. Shaped vaguely like a silhouette of Mickey Mouse, I wondered if Walt Disney vacationed here and inspired the spa. I dropped my towel and stepped slowly into the hot tub. Man, it felt good. After a total dunk and a vigorous rub of my bald scalp, I put my head back and looked at the hotel. In the light of day, it still screamed old Hollywood charm, and I could imagine Fred and Ginger waltzing around the poolside.

When the hot pool lost its scald, and my brow began to sweat, I climbed from the swirling pool and quickly wrapped myself in the towel. Boxer shorts, I learned, were not the same as swim trunks. I pattered across the concrete pool deck and took a side stair to reach the upstairs. I decided to slog through the lobby in a soaked towel, and see-through undershorts was inappropriate. Back in my room, I squeezed the water from my shorts and used the clean, plastic trash can liner as a carrier. In this weather, they'd dry in an hour in the Dodge. My free breakfast coupon gave me the directions to their sister restaurant, so I checked out and took a quick phone picture of the hotel and pool for Gina. Then I drove slowly back into my own decade. Or so I thought.

Borrego Springs was like the hotel, lost in another time that looked like a marriage of the fifties and the seventies. Most businesses stood alone, but the center of town was made up of two malls facing each other from opposite sides of the broad street. Knick-knack shops, real estate offices, liquor stores, and clothing stores offered up services to nearly empty streets. I imagined weekends were busier for this town. The road eventually connected to a large roundabout strangely named Christmas Tree Circle. There wasn't a Pine tree to be found. To my left, I found the bar I imagined. 'Carlee's' was bolted in giant, scripted letters to the front of the building, and I couldn't help but smile. In the bad old days, it would have been my kind of place. On the right, I found the Red Ocotillo Café, where the breakfast was delicious.

After a great omelet and some strong coffee, I left a big tip and hit the road. My GPS instructed me to drive straight out of town and into the hot, breathtaking desert.

I have to say even a good thing gets old, and soon I was fed up with cactus and outcroppings of rocks. Maybe because I was used to blue and green, but it seemed the closer I got to the Salton Sea, the more lonely the landscape became. When I arrived in the actual town, I had to shake my head in disbelief. Before I left, I Googled the place and stared at old photos of families waterskiing, sunbathing, and enjoying the wonder of the vast salted body of water. Other images showed beaches covered with fish bones and shacks decorated with broken machinery and old hubcaps. I expected a bit of both. I was wrong. The place looked post-apocalyptic, and I half expected a gang of marauding mutants to go by in makeshift vehicles, the likes of the movie Mad Max. One corner shined above the desolate abandonment, a huge truck stop and convenience store that looked as out of place as me at a White House dinner.

"Jesus," I said and followed my GPS toward the clinic address.

After meandering through dirty streets and past boarded-up businesses, I came to the place. Somebody had done their best to paint feathers and Indian motifs on the façade, but it only added to the place's sad and abandoned look. Even the sign, scrawled with white paint on the large glass window, did nothing to invite me inside. Only a flickering neon OPEN sign gave me reason to think anyone was home. I parked and slowly approached the front door. The interior felt blessedly cool.

"Hello?" I called.

"Hello to you," came back.

A small man that looked as if carved from gnarled wood pulled back a Navaho print blanket and came out from the back room. His grey hair in a long braid, he wore traditional Native garments, had two hearing aids, and only three teeth. But his eyes, though sunken deep in his wrinkled face, looked alert and bright.

"Hello, I was hoping you could help me," I said.

"Most do, and I can help some. What ails you beside the missing arm? There's nothing I can do to help that."

I looked down and smiled at him. "Well, I hoped you could help me find a friend." I pulled the photo of David from my shirt pocket. "He's very sick, and his wife told me he might have come to see you. She is very worried about him."

"You are a terrible liar," he said with no expression. "But I will look at the photo."

"Actually, most of that was true," I defended.

"But not your intentions. Words mean nothing if the intent is deceptive."

He stared at the picture and picked at his dark chin with boney fingers. His nails looked like shale stone.

I said, "His phone records show he called you several times. I hoped you might remember him."

"I remember him. He was very sick and hoped I could help him. I could not. His spirit was too withered and his life flame almost cold."

"So when was that?"

"You are the police?" he asked.

"No, just helping to find him."

"But not because his wife is worried. You look for him because you want to prove he is alive, am I right?"

"Not really," I said. "I'm trying to prove if he is dead or not. If not, I have people that want to know."

The old man gave me a grimace of a smile, and his eyes became smaller in his face.

"Insurance," he said and handed me back the photo. Then he stood very still, just staring at me.

"So," I said, more to break the silence than anything. "This man was alive when he left here?"

"Yes."

"And when was that?"

"That's hard to say. One day is another here. Those that arrive call and then come. Most leave after treatment, and some call again to thank me. This man did not call me to thank me. My heart tells me his flame is cold and his soul is with the spirits."

"Can you give me a guess of when he was here?"

"No."

"I see. Can I ask what kind of treatments you offer here?"

"You can."

I smiled and nodded. "But you won't tell me."

"Do you need such treatments?"

I shook my head.

"Then knowing means nothing. To know means there is intention. Intention means there are hope and faith. Without hope and faith to know is only information, and that has no power."

"I see. Look, I came a long way to…"

"Did you recognize the omen?" he asked.

"Excuse me?"

"When she crossed your path, she was sending you a message that there were no answers for you here. You ignored her and came anyway."

"What?" I felt like I was the butt of some cosmic joke.

"You see with your eyes, and you hear with your ears, but there is no listening in your heart. You are on a path, and you are so focused on the destination you do not see the ferns growing along the trail."

"Well, I guess we're done here," I said. "Thank you for your time."

"Time is an illusion. There is no time. We have now, and now is always. When we die is the same day as when we are born. What we do with the day that is our life is up to us to have love and faith."

"Okay."

"By the way, may I ask how you lost that? I sense violence," he said. "I was bitten by a rattlesnake and by the time they got me to the hospital they couldn't save the arm."

"I see," he said.

Then he smiled wide, made a gesture of finality, and went back where he came from. The blanket dropped back into the doorway, and he left me standing in the shabby lobby.

"Thank you," I called out.

"You are welcome," he called back.

The best way to put it I was freaked out. I'd put this in the same basket with Karen Carlson and try and forget about the shadows I began to feel might lurk just outside my peripheral vision.

Wait, I rationalized, the old man never said the word deer. He didn't tell me it crossed the road. He could be guessing or using some old Indian image reference that he relies on to create trust in his mojo as a cancer healer. Or maybe, just maybe?

Not a chance, I thought and nearly ran from the building. When I looked back, I realized it must have been an old liquor or convenience store. It reminded me of the Speedy Mart I used to buy gum and pop from when I was a kid. For some reason, that gave me the creeps, as if this were a symbol of lost youth and where we were all headed.

I think I was here, David's voice whispered.

"Oh, I think you'd remember this place," I said.

When I tried to backtrack out of the cracked streets to the main road, I must have taken a wrong turn. I found myself stuck heading down what was once a grand four-lane road toward the water. I eventually came to a col-de-sac that perched next to what must have once been a yacht club with no way to turn around. Nothing stood on the bleak ground, but the view had once been spectacular. The water looked gray. Not the – cloudy day at the beach gray, but like – this water is so full of chemicals nothing can live in it – gray.

"Might as well take a look." I climbed out of the rig.

Before I left home, I read that The Salton Sea was formed in 1905 when massive flooding caused the Colorado River to break through an irrigation canal. The water flowed freely into the Salton Basin for 18 months. Since then, the Sea's existence has been maintained primarily by agricultural return flows from the Imperial, Coachella, and Mexicali Valleys. The salt in the water came from the natural alkali in the soil. Then somebody had the idea of stocking ocean fish in the water to see if they could survive. Most didn't. Tilapia and Corvina thrived, and the great, salty lake became a haven for sport fishing and boating. Then time caught up with this accidental oasis, and the runoff brought in agricultural pesticide and fertilizer contamination. The saline levels increased, and the oxygen levels disappeared. When the fish died, and the lake died, the people left. Most of them, anyway. So sad.

The dead palms and dusty soil looked forlorn, and the feeling of being in a dead place caused me to shiver. Seabirds gathered on the jetty, and the gravel shore was littered with broken glass and discarded trash. An occasional fish skeleton protruded from the dark soil, and the whole view looked haunted. Then the wind changed, and my nose was assaulted by a smell so foul and acrid my eyes watered. I turned my back and coughed.

"Holy fuck," I hissed.

A quick look around showed no garbage piles or dumps of any kind. No toxic barrels of sludge sat stacked along the shore. This burning stench came from the water itself. With my hand over my mouth and nose, I quickly returned to the Durango. There I cranked the air conditioner and cleared my head with deep breaths.

"That was fucking disgusting," I said to the pouring vents. "How can anybody still live here?"

With that thought tumbling in my brain, I put the Salton Sea on my list of places I never needed to visit again. Then I found my way out of the labyrinth of streets, returned to the highway, and began my slow and tedious drive back out of the desert. Borrego Springs looked like downtown Los Angeles compared to where I'd just been, and when I climbed from the desert floor, Ranchita felt like coming home. So I tipped an imaginary hat to the Yeti as I passed and began my slow drive back toward San Diego.

I could imagine I could see the Pacific Ocean in the distance. Wishful thinking. I hit a 'T,' and the navigation told me to turn right. A mile down the road, the truck began to pull to one side, and I heard the sickening sound of rubber hissing on the asphalt. The right front tire was going flat. Soon the tire became a flopping flap of deflated rubber, so I coasted to the side of the road and stopped.

Suddenly the temperature was that of the sun. Town, any town, seemed a thousand miles away. I can do many things with a hook for a hand, but managing a lug wrench is not one of them. I called the auto club.

Twenty minutes later – it felt like an hour – a tow truck pulled up. There was a disparaging contrast between the driver and the rig. He was rough, dirty, and unwashed while the tow truck gleamed. I gave him a wave with my good hand.

"Need a tow?"

"I most certainly do."

"Ain'tcha got a spare?"

"That's not the problem," I said and held up my hook. "And it's a rental."

He gave me a yellow-toothed smile. "Lemme' check it out. I'm Clive."

Thin and tan, Clive could have been a worn out thirty or a well preserved seventy. He reeked of cigarette smoke, and my guess was he never wore deodorant. Clive looked under the truck, put his hands behind the tire, and drew back with a hiss. A small pearl of blood stood out against his grimy palm.

"Let's see what we got here." He dropped to his shoulder and craned his neck to see behind the wheel. With a pair of pliers from his pocket, he reached back, struggled for a moment, and sat up with a jagged shard of metal in the jaws of the tool.

"That's a tire killer there."

"Is it fixable?"

He scratched his wrinkled forehead. "Nope. Gash as long as my dick in that sidewall. This rig has no spare. Fuckin' rental company. Gonna' hafta' tow ya' in."

I called the rental company to report my predicament. They promised to send out a tech and a new vehicle. Clive said nothing while he hooked up the truck. Fifteen minutes later, we pulled into a small garage and tire shop that matched the driver. The sparkling truck looked like a debutant at a hillbilly dance.

"You can wait in the shop 'til the company gets here."

From the look of the shop, I suspected there was no air-conditioned customer lounge. "Thanks, but I'll wait in the car."

"Suit yourself," Clive said.

The heat was too much, so I left the Durango, loosened my tie, and took refuge in the shade of the building. The mechanic's bay roll-up door stood open like the gaping maw of a forgotten tomb. Two sketchy looking human hemorrhoids sat inside like meth-addicted mummies. I gave them a nod, and they gave me suspicious glares.

After my tenure as a cop, I can spot certain types a mile away; the lurking creep, the staggering drunk, and the ever twitching, wide-eyed crystal head. I loved meth addicts because they would sell out their mother for a rock or two. These guys were dyed in the wool tweekers. Both wore dusty jeans and cowboy boots. One had on a white wife-beater tank top and the other an old heavy metal band shirt. Both looked too thin and too awake.

"Having some trouble?"

"Yeah."

I avoided eye contact. I sensed they were looking for some good-natured agitation to take the edge off their drug-induced boredom.

"Fucking bummer," heavy metal said. "Nice truck."

"Looks new," wife beater said.

I walked to the office and called Gina. "Hello, sweetie," I said with mock happiness.

"Good timing. I'm taking a break. Are you up to no good?"

"You could say that. The best way to put it is no good is up to me. The rental car got a flat. It has no spare, so I'm waiting for them to rescue me."

"Fuck," she said with a laugh. "You and your shitty luck."

"Oh well, I'll live."

She told me about her party, how she missed me and begged me to be careful.

"Love you too. Gotta go."

I lumbered back to the truck for a drink from my cooler when I saw the two tweekers leaning against the front fender. I wanted no trouble, but my guess was these guys weren't going to give me any choice about that. I pulled my hook from my jacket pocket. "Can I help you guys?"

They both took a look at the hook and glanced at one another. "That's fucked up," heavy metal said.

"You know what? You look familiar to me," beater said. "Where you from?"

"Nowhere." I held my ground.

"Oh yeah? I hear that sucks."

"What do you guys want?"

"Coupla' bucks. You look like you can afford it."

Both were five foot ten, maybe six foot, and weighed about 150, perhaps a bit more. They were high on crystal, so they could be dangerous, but I knew I could take them.

"Sorry guys, no cash. I'm paying for everything with a credit card."

"I think that's bullshit."

I said, "Why don't you and your buddy just go back to minding your own business?"

"Fuck you," wife beater said and rushed me. Stupid kid.

Metal-head followed. I dropped back, found my footing, and put my weight into the assault. They hit me and grappled like kids in a schoolyard. Most guys know shit about how to fight. Luckily I did. I kept the hook back and pushed forward with my balled fist. Metal-head slipped on the gravel and nearly fell while wife beater got a lucky shot that bounced off my right cheekbone. I felt the sting and the rage boiled in my bones.

"That's fucking enough!"

I kicked beater's feet out from under him, and he hit the dust with a yelp. Then I grabbed metal's shirt with my hook, heaved back, and nearly tore it off. He jumped back, caught his heel on a rock, and fell back with a sickly thud.

I grabbed beater by the hair and dragged him back to his feet. He reached out and caught hold of my jacket and tore my side pocket. Franklin's photo dropped to the dirt while I pushed the beater to the ground and put my foot on his chest. He gasped and grabbed my leg, shaking his head side to side. His cheek bled from a scrape.

"I'm going to stomp your face in if you don't stop struggling!"

Metal found his feet and shuffled backward several steps when the tow truck driver came out of the office. Beater touched his cheek and looked at his bloody palm.

Then his eyes grew wide, and I realized he was staring at the photo of David Franklin.

"Hey." His voice sounded like he'd seen a ghost. "I know that guy."

"What the hell are you talking about?" I dragged him to his feet. "How?"

Beater stepped back and dabbed at his cheek with his forearm. "He came in here." He looked at metal. "Hey, come look at this."

His buddy slowly walked back, giving me a hairy eyeball. "What the fuck?"

"Look at this guy," beater said. He pointed at the photo and showed it to the wary tweeker. "Isn't that that the crazy fucker who talked to us that day?"

"What the fuck is this about?" I growled.

"That guy," beater said, holding the photo toward me. "He came in here and asked if we knew how to get some fucker whacked. He didn't look exactly like that, though. He was skinnier."

"This man asked how to get somebody killed?"

"Yeah, wanted to know how and how much?"

"Did he say who he wanted killed?"

Beater shook his head. "He just asked. I told him to go fuck himself. Didn't I, didn't I tell him to go fuck himself?"

Metal nodded.

"When was this?" I asked.

"I'm not sure. Few weeks I guess."

"That ain't the guy," metal said.

"Yeah, it is," beater argued. "That's the guy."

"It was a different dude. That's not him."

"Wait," I said. "Look close. Is that him or not?"

"Yeah," beater said, and metal shook his head. "Fuck, you, it is too."

The argument was broken up when a black Chevy Yukon pulled up. The driver jumped out and walked toward me.

"Feds!" metal screamed, and the two tweeters ran off toward the trees.

"Wait," I yelled after them, but they were gone. Their drug-driven heads convinced them they were that important. All I could do was watch them go.

"Mr. Jacobi?"

"Yeah." I took off my jacket and assessed the damage.

"Bill Henderson, Enterprise Rentals. Were you hurt?"

"No, just some punks who gave me some trouble. I'm fine."

He apologized profusely, made a production out of his presentation of the premium vehicle and a coupon for a free upgrade the next time I rented from them. His colleague made quick work of replacing the tire. I collected my stuff from the truck and put everything in the Yukon. They shook my hand and left while Clive watched the whole ordeal with a curious eye.

"That was weird," he said when we were alone.

"Were you here when this man showed up and talked to those two idiots about a hired hit?"

"I was busy with a customer, but I saw a guy who looked kind of like that show up. He bought a drink and then started talking to Johnny and Timmy. They said he asked them about a hit, but I figured they were fucking with me or too high to know the difference."

"How can I find those guys?"

"Are you crazy? They think the feds are after them now. Those two will hide in a hole for a month."

"Fucking tweekers."

"You handled those two pretty good. You a Marine? We get a lot of retired Marines around here."

"No, I work for an insurance company."

"Bummer," Clive said like that was worse than driving a tow truck in hell. He posed for me in front of the garage, and I took his picture. He seemed to like that.

I still had nothing. Wife beater swore it was Franklin, but with metal's conflicting testimony, it wasn't conclusive. I figured Franklin struck out with the bee therapy, came here, and talked to these idiots out of desperation. Hiring somebody to kill you is not suicide if it looks like murder. Thus your claim would payout. Sick but true. Or David was never here, and it was all some idiotic case of mistaken identity.

I was in no hurry, so I drove back at my leisure. A stop at the casino offered me a restroom and some sodas. This place was like Vegas. Digital billboards advertised washed-up bands in concert, free lobster buffets, and claimed the loosest slots. Gambling makes me sick, so I easily ignored the siren song of a shared million dollars in the new poker tournament. I figured Indian casinos were the ultimate revenge of the Native Americans.

I arrived back at the harbor district and had a long, leisurely dinner in a waterfront fish place. The sun went down, and the lights came out, so I took a walk along the bay. San Diego is like a small San Francisco. It's eclectic and unthreatening, like a bayfront theme park. Seaport Village offers up dining, knickknacks, and shop fronts, so I bought some frozen yogurt and watched the tourists. It was so much like a smaller Fisherman's Wharf that I felt at home.

I tossed my cup in the trash and set my head on going home. I realized I was over Franklin. Maybe it was the bee sting man, the tweekers, or the cool night air – but I was done. I couldn't wait to get home and back to my life. Carl called.

"Hey, you checking up on me?"

"Actually, no. We got another money hit down south. Franklin's account showed a payment to a place in Yuma a week before he went missing."

"Arizona?"

"That's the one. I just talked with operations, and they want you to check it out."

"That's another state. How am I supposed to manage that?"

"It's a hundred miles from you, right over the border. You've got authorization, and we upgraded your ticket to open-ended. Spend the night and leave in the morning. You'll be back before nightfall and fly home."

"I thought we were done with this."

I certainly was.

"Just this last one. I promise."

"Yuma. Jesus H. Christ. Okay, I better call Gina."

I hung up and dialed her number.

"Yuma? What the hell, Bobby?"

"Just another day, then I'm home."

"I'm gonna call Carl and give him shit."

"That's my girl," I said sarcastically. "That'll make my life much easier."

"Just be careful."

"It's Arizona, Gina, not Afghanistan."

I checked into the Marriott, took a shower, and was asleep by ten. When the alarm went off, it felt like I'd just gone to bed.

*   *   *   *

I'm sure some people find Yuma Arizona beautiful because of its history and heritage, but I'm not one of them. It has nothing to offer a northerner like me. The weather predicted triple digits, so I dressed in light slacks and a T-shirt that showed my mechanical arm to the world. I rolled into Yuma after two hours of driving through the vast and empty desert.

What a shit hole. At the gas station an old station wagon with peeling imitation wood siding pulled to the opposite pump. A bearded curmudgeon climbed out and smiled at me. His right arm was gone, and he saluted me with an old-school monster of a prosthetic hook. I returned the salute.

"Vietnam," he said in a voice sounding choked with dust.

"Desert Storm," I said back.

Suddenly I realized that in this place I was, well, normal. Truly, the general population in Yuma was a collection of people who looked as if they had left somewhere else looking for something else.

Many were older and dressed like old hippies. Mind you San Francisco is full of them, but this variety had a ragged edge to them. After gassing up I punched in the address of the High Desert Health clinic and prepared myself for anything. Again I found myself driving on the edge of civilization. Ten miles into the desert I turned down a rutted once paved road that ended at a compound. The wall and gate surrounded what looked like an old motel with an intercom wired on a post. I pressed the call button.

"Yes?" The system was old, and the word ended with a hiss that sounded like a snake with a cold.

"Hello, I have an appointment to speak with you."

"I'm sorry, can you speak up?"

"I called yesterday," I yelled.

I got no answer, but the gate buzzed and rolled back. Cactus and scrub-lined the driveway. I drove slow as instructed by a sign. Dust, you know.

Several cars were parked in a gravel lot. I pulled alongside the line, climbed out of the SUV and was sweating by the time I knocked on the front door. A Mexican woman with a kind face opened the door and invited me in. It was cool inside, and I sighed with relief.

"You said you called? Are you from the insurance company in San Francisco? Because our legal counsel told us not to talk to you."

I hadn't come all this way to be turned back without any satisfaction. I put on a weak smile and lied.

"No, I'm not from an insurance company. I heard about your services from a friend who said he visited you."

"That was nice. When did he visit us?"

"About two months ago, I think. His name was David Franklin."

"Hmm," she said and typed on her keyboard. "That name doesn't sound familiar. Just a minute, let me call the doctor."

"Thank you."

"Excuse me, doctor," she said into the phone. "It's Maria. Did we have a patient in here about two months ago named David Franklin? I see. I didn't either. Okay, thanks."

"Doesn't sound promising," I said.

"I'm sorry, what was your name?"

"Brad Matheson," I said. "Maybe I have the wrong place. He was looking for help with pancreatic cancer. I have a picture. I carry it because he recently passed away."

"I'm so sorry," she said as I held out the photo. Maria stared at it for a full minute, her soft eyes filled with compassionate hope. "I don't know. He does look a little familiar, but I just don't know. We don't keep photos of our patients and we have to be careful because sometimes insurance people come looking to see if their clients are seeking alternative help. It can cause them to be canceled."

"I think that is so unfair," I said. "I'm going through that very thing with my prostate cancer."

"We get a lot of that here," she said and glanced down at my nether regions. "We have great success with our herbal irrigation techniques."

"That's good to hear," I said, and my phone twittered. "Excuse me."

It was Gina. Back outside I stood in the shade.

"Hi there," she chimed. "Are you in Yuma?"

"I am," I said with a laugh. "This place is hot as hell."

"Jesus, Bobby. I hope this isn't going to be part of your new job description."

"I know. I've seen some country, that's for sure. There's a lake out here and a fort so I'll take some pictures."

"Sounds like fun. I wish I could've come with you."

"Trust me baby, if we were going to plan a trip, Yuma is the last place we'd come."

"Get it outta' your system because after we're married I'll have you chained to the bed. Be good and come home."

I promised I would and stood in the hot shade. There was nothing here. Most likely David called and spoke with this place but never visited. Otherwise, Maria would have remembered. She had the heart of someone who carried other people's suffering with her like photos in an album.

I went back inside. "Thank you for the information. Do you have a card?"

"I'll give you a package." Maria handed me a folder of photocopied material.

I thanked her and waited as the gate opened up allowing me to wander across the desert. Back in town I was starved and asked a store clerk if he could point me to a good Mexican restaurant.

"Miguel's," he said and pointed down the street.

I sat in the air-conditioned dining room and ate chips with strangely sweet salsa. The waitress brought my combination plate. It looked and smelled delicious. She said nothing about my arm, didn't give it a second look.

I ate and was thankful this Franklin debacle was almost over. Two dead ends and the drug-spun lunacy of two very unreliable witnesses. I pulled David's photo out of my pocket and stared at it on the table. So what if you visited these places, you're dead now, right?

The waitress came around and refilled my water glass. She looked down at the picture and smiled wide. "I remember him."

"I'm sorry?"

"Yeah, I remember that guy. He said he was a reporter doing a story on alternative cancer techniques. Said he worked for a newspaper in San Diego."

"Did he mention his name?" I said.

"I don't think he told me his name. He left me a huge tip, though. I always remember the big tippers."

"His name is David," I said. "He's a friend of mine. He actually has cancer, and I am looking for him. His wife is worried sick, and his kids miss him. Did he say where he was going after here?"

"Yeah. He said he was going to talk to some place over the border that does microwave therapy, or some such shit. Oh, sorry about the mouth."

"No problem."

"Yeah, I think that was him. Maybe not," the waitress said and dropped my bill.

"Maybe not?"

"Well, it was a while ago. It looks like him."

"Thanks."

This was getting stupid.

See, Maybe I was here, David's voice whispered.

I slowly finished my meal, left her a big tip. I stopped at the fort to take a couple of pictures, and then I drove out to Lake Martinez and took some quick shots around the boat dock. A quick access of my files by phone brought up the very clinic she mentioned. David visited their website three weeks before going missing. San Luis, the town I needed to reach to cross over into Mexico, was twenty-five miles back toward San Diego. I'd take a look.

Thank you, David said.

I ignored him.

An hour later I found San Luis and the small town surprised me. Being on the border I had imagined a dusty one-minute stop with an American border patrol office and a guard shack headed into Mexico. Instead, I found a small but clean burg with paved streets, a small but classic governmental building and a school. Granted, the entire community was in about a ten square block cluster, but very nice. There were not many white faces, but this close to Mexico that was understandable.

I parked the truck at a curb and got out to document the small town with the camera. With each click, I got a small sense of dread, as if I was documenting David Franklin's death. This must be what true crime writers feel like when they collect references for their stories. Lou Drake, my favorite true crime writer, once said it was like walking a trail of bones and tears.

A small guard shack was bordered by fencing that I was sure ended a quarter mile out of town. From there barren and deadly terrain acted as a deterrent for illegal crossings. One of those red-and-white-striped mechanical arms was across the access. There no return and I realized this was a one-way journey.

A sign said all traffic into Mexico must first stop and check in at the county office. I rolled into the parking lot and took one of the ten empty spaces. A light wind blew, and the warm breeze helped dry my sweaty back.

Automatic doors slid back. Two uniformed men behind a glass-faced counter occupied the clean office. It looked bulletproof, like in city banks. One of the men smiled and asked me what he could do for me. His nametag said 'Wallis.'

"Everybody has to check in here before heading across the border?"

"Yes," he said. "First, what is your reason for entering Mexico?"

"Oh, I'm not going in. I'm trying to find a person that may have come through here. Would you have records of anybody that came through in the last month?"

"No, we're just here to hand out information and make sure anybody going down knows the risks."

"And it's one way."

"It is. You come back through Mexicali."

"And those risks you talked about. You mean drug cartels, severed heads, and people strung up under bridges. I've heard the stories."

"They are more than stories sir," he said gravely.

His partner spoke up. "Thousands of people have been killed and now kidnappings are very common. People need to know what they may be walking into down there."

"Do you know where this guy was going?" Wallis asked me.

"Del Raya," I said. "About twenty miles down."

"Del Raya is a war zone. Fourteen people died two weeks ago when masked men shot up an alternative cancer treatment center. They killed everyone."

"Any Americans?" I asked.

"No, thank God."

"Thank you, that's all I need to know."

I didn't die there, David said.

I scratched Del Raya off my list and pushed north back to the main highway. A few miles up two National Guard Humvees passed me heading to San Luis. Besides the violent horror show between the cartels and the rampant illegal immigration, I also heard about the National Guard's impotent presence along the border. It was a show of mock force. The soldiers had unloaded weapons and orders to not engage unless under direct attack. Contrary to the left-wing sway of the city of San Francisco, I have my own ideas about immigration and defending our land. My radical ideals have granted me many lectures from my more liberal friends. I usually just nod and let them talk.

Carl called. "Any luck?"

"No, they wouldn't talk to an insurance guy, so I had to pretend to be a friend looking for treatment. Now I'm admiring the vast and majestic vistas of the American desert."

"Then you're done. Head on home."

I set the cruise control and pointed myself west. This was a snipe hunt if I'd ever seen one. Nobody could positively identify David and there were no definitive records of his being anywhere. My cop brain surrendered to defeat.

"Sorry David," I said out loud. "You're just a ghost. You can stop whispering in my ear. This is a lost cause."

Don't give up. Look at your notes. What haven't we tried?

I took his photo out of my pocket, now bent and scratched from travel and tumble. "Sorry buddy. We've tried everything and we're at a dead end."

Please!

"Claire put your thumb in an urn, the kids have gone into therapy and your family has the money. The bosses have forgotten you and when I get back they'll assign me another case. You are in the drawer."

What about everything we've found?

"What we have here is what is known as an orgy of circumstantial evidence. You're dead, it's done and I'm going home."

Please...

"No, I've put too much on the line to keep doing this. I'm going home."

David went silent. I put on a country western station and hummed along while the air conditioning kept me cool. My heart felt light. I folded David's photo in half and tossed it on the passenger seat. Two hours later I dropped the rental off at the yard and jumped on the shuttle back to the terminal. After another pat down I bought a Diet Coke and waited. It was an uneventful flight home. Gina picked me up at the curb at SFO.

"Well, hello there young man," she said with a teasing voice. "Need a ride?"

"My mother told me never to take rides from strangers."

"But I need help finding my puppy and I have candy."

I slipped into the passenger seat and she gave me a fierce kiss. "I missed you."

"Let's go home."

"That sounds great."

*   *   *   *

The following day I sat at my desk and kept my decisive attitude that Franklin was dead, and so was the case. My hand flew over the keyboard while I finished the brief report. Then I printed out two copies – one for me and one for Carl. I left him a message to meet me in the lobby ten minutes before the meeting. While I rubbed my temple, it dawned on me I had not taken any vacation time in a year and a half, and the idea of taking Gina to someplace warm with clear blue water sounded like a great idea. I knew how to convince her. All I had to do was remind her how great she looked in a bikini.

"Hey big guy," Janice called through.

"Yeah?"

"I got Claire Franklin on line two asking for you."

"They just agreed to give her half a million bucks. She doesn't know that yet, but she will by the end of the day. What more does she want?"

"Ask her yourself."

I scratched my chin with my hook. Watch yourself, I warned myself. "This is Robert Jacobi."

"Hello Mr. Jacobi. It's Claire Franklin." Her voice sounded agitated.

"Yes."

"I want to apologize for missing our appointment."

"That's perfectly understandable considering the recent developments. Once lawyers are involved, my job is finished. Besides, I was out of town."

"Something has happened."

"Mrs. Franklin, with the current state of your husband's case, it isn't appropriate for us to speak. If you have questions, they should come through your lawyer."

"So they are settling?"

"That is not my question to answer. That decision comes from another department. I know your case is in final evaluation, and we'll contact your attorney with the decision once it's made." I hoped she got the hint.

"Can I talk to you about something else?"

"You can stop worrying about what happened before. I know you're sorry. Ask anybody, it's hard to hurt my feelings."

"It's not about that," she whispered.

"What can I do for you that your lawyer can't answer?"

"I had to hire the lawyer. I had to make sure the policy settled," she said so softly I could barely hear her. "I don't have much time. I didn't know who else to call."

"I'm confused." But that was a lie. I knew what this was about. She'd had a visit from Rizzo the rat. "Why can't your lawyer handle this for you?"

"Oh my God." Her voice sounded full of fear. Here it comes, I thought. "I have to tell somebody. I'm so afraid."

I stopped her. "Take down this number and call me back. Give me five minutes."

"Okay."

I left the office and headed for the elevator.

"Where are you going?" Janice said as I passed by.

"I have an audience with the Pope."

"What's her name?" Janice yelled.

I walked into the San Francisco sunshine and found a private place. Five minutes on the dot, she called back.

"Jacobi," I said.

Claire's voice was desperate. "I'm sorry. I need help and didn't know who else to call."

"Okay, listen," I said. "Whatever you feel you need to tell me, I have to warn you if I am put in a conflict regarding your claim, I would have to take the side of the company."

"It's not about that."

I closed my eyes. "Explain this so I can understand what we're talking about. Be as clear as you can, and I will stop you if we are drifting into dangerous territory."

"I got a call yesterday." I swallowed hard. "A woman said she was calling about a loan David took out and failed to pay back. I asked her what company she was with, and she said it was a private loan for ten thousand dollars. She said David promised to pay it back, and they never saw him again."

"It's probably a scam." I knew it wasn't. "Your husband's story has been in the news, and this is somebody that got your information and suspects you're getting a settlement. They're trying to scare you into paying out some money. Was there anything distinctive or official about this person?"

Her voice grew shakier. "She sounded foreign."

"What would you guess the accent was?"

"It sounded like Russian."

"Did she call on your landline or your cell?"

"The home phone."

"Did she ask where you live?"

"Yes."

"What did you say?"

"I said I knew nothing about it and hung up. When she called back, I didn't answer." Then Claire started to cry.

I thought of Rizzo and how the trouble started when I mentioned the name, David. They put the media coverage with a face, and my question eliminated any doubt they had.

"Have they called back?"

"Yes, this morning. This time, it was a man."

I touched the cold curve of my hook to my cheek. "What did he sound like?"

"Kind of a high voice, but it sounded strained like he had trouble talking. Like he was talking with his teeth clenched."

I must have broken his jaw. "Well, I think it still may be a scam. I'd take this up with your lawyer and tell the police. You'd be surprised how many old friends and scammers come out of the woodwork when you come into some money."

"But I haven't received any money," she said.

"Trust me," I said against my better judgment. "You will."

"He told me not to call the police."

"What else did he say?" I asked and wished I hadn't.

"He said he knew where my kids went to school, and then he gave me my address."

"Why call me?"

"Because you're the only person I've ever met who looks like he knows how to handle situations like this."

"Meaning what exactly?"

"You look, well, tough," she whispered.

I was in a quandary. If I left her with pat answers and these assholes came calling with baseball bats, I'd have to live with that for the rest of my life. I felt an

210

obligation to give her some gritty reality and some solutions as well.

"Just in case this is a real threat, do you have someplace you can go for a day or two?"

"Am I in danger?"

"I don't know," I said. "You never know with these situations. I'll look into this for you, and in the meantime, make sure you're locked in and safe. Don't let anybody in and call the police if anybody comes knocking. I'll call you later today."

"Then what?" She sounded like she was falling apart.

"If I find out this is credible, you'll want to pack up your kids and go someplace out of the city. Make sure you only use a cell phone to call anybody. What's your number?"

I jotted it down and tucked it in my pocket.

"I'm sorry to involve you in this," she said.

"I'll call you in a few hours."

"Thank you, I…"

I killed the line. My scalp tingled, and I ran my hand through my goatee. The high strained voice sounded like Rizzo. The woman calling was a soft touch tactic. If that didn't work, they got nasty. My visit tipped them off. Man, did I screw the pooch. Now I had a responsibility. Damn, my fucking need to be right!

Carl called. "Hey Bobby, you wanted to meet before going upstairs?"

"Just to look over the report."

"You sound stressed. You haven't changed your mind about this, have you?"

"No. It's just feeling the finality of this case. I know I got too personally involved in this one."

Carl laughed. "Just a little bit. See you downstairs."

In the elevator, I thought of the mess this became and how this was far from over. Carl sat in one of the lobby couches by the executive elevator. He waved me over.

"I take it back. You looked more stressed than you sound."

"I'll get over it. Here's the report."

I sat while he read through it. "Looks great. Now let's go see the suits."

We took the elevator to the executive floor, and I followed Carl into the conference room. Again I thought of Claire Franklin running scared and felt my neck muscles tighten. My head began to pound. I needed to calm down, or I'd lose it if Henderson fucked with me. We took our seats, and I thumbed the cover of my report. Carl nudged me under the table and gave me a questioning look.

"You look sick. You up for this?"

"Yeah. I'll get through this, and then I think I'm going to take some time off."

"I insist," he said.

"Well, let's get this shindig underway," Henderson said. "Talk to me about Franklin. The wife has hired a lawyer, I'm told."

Carl opened his folder. "Yes."

"So what's the verdict?"

"After examining the facts, we're convinced that David Franklin was the victim of foul play and is now deceased," Carl said. "There is no body, but we have his thumb and circumstantial evidence that he was the victim of torture. We believe it was a case of mistaken identity, and his body will never be found."

"Do you concur?" Henderson asked me.

"I do."

I sensed that Carl relaxed.

"So, death in absentia," Henderson said. "How long until we can get a death certificate?"

"I spoke with the coroner's office this morning," Carl said. "They have all the evidence, and they agree that under the circumstances, we can safely say that David Franklin, if not dead upon his alleged kidnapping, would be and is dead now from foul play or his advanced stage cancer. We should have a certificate by the end of the week."

"Works for me," Henderson said. "And it's only five hundred K, so nothing to lose sleep over. You're in agreement, Jacobi?"

"Yes, and I apologize for interrupting the meeting, but I'm feeling like I'm coming down with something. I don't want to infect everybody in the room. I need to excuse myself."

Henderson gave me a limp-wristed wave. "By all means."

"Thank you."

"I'll call you later," Carl whispered.

Claire Franklin called me an hour later to tell me she was safe at a friend's house out of the city. I called Joe in Oakland and asked if he had found anything about the Tavern Russians.

"Yeah, badass shit," he said.

"I learned that personally, remember?"

"Bull's Eye on Hardy Street, right?"

"Yeah."

"OPD patrol responded to a 'shots fired' call on that one. The owner said it must have been a mistake. That was you." It was not a question.

"I didn't shoot the gun. Rizzo The Rat did."

"Who?"

"Pock marked guy in an expensive suit."

"Yuri Bolteketch," Joe said. "Small time. Makes loans and does some work in prostitution and drugs."

"You know that for a fact, and he's still on the street?" I said. "What has happened to law enforcement?"

Joe laughed. "Yeah, I know. But I also know Elvis is alive, but nobody will listen. So what happens now?"

"My guess is Franklin took the money and bolted. They were looking for him, and I showed up, mentioning his name. Yuri contacted Claire. She's out of town now until Bayside settles the claim."

"So it's Claire now?" Joe chided. "Mrs. Franklin is Claire? Won't Gina kill you and then go after her?"

"You're as bad as Janice. Once she has the cash, I'll advise her to pay off the scumbag and get on with her life."

"Good plan. So Franklin is officially dead?"

"As far as we're confirmed."

Carl called, and I said the paperwork was filed, my day was done, and I was taking my two weeks.

"I dropped the line to HR an hour ago. I'm taking Gina to Hawaii. She doesn't know it yet, but I am. I'll take two sick days, go through the motions until next week and then boogie out of town."

"You'll last three days and be Jonesing for the action."

"Nope, I'm going to forget about this place for fourteen days."

"I went to space camp on my last vacation," Carl said. "I resent your fabulous life."

"Talk to your sponsor," I said, and we agreed to connect at a meeting later.

CHAPTER TEN

I paced my place like a bear in the zoo until Gina's day ended. Someplace warm and away from home was what I needed. Getting away would do us both good. I took her to Bay View Bistro. As usual, Wally spoiled us rotten. While waiting for dessert, I took Gina's hand.

"I want to talk to you about something."

Her eyes widened. "Oh shit."

"What?"

"Nothing. Sorry. Go on, what did you want to ask me?"

"Wait, what was that all about?"

"Ignore me, ask me what you wanted to ask me."

I shook off the shock of her reaction and opened my mouth. "This last case has been brutal, and I know you've been working like crazy, so I want to do something special. Let's take a week and go to Hawaii."

Her face held a frozen smile, but her eyes betrayed her emotions. At that moment, I realized she thought I was going to ask her to marry me. My face must have betrayed me because she suddenly looked down.

"Yeah," she said, "I would love that."

"Okay, great. I'll look into it, and –"

"Babe, look, I can't go away for a full week," she interrupted. "Business is nuts, and I just can't do it. I'm sorry, baby."

"I understand."

Silence haunted the space between us. I felt like there was a shift. Gina and I have always fought – passionately, emotionally, and ferociously. But we always stayed honest, dedicated, and forgiving. As former alkies, we have to have no secrets, but this misunderstanding suddenly divided us.

"Maybe we can take a long weekend. Go to Catalina and stay in a bungalow and relax for a couple of days."

Her offer felt forced, and I knew she was hoping to bridge the gap we both felt. I tried to fix it. "Gina, I want to say something. I know this went fucking sideways somehow. I'm sorry if I—"

She put a hand to my mouth. "This is my shit. It's been a wonderful night. The food was great and your wanting to take me away is so sweet. Don't worry; I'm just being a girl. We'll go to Catalina this weekend, and it'll be fun."

"Great," I said with a smile.

Dessert came, and we shared Wally's famous chocolate pie. With each bite, I tasted the bitter, dark chocolate and the sweet caramel topping and felt the same mixture in my heart. She was wrong; this was my shit. I should have known Gina was hoping I'd make an honest woman out of her. Over the next few days, I went to meetings and spent extra hours down at the meeting hall. Soon I found the insane blather more than I could stand.

Since Claire's call, David Franklin had begun gnawing at me again like a rat in a wall. His voice whispered and nudged at me until I wanted an exorcist to remove him from my psyche. This time off was suddenly a nightmare. Plans were made, and I booked the bungalow. Gina and I smiled at each other, but our lovemaking felt different. She worked long hours to justify the time away. Friday morning rolled around, and I picked her up from her place. I put her bag in the back of the truck.

"I so need this weekend. I'm so excited," Gina said.

"Me too. It'll take about half the day to get to San Pedro and an hour to the island."

"That will give us plenty of time," she said. "Just one rule on this trip."

"What's that?"

"No talking about work. Either of us."

The next four hours felt like eight. Our moods lightened on the jet boat ride to the island. Flying fish surprised the passengers, and distant whale spouts made Gina act like she was sixteen. We hugged and kissed, and I nearly cried to feel the old us come back.

"God, it's beautiful," Gina whispered when we cruised into the harbor. "You know, I've never been here sober."

"Me either."

With no cars on the island, we climbed onto a golf cart shuttle that took us to our bungalow. After we checked in, Gina threw herself at me, and we lost ourselves in each other. In the passion, I felt forgiven for not asking the question she wanted. Afterward, we walked to town, ate ice cream, and browsed a gift shop. While Gina looked over boxes covered with shells and tried on seahorse necklaces, I struggled with my feelings.

I loved Gina, something I was sure I'd never find again. But was that our destiny? My head hurt, but my face showed only happiness for being away with her.

"What do you think of these?" Gina tossed her head to show off pearl earrings. I hadn't noticed her pick them up.

"They're great. I'm buying them for you."

"I'd accept nothing less."

Our weekend went on the same way. When it ended, I was no closer to a decision on what to do. This was one I wanted to talk about with Carl. On the boat back, we hit rough water, and many of the passengers felt sick. Gina braved it, but by the time we reached our harbor, she was green.

"Let's get something to drink and let our stomachs settle," I suggested.

After some soda and crackers, Gina's color returned. A walk around the harbor made her right, and we began the four-hour drive home. We drove up Highway One, and I concentrated on the winding road. Gina was quiet, and I sensed the tension from the restaurant invade the truck.

Gina finally broke the silence. "Baby."

"Yes, sweetie?"

"I've been thinking," she said.

That meant the unspoken words would finally be said. I swallowed hard and took a breath. "Oh yeah, about what?"

"Us."

"What about us?"

"About what we're doing. You know?"

"I thought we are doing is what we both agreed we wanted. Or am I wrong?"

"No, you're not wrong. But it's been, what, three years?"

"And?" My heart beat like a kid on crack with a bass drum.

Gina looked at her hands folded in her lap. "I just think we should talk about what we ultimately want."

"Baby, stop dancing around the issue. That night in a Wally's you thought I was going to ask you something. Tell me what's on your mind, or I'll drive this truck off this big scary cliff and kill us both."

"The truth?"

"Uh yeah."

"You know what I'm getting at," she said.

"No, I don't." Yes, I did. "What's up?"

"Just forget it." Gina looked out the window.

I saw an overlook and pull-off with the truck pointing out over the frothing sea. Pelicans drifted on updrafts and the kelp undulated with the seething swells.

"Okay," I demanded, "what the hell is going on?"

Gina bit her lower lip. "I said forget it."

"I know I'm saying this all wrong, but we've always told each other what the real deal is, and right now I'm lost. So, please don't play games with me. If you have something to say or something you want, I need you to tell me what it is."

She crossed her arms. "How romantic."

"Oh my God!" I got out of the truck and walked to the edge of the cliff. It dropped three hundred feet to the rocky beach. Did I think about jumping? Yeah, at that one single moment, I thought of the release I'd experience eating those rocks. The cold ocean could then pull me out to sea so the local sharks could have me for dinner.

Gina walked up behind me. "Bobby?"

"What?" I turned, and Gina stood hugging herself. Her hair moved with the wind, and I gave her an expression of pure masculine frustration.

She looked cold. "Why are you so mad?"

"You're kidding, right? If you have something to say, just say it. I'm thinking breakup, babies, you drank? I may know a lot of shit, but I'm not a psychic." I thought of Karen and shivered. "If you make me guess, I'll probably be wrong and piss you off."

"I guess I'm afraid to say it."

"Why?"

"I don't know." She actually pouted. I had never seen her this way.

"We're grown people. Just tell me…"

"I want to marry you!" she blurted.

I walked in a circle. "Are you sure this is what you really want? And don't say no because you're pissed. Put the anger and temporary hatred and embarrassment aside and tell me the truth. Do you want to marry me?"

"Yes," she said.

"Why?"

Gina lowered her voice. "Because I love you."

My last wedding flashed through my head, and I found it hard to catch my breath. "Okay, let's get married."

"Seriously?"

"Yeah, whatever you want. Just tell me when to be there."

Gina ran and hugged me, she hit me with a bone-snapping embrace, and I could only return it.

"So, was that a proposal?" I asked.

"Guess so," Gina said with a huff in my neck.

"Wasn't that my job?"

"We'd be dead of old age before you'd get around to it."

"We alkies sure know how to make everything dramatic and difficult, don't we?"

"Yes," Gina said and leaned back to look at my face. "Wouldn't have it any other way."

After that, Gina couldn't stop talking. She blathered on about wedding dresses and friends who recently tied the knot. She kept smiling at me and telling me how happy she was. I smiled and nodded, keeping my eyes on the road. We got home, and the first thing I did was call Carl about the engagement.

"Hey!" Carl screamed in my ear. "That's great. She'll make an honest man out of you. Congratulations."

"Thanks, I'm glad you're so happy. I'm still a little freaked out."

"Oh, let that shit go. You know the guys at the home group are going to want to throw a bachelor party. Women and song, no wine."

I laughed. "Knock yourself out."

"Gina's happy as shit, isn't she?"

"She is."

"So when did you propose?" Carl asked.

I told him the whole story. "So it was I jump off the cliff or say yes."

"Oh man, you crazy kids. What did you do about a ring? You gotta' have a ring."

"I called Johnny from the Monday night men's group. We're going over to his pawnshop tonight and pick one out. He says it's on him."

"Pawn shops and cliff jumping threats, and they will live happily ever after," Carl said. "Johnny's got some great stuff to choose from because of the economy, you know."

He did, and when we left, we had matching bands. I wanted to wear mine right away, and Gina said that was fine.

"It'll let the ragged hordes of divorcées know you are off the market," she said.

Over the next two days, Gina worked her shop while I imagined the next phase of my life. Within days the word got around to everyone. My A.A. friends smothered me with sloppy love and good wishes. But when Janice called, she was as mad as a hooker done with a broke John.

"You're getting married?"

"Well, thanks for being happy for me."

"I'm pissed that I had to hear about this from somebody else. Carl told me. I can't believe it."

"It's true. Jesus Janice, give me something good, or I'm hanging up."

"How about this, we'll be making a wire transfer into Claire Franklin's account tomorrow. She authorized us to pay off her tax debt and bring her mortgage current, so she'll be getting a lump sum of four hundred and sixty-eight thousand dollars. That should make her happy."

"I'm glad," I said.

"Does Gina know about the little tryst you had with Franklin's wife?"

"Be nice."

Janice gave him a snarky look. "Too hard to start new habits. It won't be the same, you know? You married? I'll have to watch myself, or she'll come in and kick my ass."

"Maybe."

"Congratulations, I guess."

"That means a lot to me, Jan."

So the settlement was in, and all the Franklin family's troubles were over, financially anyway. That meant I could expect a call soon. But I didn't hear a thing.

Gina and I talked about the wedding, and I wasted time. The problem with too much time on my hands is my brain gets busy. It's hard to explain, but you have this sense that everything has to have some concrete resolution when you're a detective.

Bad guys do bad shit, and we track them down and put them away. If there's no finality, it's like unresolved anger from some past trauma you can't remember. I once heard that if a greyhound dog catches the fake rabbit, the experience ruins the dog's desire to run for life. If a detective doesn't capture the bad guy and the case is never solved, they will spend their lives working it. Some go crazy. Some kill themselves and leave pathetic notes of failed lives.

I was not that far gone. I accepted that David Franklin was dead, but my mind kept turning over the need to prove that when everybody thought he was dead, even his wife, he wasn't. I knew that if Russians had grabbed him for not paying back the loan, they would have taken his driver's license, gone to his house, and taken everything he had. And I believe David was searching for the miracle cure and hoping the Russians wouldn't track him down.

To find some peace, I decided to wrap up the last remaining strings of evidence. One was Rita, the supposed mistress at the advertising agency. A flip through my records gave me Rita's number. I introduced myself when she answered, and she nearly squeaked with fearful surprise.

"Paula said you'd be calling."

"I appreciate you taking the time to answer some questions."

"I'm worried about this," she whispered. "Paula said I could be in some trouble. Should I talk to a lawyer?"

"No, nothing like that, I promise. We're trying to wrap up the investigation of Mr. Franklin's disappearance. I just need to follow up with a few people who were peripheral to the case."

"So he's dead?"

"Yes."

"Oh, that's terrible. What do you need to know?"

"There were rumors you and David were involved somehow. Not that we care one way or another about that in particular. We were hoping you could help shed some light on his state of mind after he was diagnosed."

"David and I were not having an affair," Rita said indignantly.

"I understand. Nobody is accusing or judging."

"I liked him, and we were friends, but it was nothing more than that. He was really in love with his wife."

"I've spoken with Mrs. Franklin, and I agree. Can you give me your impression of his state of mind?"

"He was so afraid for his family." I could hear the distress in her voice. "I know they didn't have health insurance, and if he got treatment, it would eat up his life insurance. He was afraid his family would have nothing. It was so sad but so sweet. I admired David for that. I…" She took a moment to collect herself. "I'm okay now."

"Did he share anything about any plans he might have had?"

"He was going to try and find alternative care. He said he was going to make sure his family was provided for."

I asked gently, "Did he give any examples of that?"

"One day, he was online and asked me what I thought about bee sting therapy." She coughed, holding back a laugh mixed in with her grief. "Crazy, desperate stuff. I felt so powerless to help him. Then he quit coming in, and I heard about the car and the bullet holes, and I was so scared. I took a day off to just cry."

"Did you reach out to his wife?"

"No," she said nervously.

"Did anyone from the office reach out to her?"

"The partners sent flowers and a card. I know we made sure she got his final paycheck and some extra. So, yes, we reached out."

"Well, that answers all my questions," I said. "Thank you so much for taking the time. And I assure you it all ends right here, you'll never hear from me again."

"Thank you."

My gut told me she probably flirted shamelessly with the guy, and when he announced he was sick, she knew it was over. That was one more item checked off my list. Closer to closure. Then there was Karen Carlson. I could put this one to bed with an online search. I Googled Karen Carlson psychic 1937. Her name was everywhere. One site listed famous psychics through the ages, from Nostradamus to Jean Dixon, and there she was. A link to a Wikipedia post brought me to her bio.

Karen Eleanor Carlson (1901 – 1937). Best known for her early work in traveling shows. The daughter of Thaddeus and Alice Carlson, known for their mind-reading act that elevated them to brief stardom from 1901-1904. The American Psychic Foundation recognized Karen for her skills as she was mentored by some of the best mind experts of the era. She died under mysterious circumstances in her flat in Soho, New York, on January 2nd, 1937.

She never married but had one child, a daughter Freda. The summary explained Freda Carlson was still an active psychic in California. So Freda Carlson would be in her seventies today, and I bet she had a voice like a chain smoker. It was a great bit. Channel mom and make some cash. Perfect. Did I find closure in this exercise?

Hell no. It seemed to make things worse. Thank God Gina called and broke the insane spell.

"I've been swamped today and could use a break," she said. "Want to come and take me to lunch?"

When I pulled up to her cupcake shop, the line of customers was out the door. Gina was bustling around like a one-woman tornado, packing party orders and wrapping them for delivery. She seemed to know all her customers by name.

"Just a minute, babe." She handed me a cupcake. "We just got slammed."

"I'll wait."

The bite of the sweetness almost made me swoon.

"Oh baby, can you give me a hand?"

"Only got one," I joked, "but I can help."

"Could you take that tray and run it out to that minivan out front?"

When I approached the woman, her eyes grew wide. Then she stepped in front of her children. I gave her a big smile. "Your cupcakes ma'am."

She opened the rear of the van, and I put them carefully inside. I must have looked a site to Mrs. Average Housewife – a beast with a hook sauntering out with her five-year old's birthday sweets. I gave her a smile and a tip of an imaginary hat.

"Have a nice day and a great party."

"Thank you," she said with a desperate smile. "Bye now."

"Mommy," the little girl said. "He was scary."

The mom shushed her, and they sped away. Half an hour later, the crowd thinned. Gina washed her hands. "Almost ready."

I bit into another chocolate wonder. "You know, you probably shouldn't send me out to drop off the product like that. I'll scare off your customers."

"What, babe?" Gina came drying her hands.

"I think I just scared the shit out of Mrs. Middle Class there."

Gina laughed. "Yeah, well, if I know these moms, she'll probably go home and rub one out thinking about you."

"You are a seriously nasty girl."

"You know it." She kissed me, and her lips tasted like butterscotch frosting.

In the middle of a soup and salad, she announced she had to go to another women's retreat. "This time in Yosemite."

"You just got back from one."

"Yeah, but their main speaker just canceled, so I'll take her place. Sorry baby, I feel so bad."

"So I'm going to be all alone with all this time off. Imagine the trouble I'll get into."

"Well, if I'd known about this vacation of yours earlier. I should call Carl and give him some shit."

"No, he's under enough stress as it is," I said. "With me gone, he's got more on his plate. Trust me; he felt bad about the timing and the lack of warning."

"I'm so sorry. Guess you'll have to figure out a way to keep yourself busy during the day. Besides, it's only for the weekend. We'll do something when I get back. We can run off for another long weekend."

"What did you have in mind?"

"Carmel by the Sea," she said. "Three days, two nights. We'll make it fun."

"What about tonight?"

We agreed to a movie, so when she got off work, we took in a new action flick filled with over-the-hill stars still trying to be tough. I found myself relating a bit too much, and Gina must have sensed it. She took my hand and made a production out of feeling my right bicep. Between the firefights and the explosions, David Franklin occupied the empty seat beside me.

So where did I go? He asked. How did I get by? Okay, my story was bullshit, but I still had cancer. What did I do about my pain, how did I stay hidden in plain sight? Who recognized me or ignored me completely? C'mon Bobby, answer these questions for me.

I tried to pay attention to Sylvester and Bruce and Arnold as they swaggered and told shitty one-liners, but David wouldn't shut up. The movie ended with a spectacular explosion and a bullet-riddled aging movie star blowing up the hatchet-faced newcomer bad guy with an RPG. When the smoke cleared and the credits rolled, I couldn't have told you the thin plot or why they were all hurling grenades.

"What did you think?" Gina asked.

"It was a bit corny," I said.

"It was supposed to be."

I laughed. "Let's just say I won't need to see it again."

We went to her place and made love amongst the transient smells of vanilla and melted butter. Gina always worked out her creations in her home kitchen. We slept afterward, and a dream plagued me. I was digging through a massive pile of garbage because I knew Butch was lost somewhere in it. I could hear him yowling, his voice disembodied and growing dimmer. I called his name.

"Can I help you?" A voice asked.

I looked around for the source of the question. Beside me was a young woman wearing white. She had small angel wings growing out of either side of her head. As she smiled at me, the wings slowly flapped and stirred her hair.

"My cat is lost under all this shit."

"He's home sleeping on the couch."

"But I heard him," I said. "He's under here."

"That's David Franklin weeping," the angel girl said.

"How would you know?" I asked. "Who are you?"

"Karen Carlson."

"Psychic Karen?"

"Yes," she said.

I woke up to Gina's smiling face. "You were dreaming. You talked in your sleep."

"Hope I didn't bother you."

"No, but it was cute." I rolled over and kissed her neck. My arousal made her laugh, and she guided me inside her. "Just a fast one. I gotta' get going."

Then she went to take her shower. With no place to go, I stayed in bed until she came out and started to dress.

"Are you getting up, lazybones?"

"In a minute." Nothing is sexier than to watch Gina go about her Business and not realize how gorgeous she is. To watch her dress is the sexiest reverse striptease I've ever known.

"What?" Gina asked.

"You're so damn sexy, babe."

"I'm struggling to get my fat ass into a pair of pants. How is that sexy?"

"You'll never know how much."

She kissed me. "Gotta' go."

"I'll lock up."

I used the shower, dressed, and went home. Butch met me at the door and offered some uncharacteristic affection. The more I ignored him, the more he mewed and acted desperate.

"Butch, you wimpy-assed freak. What do you want from me?" He answered with a pathetic whimpering meow. "What?"

I crouched down, and he ran to me, rolled on his back, and closed his eyes. I gave his furry tummy a quick rub with my hook, and he gave a satisfied purr.

His hind leg was no longer bandaged. He probably ripped the bandage off himself.

"You crazy cat," I said. He stayed on his back.

I changed into jeans and a short-sleeve shirt that exposed my entire prosthetic from the elbow down. My phone rang, and I was surprised to recognize Karen Carlson's number. With humorous swagger, I answered.

"Mr. Jacobi," she said with no gravel in the voice.

"Hello, Karen."

"It was interesting to visit with you last night. Did you find David under all that emotional debris?"

"Uh," I was genuinely shocked. "What can I do for you?"

"David's voice called out to me as well. He is not at rest."

"And?"

"His flesh is not at rest."

"And?" I asked again.

"What did the man tell you by the dead sea?"

"Now wait," I retorted.

"Hello?" Gravel tongue said. "Do you want to make an appointment?"

I hung up, my mind swirling with the impossibility of what had just happened. How could she possibly know about my dream or my visit to the Salton Sea? I needed to talk with my sponsor. I hadn't touched base with Carl in two days, and with Franklin's voice back in my head and calls from dead psychics, I was feeling pretty spun.

Should I confess all this to Carl? I decided this was just post-case crap and too much downtime detox. As if reading my mind, Carl called on me. The spooky coincidences were piling up at an alarming rate.

"How are you doing with all this time on your hands?" he asked.

"Sane and sober," I said. Well, sober anyway.

"Glad to hear it. The Franklin case is closed, and the wife's been paid. There's a weekly meeting to summarize the closed files. You want to take an hour and be there?"

"Not unless you really need me there."

"We'll get by. What's your plan, then?"

"Probably just gain weight and watch sports."

"Sounds like fun," Carl said.

"Have we had any correspondence from Mrs. Franklin?"

"None," Carl said. "Any fallout from the Russian you pummeled?"

"No. I'm glad it's all over."

"Me too. Have a good day and be good."

With week one of my vacation nearly gone, Gina and I spent Thursday night together. She left for Yosemite in the morning. I tried to forget about my odd psychic phone call, and I made a conscious effort to be as present as possible. We ate and wrestled in the sheets and slept like babies. Saturday morning, Gina kissed me and hurried off to meet her sponsor to drive to the mountains.

"I'll call when we get there," she said.

The gym sounded like an awful idea. After a meeting where I heard nothing, I went home to vast emptiness. I watched three hours of mindless T.V. until Gina called.

"Hi, we're here."

"You made good time. How's the weather?"

"The weather? Really? I'm calling to tell you I'm looking forward to Carmel."

"Me too."

"Okay, gotta go. I'll lose my signal in the park. Love you!"

"Me too."

The void returned. While I sipped a Diet Coke and ignored Butch rubbing against my leg, my phone rang. It was Buddy.

"Hey you big fuck," Buddy chimed.

"Hello to you too, you short fat asshole. What's up?"

"I found out you're on vacation. You lookin' to earn a little extra cash?"

"Doing what?"

"Recon work for me," he said. "I got a couple of jobs in house, and I could use some help. Two hundred a day plus expenses."

"Sounds like something that could get me into some trouble."

"Nothing dirty or seedy, just follow a couple of wayward spouses. Oh, my gal found out about that Mexican number you wanted me to trace. It had been disconnected, but I was able to track down the former user."

"Okay, shoot."

"It was listed to a place called 'The Compound', an alternative health center near Guadalajara. I looked the place up, and it's a faith healer who calls himself Charro de Cristo. The Internet says he does psychic healings, and people come from all over the world to see him. Kind of like that guy down in Brazil."

"Interesting."

"Some say this guy is for real," Buddy said.

"I'm sure that's why Franklin was looking it up. Just a second." I fumbled through my stacks of paper. "He made several calls to that number. He also visited a website with a Mexican URL, but when I tried to go to it, the site was down."

"Soon as I got the target on the number, I got the rest from Google. This guy's all over it."

"Thanks."

"Glad to help. What about the freelance? You want the job?"

"Better not. Gina and Consolidated might frown on that sort of thing."

"Pussy. Call me if you change your mind."

I Googled Charro de Cristo and found several links. Some said he was a fraud, and others vehemently declared him to be the real thing. More than that, I found a site that showed a photo of the man himself. It included testimonials and a description of his services. A grainy, short video showed him grab a woman by the head and then throw his hands in the air. The patient swooned and had to be supported while taken away. I'd seen it before, in every tent revival and faith healing man of God that ever bamboozled a congregation.

My phone rang. Damn, I was a popular man today. I sat back and frowned. Claire Franklin's number flashed on the screen. It meant one of two things, either she was calling to thank me, or the Russians called her.

"Jacobi." I tried to sound officious.

"Hello Mr. Jacobi."

"Hello Mrs. Franklin. What can I do for you?"

"They finally called me again."

"They, meaning the Russians?"

"Yes."

"Well, tell them you can pay the debt, and ask them how much and how to do it."

"It's ten thousand dollars, right?"

"That was the original loan. These people charge high interest. They may hit you up for as much as twice that."

"They didn't say that," she said. "They only mentioned the ten."

"It's a ploy. They get you talking, and then they up the ante. They hope to intimidate you enough to be willing to pay anything to get them out of your life. Especially if they know you're frightened, grieving, and flush with a recent settlement."

238

She was genuinely freaked out. "How do I contact them?"

"You have to let them call you."

"Oh God," she barely said.

"You can go always go to the police."

"But my kids," she said.

"That's why you have to settle this thing. Life is pretty cheap to these people. Leave the kids somewhere safe and go home and wait until they call – and they will. Tell them you'll have the money in a week, and you need to know how much and how to deliver it. They can be pretty savvy and may have you wire it."

"Shit," she said with a frightened chuckle. "I am so fucking scared. What if they don't want the money and they want to hurt me instead? What if I pay and they want more?"

I soothed her. "Listen, this may sound bizarre, but they are business people. If they strong-armed or hurt anybody willing to pay, the word would spread, and then they'd have no business left. Just because they operate below the street level doesn't mean they're not looking for customers. You give them their money, and they'll go away."

"It's all so sordid," Claire said. "I'm so confused about why David would take out this loan and not tell me."

"Pride," I said without a thought. "A man wants to take care of his family. I'm sure he borrowed the money to make sure he could pay the bills. Did you pay the bills, or did he?"

"He handled all of that," she said.

"Then he was keeping the truth from you about how bad things were. David may have been juggling money to try and keep everything balanced. Taking this money was his last desperate act to try and hold everything together."

"If he had only told me the truth, then we could have worked it out together," Claire whispered. "I would have understood."

"Pride," I said again. "I suggest you talk to these people right away. If you need any help, you can reach me on my cell for the next week. After that, I'm out of town."

"Can I say something out loud, for my own sake?"

"Sure."

"Damn David for keeping this from me. Now he's dead, and my kids have no father, and all this was going on behind my back. I feel cheated. I really do."

"Take it easy on the poor guy. He may have lied to you, but at least he didn't run off with another woman. If anything, David made sure he left you with a great deal of money and no bills."

"It makes me wonder if he ever loved me."

"Trust me," I said. "A man wouldn't go to this much trouble unless he loved you more than his own life."

"Thank you for that. We're having a memorial service for him. I bought an urn, and everything and the only thing going in it is a tablespoon of ash. That's all I have of him."

"It's better than nothing."

Claire's voice went up an octave. "Janice was right, you're not nearly as scary as I thought you were."

"Thanks."

"Can I ask one more thing? When I talk to these people and if they want to meet me, will you go with me? I mean, if you are around? The idea of meeting with people like this will be too much for me. I can pay you."

"Of course," I heard myself say.

"Thank you."

I wasn't surprised I said yes. I asked myself what Carl would say. His answer? Allowing this woman to take this chance alone would be selfish and cruel.

"Here we go," I whispered. I prayed those Russian bastards would give her a Western Union quick pay I.D. and be done with it. Gina called, and I listened to her go on about the retreat.

"I'll be home Monday around dinner time. I'll be starving, so think of someplace good to go when I'm home."

"After that drive, I'd think you'd want burgers and a bed."

"Sounds good to me."

I watched T.V. to distract my brain until I got hungry. Fish and chips, then a meeting sounded good, so I headed for a little place near home, then a men's comedy speaker meeting called Soberday Night Live.

The fish was great, and then the speaker was hilarious. A few minutes with some old friends had me settled. Then I headed for home.

CHAPTER ELEVEN

Sunday morning broke gray and somber. My serenity from the night before snuck away while I slept, and I imagined it out prowling the alleyways and back lots with Butch. Despite my morning meditation and daily readings, my mood stayed as cloudy as the sky. Coffee helped, but I suddenly missed Gina. I wanted nothing more than to have all the threads of my life tied up in a neat little bow again.

David Franklin's voice invaded my thoughts, and I found myself fighting the urge to revisit his desperate search. Mexico and its faith healer whispered to me. I tried to shake off the insanity. Butch suddenly jumped through the window with a dead lizard in his mouth.

"Sorry pal, but you gotta eat that outside." He looked at me with a sneer, so I stomped my foot and he retreated. "Keep that shit outta' here!"

The sound of him crunching on the corpse made me cringe. When my phone rang I nearly smashed it against the wall. Claire Franklin. God, how did it come to this? My voice sounded as empty as the space I wished Gina filled.

"Hello Claire."

"They called," she said in a harsh whisper. "They want the money by Monday, or they said they would hurt the kids. They want it by ten in the morning."

My heart went cold. "What did they ask for?"

"They want thirty thousand dollars. Thirty thousand, why would they want so much?"

"Because they're crooks," I said. "The normal vig on a loan like this is about ten percent a month."

"Vig?"

"Exorbitant interest. Sometimes they call it juice. So if David had handled it normally, he would owe another five grand, something like that. But he jumped ship, and they likely got mad, so it sounds like they're going after an extra fifteen grand. They think they're dealing with a scared woman with a fat bank account. Did you tell them how much the settlement was?"

"No."

"Did you mention me?"

"I said I had somebody who was helping me to handle the payment. When I asked if I could do a wire transfer, they said no. In fact, they laughed."

"That means these people are small time. Don't worry, we'll handle this, and I'll make sure you pay only fifteen thousand. What do they want you to do?"

"They said they'd call back in two hours and tell me where to meet them. They want cash in a brown paper bag."

"Did they say no cops and all that happy horse shit?" I was losing my temper with these fucks.

"Yes."

"Are you home?"

"I am. Should I leave?"

"No," I said. "In the morning, go to the bank and withdraw the cash. Tell them you're buying a car, and the owner will only take cash. They'll try to convince you to get a cashier's check but say the seller got burned that way once before, and he wants cash. Buy one of those zipper bank bags and then put the money in a paper lunch bag. We will meet at the Bay Bridge Park. Do you know where that is?"

"Yes."

"This is a strange question, but do you have any sedatives?"

"Yes, some Valium. Why?"

"You're going to take one before we go in there. Just something to mellow you out, Okay?"

"I understand," Claire said.

"Call me in the morning when you leave the bank."

"I'm so scared."

"They won't bother you tonight. They know you're scared shitless, and they know you're taking their threats seriously. Lock your doors, take a Valium and go to bed. I need you sharp when we do this."

"I know, but– "

"Claire," I interrupted, "there's a saying. Everything after 'but' is bullshit. It's going to be okay. I promise you that. Just be ready to follow my instructions."

Her voice sounded like it was coming from the bottom of a well. "Yeah."

"Good girl. Call me when you leave the bank." I hung up.

I went to the small safe in the back of my closet and pulled out my Glock nine-millimeter automatic. My little five-shot .38 peashooter wasn't adequate for this rodeo. I loaded the Glock with hollow points and tucked the gun into a small shoulder holster that fit snugly under my prosthetic. Even a pat-down could miss it from all the hardware under there.

My agitation was gone, replaced by a cold void. When I was a cop, I had this thing I did, a type of meditation. The night I lost the arm, I was in that zone, disconnected from fear and emotion and expectation. In that space, I could follow my training and my gut. Emotions can't guide you, only calculated focus can. I found that place again for the first time in almost four years. When the phone rang, it could have been a machine that answered.

"They want me to come to where David met them. A bar in Oakland," Claire said.

"The tavern. I know it. I'll drive tomorrow. Thanks." Then I called Joe.

"Hey Buddy," Joe said. "Calling on a Sunday? I hear you're getting married. She pregnant?"

"Listen, Joe, I have something I have to do, and I may need your help."

"Oh shit. I know that fucking voice. What the hell are you up to?"

"What was that shithead's name at the bar in Oakland?"

"Yuri Bolteketch," he said. "Why, you going to kill the little cocksucker?"

"Not if I can help it. I'm seeing them tomorrow."

"So if Bolteketch ends up dead, you're the guy who killed him?"

"And If I end up dead or missing?"

"He did it," Joe said softly. "Don't worry, either way, he's a dead man."

"Thanks."

"Need some backup?"

"Maybe," I said. "If I do, I'll call."

"Always, my man," he said. "You can't tell me anything?"

"I'm convinced he's the one who killed Franklin." I hoped that was true.

"Understood," Joe said.

I prayed Gina wouldn't call because the man who answered would be unrecognizable. After four years of recovery, I had forgotten this side of me. I might as well have put my heart in the safe when I pulled out the gun. When I caught my reflection in the window, I barely recognized the face staring back at me.

*   *   *   *

Stone doesn't sleep. When I opened my eyes, I hadn't lost a moment of consciousness. The night passed in an instant while my eyes stared at the back of my lids. Dressed and alert, I drove to the Bay Bridge parking lot and sipped coffee, waiting for Claire's call. As if sensing her desperation, I pushed the talk button the same instant the phone began to ring.

"Hello Claire."

"I have the money."

"Meet me where we agreed."

When she entered the parking lot, I flashed my lights, and she parked next to me. I rolled down my window. "We're taking my truck. I'll have better control of the situation if I'm driving."

She looked nervous as she collected her things and came over. I helped her into the truck. She dug into her large purse and pulled out the bundle. It looked smaller than I expected.

"All large bills," she said. "Like they asked for."

"Did the bank give you any trouble?"

"No, they just smiled and counted it out."

"Did you bring the tranquilizer?"

"I did, and I know I need it. Should I take it now?"

I nodded, and she pulled the pill from her pocket. I offered her a bottle of water. She swallowed it in a quick gulp.

"The doctor gave me these after David first disappeared. Never thought I'd need them for this kind of thing."

"Now I need you to listen and follow my instructions very closely," I said while I drove out of the parking lot. We merged onto the road leading to the bridge. "The Valium is to keep you from freaking out. This will be a tense situation. I have to let these people know you're paying fifteen thousand and nothing more. It could get confrontational, especially since I fucked this guy up when I saw him last. He tried to shoot me, and I busted his face."

"Oh God," Claire said and slumped. "I don't think I can do this."

"Claire, I need you to find some spine, okay?"

She gave me a shocked look. "I –"

"I apologize for speaking to you this way, but I can't have you fall apart on me until this is done. Please tell me you'll hold it together."

"I don't know If I –" she started but must have seen the expression on my face. "Okay."

"Good girl."

While we crossed the Bay, she whispered, "I'm sorry to say this, but right now, I'm not sure if I'm more scared of them or you."

"I don't blame you."

Once across the bridge, we dropped out of the commuter lanes and entered the neighborhoods. The streets became less well-kept and the houses more threadbare. Soon we were back in shit town. Claire seemed calm, and I was sure she was floating from the

Valium. I turned up the ragged street and stopped at the curb in front of the tavern. She gave me an anxious look.

"This is it." I climbed out of the truck and opened her door. "Remember. I'll do the talking. You stay behind me."

She stayed directly behind me, and I listened to her shallow, nervous breaths. I stopped outside the door and looked her in the eye. "I need you to be ready for this."

"Okay," she whispered.

I pushed open the door, and we entered the tavern. While my eyes adjusted to the dark, a heavyset man locked the door behind us. My shoulders coiled like springs, and I was ready for anything. I made out Bolteketch sitting at the back of the bar surrounded by six men holding guns. If Claire had walked into this alone, they would have cleaned her out.

"Hello Mrs. Franklin," Bolteketch said. He gestured for us to come closer.

Claire stayed behind me and took tentative steps while I strode up and dramatically dropped the cash on the table. I set my hook beside the stack of bills and opened and closed it slowly. It caught everyone's attention.

"You aren't doing business with Mrs. Franklin today," I announced.

Bolteketch touched his cheek and spoke through his wired jaw. It sounded like a pansy trying to sound like Jed Clampett, from the Beverley Hillbillies.

"I have no business with you. This is between her and me. I'll deal with you later after I take her money."

"There's fifteen thousand here," I growled and tapped the cash with my hook. "It's more vig than she owes, and what is between us has nothing to do with her loan."

"It has everything to do with it," Bolteketch said and leaned forward. "You came here and did this to me for her."

I laughed. "Don't flatter yourself. Word on the street is you're too small-time for the cops to give a shit. I came here looking for a guy I thought you might have killed. It was too bad it turned out you were the fuck he took the cash from. Now he's dead, and she's here to pay. Fifteen grand, that's all, and then we're done. After that, anything between you and her, and you and me, is over."

"I don't think so."

I heard Claire squeak behind me. Oh shit, hold it together, girl. Don't freak, don't scream, and don't even speak.

"I can get you more," she said breathlessly.

"Claire," I said sternly.

"I can. I can get you what you want if you promise this will be over. Please, I can get more."

"You see?" Bolteketch stood up and pointed at the money. "I'll take this as half. I want the rest tomorrow. If not, I'll—"

251

"You won't do shit," I said, but Claire moved around me. It was too late. Bolteketch moved back, and his goons pointed their guns while Claire screamed. If I didn't act fast, someone would die.

"Grab her," Bolteketch yelled.

I told Claire to run, but she was too scared to move. I threw my weight against the table and drove it into Bolteketch's legs, knocking him back into his chair. Then I lunged across the table, and we both fell in a tangle on the floor. Before his goons could react, I had him on his feet with my hook at his throat and my Glock at his temple.

"Stop!" Bolteketch screamed through his teeth.

Six men pointed guns at me, and the bartender aimed a shotgun at us from behind the bar. I knew it was an attempt at intimidation. From that range, he'd pepper everybody, including his boss, with buckshot. Claire had her fists to her mouth and her eyes closed. The air smelled of sweat and fear.

"If anybody moves a fucking muscle, I will paint that back wall with his brains," I yelled at the top of my lungs. My voice was like a cannon shot. The sound reverberated off the walls. Bolteketch's wet breathing seethed through his clenched teeth.

"Let him go," the bartender demanded.

I laughed coldly. "Fuck that. This is the way this is going to go down. Bolteketch will gladly accept this nice lady's offer to pay him more than he deserves because her husband went and died and didn't pay back his loan.

We will thank him for being so understanding we'll leave here without any more trouble."

I saw the gun barrels wavering and the gaping maw of the shotgun across the room. Claire stood paralyzed with fear.

"And if I don't agree?" Bolteketch asked.

"I will kill you and walk this woman back to her family with her money."

"That would be a good trick," he said. "My associates would kill you."

"Oh, I don't think so," I hissed in Bolteketch's ear. "They'll let me leave here, I promise." My hook scratched his throat, so I opened the pincers and placed them on either side of his jugular vein.

"You bluff," he said quietly.

"No. See, I know you're small shit, and these guys know it too. If I kill you, they'll take over this place and run it better than you ever did. They'd probably thank me."

"Fuck you!"

"No, I'll fuck you," I said with a sick smile. "So accept this nice lady's offer, and we'll all shake hands and go home. Or I'll tear your throat out and watched you bleed to death."

Claire found her voice. "Robert?"

"Ask him nicely," I said.

Claire gave me a confused and fearful look. "What?"

"Ask Bolteketch to accept your money," I said. "Do it now."

"Please do what he says. I don't want your blood on my hands. I've lost my husband and my children lost their father."

"Tell him," I urged.

Her voice grew in volume. "I'm a housewife from San Mateo! I shouldn't be here, I am not like this, how did this happen? Why won't you just take that fucking money and leave me alone?" Her voice ended with a shriek.

"What'll it be?" I asked Bolteketch.

He looked into my eyes and must have seen the cold. He knew I would gladly kill him and lose my own life in a spray of bullets and care nothing as long as he was dead.

He let out a nervous laugh. "Okay. Yes, the money is fine. I was greedy. You are right. Fifteen is fine, now can you let me go?"

"Put the guns on the table next to me," I growled. Bolteketch nodded and each man obeyed. "And you Bruiser. Put down the scattergun."

"Do it," Bolteketch hissed and the big bartender complied.

"Now, everybody back by the dart boards and keep your hands in the air." They all did. "Claire, move to the door."

"I'm afraid to move. Mr. Jacobi, I'm…"

"It's okay Claire, just walk slowly toward the exit."

With careful steps, she inched her way until she stood with her face to the door. I dragged Bolteketch with me until I was beside her.

"Listen up Rizzo," I hissed in his ear. "I called the OPD before I came here and they're watching this place. If anybody follows they'll come down on you like the wrath of God. Until now they've left you alone because they hoped you'd lead them to bigger fish. One call from me and you'll be plenty big."

"Bullshit. You're a hired thug. You know nobody."

"Claire, pull my phone and scroll down to Joe. Put it on speaker."

She found the number and pushed the call button.

Joe's voice broke through the tension. "Hey, you big fuck! Did you blow Bolteketch's fucking head off?"

"Not yet. I'm here with him now. Wanna' say hello? I was just making the point I have friends in high places."

"Say something, Bolteketch," Joe urged.

"Hello."

"Now listen to me. The man who you're with? He's a certified psycho. He used to be a cop, and they threw him off the force because he lost his mind, as well as his hand. Do what he says, or I can't do anything for you. Understand me?"

"Is this a trick?" Yuri asked.

"Listen carefully. My name is Detective Joe Santos of the Oakland Police Department. We are speaking on an official police issue phone, and you are lucky to be alive. If you don't let this man and the woman go, we will kick down your door and arrest you."

"Okay," Bolteketch said.

"Thanks, Joe," I said and hung up.

"I am sorry," Bolteketch said through his teeth. "I promise you are forgotten. You have my word as a gentleman."

I pushed him away. "Good enough. We're leaving. Remember, the cops are watching, and if anybody leaves this place in the next hour, they will come down on you, and this shit hole is closed."

Bolteketch rubbed his neck. "Just go."

We were halfway out of the neighborhood when Claire suddenly made a frantic gesture for me to stop. She opened the door and vomited violently into the street. I waited for her to finish.

"It's okay," I said.

Claire shook her head. "It's not. I–" She erupted in tears.

I drove away from Oakland while she sobbed. She cried across the bay and finally settled into deep breaths by the time we reached her car. Now on safe ground, I felt the ice melt in my veins, and I felt flush.

Claire's eyes looked wild. "How do I forget what just happened?"

"You don't. That's like the day I heard the shotgun blast and realized my life would never be the same. You can either lose yourself in it or become stronger as a result of it. I see you being stronger."

"Would you have killed him?"

"To save us? Yes, I certainly would have."

She put her face in her hands. "That was insane."

"Yes, it was."

"How do we know they won't come after us?"

"They won't," I assured her. "Rizzo is small-time, which is probably why David went to him in the first place. After hearing Joe's voice, he'll probably catch the next boat back to Ukraine."

"Why do you call him Rizzo?"

"Rizzo the rat," I said. "Dustan Hoffman in Midnight Cowboy?"

She suddenly laughed. "Oh my God. He was like that, wasn't he?"

We both laughed nervously and then went quiet.

"Can you drive?" I asked. "Or should I get you home, and you can make arrangements to come back for the car."

"No, I can drive. Between the Valium and the crazy shit back there, I am just kind of numb. Is it really over?"

"I guarantee it."

She gave me a long stare. "Okay."

I helped her to her car and watched to see if she was steady enough to drive.

"Call me if you need to," I offered.

She lowered the window and looked at my hook, then at my face. "Robert, I'm not sure if you're an angel or a devil. Either way, I'm so grateful for your help with all of this."

"You're welcome."

"Goodbye, Mr. Jacobi."

She keyed the ignition and started to slowly drive away. Then her brake lights came on, and she tossed something out her window before speeding off.

I walked over and picked up a brown paper bag. Inside was the other fifteen grand. She had it all along. I put the cash in my jacket and went back to the truck. Funny way to thank me, I thought. She made sure I couldn't refuse it. Or maybe she wanted to be rid of it because it was part of the whole nightmare she just lived through. As for me, I couldn't give a fuck where it came from. It was an excellent windfall, and it would pay for a lovely wedding. I was beat when I got home, but I called Joe to tell him what went down. I left out the fifteen grand thrown at my feet.

"Holy shit. And she held up through it?"

"She held it together the best she could. I told her she would be a stronger person as a result."

"Good line. Do you need me to drop in and make sure Bolteketch keeps his promise?"

"I think he got the picture."

"That was a stroke of genius, by the way," Joe said. "But what if I hadn't answered the phone?"

"After my last call, I knew you'd answer no matter what."

"So, you okay big man?"

"Yeah, I'm just whipped. I think I'll sleep for a week. Hold on, Claire is calling. I better take this."

"Okay, see you."

I took a deep breath. "Hello?"

"I hope that," she said and stopped. "What I mean is…"

"Have a good life," I said.

After a long pause, she said, "Thank you."

It was enough.

Gina called, and I let it go to voicemail. I put my gun and the cash into the safe, set the alarm to go off in three hours, then went to bed. An hour later, a call from Gina woke me, and I groped for my phone.

"Hey baby, did you get my message?"

"No, I was asleep. Where are you?"

"You're asleep? In the middle of the day?"

"Bad night last night. Hey, I'm on vacation."

The ice melted, and the trauma and drama of the last two days had left me exhausted. But I felt like myself again.

"Hope you're rested up because I want to see my man when I get home."

"I'm up for that."

"I'll be home in about an hour. See you then."

I rolled out of bed and lumbered into the shower, where I pelted myself with water hot enough to sting, then switched it to cold and almost screamed – an old hangover remedy that also works great for waking my ass up. After a towel off and change of clothes, I trimmed my goatee, brushed my teeth, and picked up the apartment. I looked forward to losing myself in Gina's love and forgetting all about the Franklins and the Russians in Oakland. My cell displayed a blocked number. I answered with a careful hello.

"Hello, Mr. Jacobi. This is Karen Carlson."

What the fuck? "Hello Karen, what can I do for you in this realm?"

Mean, yes, but I suddenly felt like my old pissant self.

"You have quite the sarcastic and irritating sense of humor," she said.

"People weren't like that in 1937?"

"I pray you find peace from the antagonism you feel when confronted by what you don't understand."

"Enough therapy," I said with a laugh. "What can I do for you?"

"David's flesh has called out to me. His wife is in transition, and his soul struggles with his own conflict. I wanted to tell you I feel his need to reconcile what is left of him."

"What is left of him is a thimble full of ash in an urn on his wife's mantle. Can we get real here, and can I talk to the gravel-voiced woman? She's flesh and blood, right?"

"She is sleeping while I speak with you. Will you listen?"

"I'll listen to reason and sanity. Anything else is a waste of time. David has been screaming in my ear for days, and I won't listen to him either. Not anymore."

I couldn't believe I was even bothering with this conversation.

"Please, Robert," Karen's smooth tone said. "Let go of your anger and closed-mindedness and embrace what scares you."

"David Franklin is dead, and his thumb proved that. That's all that's left of him."

"You're wrong. His spirit still lives. I sense his soul in Mexico."

"So?" I demanded with obvious disdain.

"Listen to him, if only for your sake."

"My sake?" I laughed. "What does this have to do with me anymore?"

"Hello?" gravel voice was suddenly on the line. "Would you like to schedule a reading with Karen?"

"Just had one, thanks!" I killed the line.

Please, David's voice whispered.

"Fuck you, Franklin!" I yelled. "I'm not going to Guadalajara. I don't have that kind of time. Besides, every other clue has been shit."

Please!

"No! I'm not going to fly down to Guadalajara Mexico to chase down a ghost!"

An hour later, Gina knocked at my door.

"You look good enough to eat," she said, "and you smell good."

I hugged her with my good arm. "Just got out of the shower. How was the retreat?"

"Serene and spiritual and fun and necessary. Now all I want is you to myself."

"Yes ma'am."

We wore each other out. Afterward, we walked to a nearby burger joint and ate grass-fed burgers with organic sweet potato fries. After dinner, we enjoyed gelato, and she rambled on about the retreat.

"Sounds like good, sober fun," I said.

"And what did you do?" she asked.

"Nothing much." What Gina didn't know would keep her happy.

"Did you go to meetings?"

"I did. And I ate and breathed and slept and lived like a normal person."

"But Bobby," she said, "you're not a normal person. I don't have to be back in the shop until Thursday morning, so let's go to Carmel By The Sea and come back Wednesday night."

"You're still packed," I pointed out.

"We don't need much."

"I'll spoil you rotten." Why not? I had fifteen grand in my safe.

We slept, and my dreams were erratic, convoluted masses of images of carnivals, brash music, and David's face. In the morning, the thoughts disappeared and became the things of shadows.

"You okay, baby?" Gina asked.

"Perfect," I lied and carried our suitcases to the truck.

Three hours later, we checked into a quaint B&B, shopped, ate, walked, and talked. My mind was clear, and I thanked God for that. Tuesday night, we dined in the nicest place I could find.

"Bobby, there are no prices on these menus," she whispered.

"I got it. Just order what you want."

"I should go away more often. I like it when you spoil me."

Later we walked on the beach, and Gina talked about the wedding. "I don't need a big fancy deal, but I would like to have something nice."

"Like what?"

"I was thinking about Napa Valley or someplace else in the wine country. Not too many people. Just close friends and my kids."

"All our friends are recovering boozers," I joked. "Wouldn't the wine country be a bit inappropriate?"

"It doesn't have to be at a winery, but someplace nice."

"What about a honeymoon?"

"I've never been on a cruise."

I liked the idea. "To where?"

"Someplace warm and tropical."

"Look into it and find out what's available, and we'll do it."

"It will be expensive," she said. "Worried about the money?"

"Not at all. I got it covered."

"I like that plan. I thought we could do a January or February wedding, so it's cold here, and we go where it's warm."

"Plan it, and I promise I'll show up."

"You're too easy. What's up with that?"

"I'm surrendering. Besides, I want you to be happy."

"Perfect," she almost squealed.

Wednesday morning, I woke to my intuition and Karen Carlson screaming in my head. I was fucked. Detective Bobby Jacobi arrived while I slept and was currently occupying the seat at the head of the table. The when, where, how, and why of David Franklin roiled in my head like an angry, confined snake.

Luckily Gina was so distracted with wedding plans that she barely noticed. We spent our final day shopping in antique stores and knickknack shops. After lunch, we had ice cream while overlooking the ocean, then checked out and headed home.

"Thanks for being so understanding about my new craziness with the wedding," she said. "You sure you're okay with all this?"

"Perfectly," I promised.

Twice on the way home, she looked at me and cocked her head. Her expression was oddly questioning.

"What?" I asked.

"I'm afraid you're over there quietly freaking out."

"I'm not, I can guarantee you. They settled on the Franklin case, and I always spend some time processing the evidence in my head to finally let it go."

"So the widow got her money?"

"Everybody got everything that was coming to them."

Gina smiled. "Okay, I've been through this with you before. You just seem a little farther gone today than ever before."

"Heavier case," I said. "It brought up a lot of stuff for me—old shit. I talked to Carl, and he gets it. I'm shaking off some old ghosts."

And psychics and voices, I thought.

"As long as you're okay."

I dropped her at home, then went to my men's meeting but heard nothing. Carl and I went for coffee, and I stared at my cup.

"Want to talk about it?" he asked.

"I do. But you're not going to like it."

"Try me."

What came out of me was a steady flow of honesty regarding the Russian loan, the psychic calls, and Franklin's voice in my head. Carl stared at me while I spilled my guts about the Mexico hunch, the desperate screaming of the old cop in me, and the irrepressible need to board a plane and fly down to Guadalajara. I needed to find out if David had ended there, begging for last-hope help from a faith healer. I finished with the fact I nearly killed Claire Franklin and myself in the violent confrontation with Russian loan sharks. I left out the fifteen grand sleeping in my safe.

Carl exhaled. "Anything else?"

"No, that's about it."

"Holy fucking shit Bobby. What the hell?"

"I know, pretty fucked up, huh?"

"So I guess the next question is, was that a confession or a declaration of intent?"

"That's what I'm trying to figure out."

Carl folded his hands. "Here's the problem. As your sponsor, I can say that confessing all this is a good thing. It gives me a clear understanding of what you've been going through. As your boss, I can say that all of this is completely nuts and borders on mandatory firing. A lot of what you've talked about is in direct contradiction regarding the client-insurer relationship and company policy. So from both positions, I have to ask, what is your intention?"

"What if I went?" I asked.

"As your sponsor, I'd try to convince you not to. But as your boss, I'd have to put you on disciplinary leave until the completion of an investigation. Then I'd have to discharge you."

"What about as my friend?"

Carl dropped his head and hunched his shoulders. He looked up at me through his eyebrows. "I'd say if this was something you had to do to put this behind you, make sure it was left behind in Mexico and never discussed again."

266

"I'll give that some thought."

"If you choose to act on this, you will tell Gina." It was a command.

I swallowed hard. "Yeah."

Carl patted my shoulder, wished me luck, and left me to stare at my cooling coffee.

*   *   *   *

Gina and I sat at a picnic table in Golden Gate Park. She mangled a paper napkin while I told her the same story I had told Carl. Her eyes were glazed steel, and her brow was as wrinkled as crepe while I told her everything. Again, I left out the fifteen thousand dollars.

Her tone was flat. "So while I was at the retreat, you were holding Claire Franklin's hand and threatening to kill Russian criminals with guns."

"That's about the gist of it, yeah."

"And now you're telling me you're going to fly down to Mexico to chase this ghost of yours, a man that everybody knows is dead. His wife has moved on. The company has paid out based on your investigation, but you can't just move on?"

"Yeah."

"What the fuck? Bobby. What did Carl say?"

"He says he'll look the other way as long as when I get back. I leave this all behind me."

"And what about us? If you go down there and, I dunno – get arrested? Get killed? What if you find out the truth? What then? Why is it so important if this asshole died?"

"It's more than that."

"Bullshit, baby. I need to know right now. What's this really all about?"

"I don't know. I—"

"Tell me the truth!" Gina nearly screamed.

I yelled back, "This is haunting me like the devil! You don't get it. I have spirits calling me on the phone. His wife's face is in my head and what I put her through. I have this irrational need to know what the fuck happened."

Gina's face went white. I'd never acted like this before. "Okay, but—"

"There is no 'but,' Gina." I lowered my voice and held up my hook. "It's about this, about us, about who I am and what I do. If I don't get closure on this, it will haunt me."

"Meaning what?" Gina said.

"I have to know. The cop in me needs to have this solved, figured out, and put to bed. Otherwise, this is going to bug me forever."

She put the wadded napkin on the table. "What do you mean by spirits?"

"You'd never believe it."

"Try me."

I explained the calls from the psychic and the creepy coincidences surrounding the case. Gina nodded. "You're right. It's hard to believe. But I know you well enough to know if this shit has you this worked up, it must be pretty crazy."

"Listen. I—"

"No, you listen. This is your shit, Bobby. This is the past, and the bullshit of losing your arm and your career and this needy housewife brought it all back. They gave you a medal, and you were a hero. Isn't that enough?"

"It isn't about that," I whispered. "Or maybe it is. Whatever the reason, all I know is I have four days before I have to be back at work, and if this isn't over for me, I'm worthless."

"Then go," she said.

"What?"

"Go. But I get to say something now."

"Okay."

"Bobby, this scares the hell outta' me. I don't know the man sitting in front of me. This asshole Franklin and his wife took Bobby Jacobi and replaced him with you. So do what you have to do and find him. But when you get back, if this man," she pointed at me, "is still here, I'm not interested."

"I get it."

Gina slowly pulled off her ring and handed it to me. My hand trembled while she put it in my palm. "I don't want to be a widow before I'm a wife. I'll pray for you. Fuck, I'll pray for us. When you come home, if you come home, and I recognize the man I love? Then give that back to me."

"Baby, I—"

"Goodbye Mr. Jacobi. Have a safe trip."

Gina walked away, and all I could do was watch her.

Around me, people laughed and enjoyed the sunny weather. Children played, and the bay looked as smooth as opal glass. It should have been a perfect day.

My cell rang. A blocked call. Fuck Karen Carlson and her bullshit. Fuck David Franklin and his desperate bullshit and this convoluted mess. Fuck it all. I wanted my life back. The phone rang again, and I put it to my ear.

"Hello, Karen."

"Thank you for doing this," she said.

"Someday, you'll have to tell me who the hell you really are and how you do this crap."

"If I knew that, I'd have the answer to all things," she said.

"I never want to hear from you again."

"Yes, you do." I could sense the laughter that almost broke through in her voice. "Your future depends on it," she said.

"If you'll excuse me, I have to go get a CAT Scan."

CHAPTER TWELVE

As carl drove me to the airport, I listened to his concerns and warnings about how sideways this could go. All I could do was nod and nod some more. With no luggage and enough cash to cover my insane quest, I climbed out of his car, and he gave me a hard stare.

"Be careful."

"I promise."

"I love you, Bobby," he said. His voice cracked.

"Jesus Carl, I'll be back in two days."

"Oh, that's not it. I'm just thinking how hard it's going be on me to fire you if you fuck this up."

"I love you too. Now go."

He merged into traffic, and I watched until he disappeared into the lanes. Janice called, and I answered with a happy hello.

"Carl just told me you're going to Mexico for a couple of days. First, you're engaged, and now you're off gallivanting across the southland? I think you don't love me anymore."

"I'll always love you, Jan, in that sick and special sort of way."

"Have a shitty trip," she said and hung up.

Thank you for doing this, Franklin's voice whispered.

Fuck you, Franklin, I thought. I'm doing this because my cop instincts need to know the truth.

I got in line for security. Like a good sheep lining up for slaughter, I showed my ID and boarding pass, took off my shoes, emptied my pockets, and waited to be called through. I might just as well have worn a sign on my chest that I was up to no good. Even though I agreed to the full-body scan, I was still sent to secondary.

"Please remove your prosthetic," the uniformed security agent asked. I shrugged out of it and placed it on an aluminum table. "I'm going to give you a pat-down now."

"Knock yourself out."

His hands caressed me, and his fingers probed my gaps and crevices. I stood perfectly still and clenched my jaw. While I was manhandled, I saw two Middle Eastern youths pass by the one-way mirror without so much as a second glance. I must have stiffened because my groper stopped and waited, then moved on. When he was sure I had no bombs up my ass, nothing behind my dick or in my armpits, he gave me a once-over with the wand. It screeched as it passed over my left elbow.

"Buckshot," I said.

"Excuse me?"

"I lost this hand in a hunting accident, and those other scars are from buckshot they removed. There's a piece of it still in my elbow they couldn't get."

"I see." He waved the wand over the spot a few more times and got a small beep each swipe. "Okay."

"It sets off the metal detectors whenever I fly."

"I'll make a note of that." I was allowed to move on.

I went to the men's room to attach my hook. I got a few wary glances from men suddenly in a hurry to finish at the urinals. I just smiled. Then I joined the uneasy masses awaiting their flights. Joe called.

"Bobby's meat market," I said. "You can't beat Bobby's meat."

"Real funny, asswipe," he said. "Where the hell are you?"

"Airport. I'm taking a couple of days and going to Mexico."

"Good fishing down there. You going to get out and throw a line?"

"Maybe," I lied.

"Okay, well, all is cool up here. I kept an eye on Bolteketch, and he's been keeping a low profile. You'll be interested to know the Franklin house is up for sale. Guess she's moving on."

"I hope she finds solace and happiness."

"Uh, am I talking to Robert Jacobi, the guy who thinks all people are scum until proven otherwise?"

"Give me some slack. I had some empathy for her. Is that a crime?"

"Yeah, whatever," Joe said. "Have a good trip."

"I appreciate that."

I was so far off the map I was in that place where they write, 'Beyond here, there be monsters!' I shook my head.

"I must be fucking nuts."

I may have died there, David said.

You cannot destroy the spirit, Karen said.

It was getting crowded in my fucking head. My phone beeped that I had a text message. Gina. Have a safe trip was all it said.

The flight was called. I handed over my boarding pass and followed the line of travelers down the ramp. Smiling attendants greeted us, and I found my seat. Thank God I was by the window. A woman traveling alone stopped and looked down at me, then at her ticket. She didn't look happy. All she carried was a small rolling case, and she struggled to stow it. I helped her, and we both took our seats.

"Thank you." She fanned herself. She was heavyset, probably in her fifties, and obviously nervous.

"Hate to fly?" I said.

"Terrified."

"Careful," I joked. "That sounds like 'terrorist,' and you might get into trouble."

She giggled. "Wouldn't want that."

I made small talk, and she calmed down. By the time they made the announcements, I learned her name was Alice, and she was a schoolteacher joining a group on an educational goodwill tour starting in Guadalajara.

"We're going to underprivileged schools so we can make recommendations to our benefactors regarding donations."

"That sounds great."

"What about you?"

"Vacation. I'm going down to do some cave climbing."

"With that arm?" she asked. "Sorry, but I have a brother-in-law with the same disability. He has the hardest time with so many things."

"It's only a disability if you let it be one."

She gave me a proud smile. "Mind if I ask how you lost it?"

I was going to say in a plane crash but decided against it. "Cancer."

The engines wound up, and the plane started moving. The captain told us there were thunderstorms over the desert, and we would experience some turbulence.

Alice turned white. "Dear God."

The plane finished its roller-coaster ride through the high clouds and slowly descended to the Guadalajara Miguel Hidalgo y Costilla International Airport. Alice finally exhaled, and her color went from pale to bright red.

"That wasn't so bad," I said.

"No, well, maybe it was," she said.

We finally spilled out and went through Mexican customs. A scan of my passport had me through the terminal, and I rented a Buick sedan. Before leaving the parking lot, I programmed the navigation system to guide me through the one hundred and fifteen miles to the health compound.

Guadalajara is a big city, and the directions were straightforward. I followed Mexico highway 80 for miles through rough business districts, clusters of residential areas, and finally to the edge of what I could only describe as desolation. It looked much like the California desert, only bleaker.

After fifty miles, the brown shifted to green. Trees seemed to explode from the ground, and the sand and rock drew back to give way to life. I'd been driving two hours when the quiet navigation voice suddenly came to life and told me to turn onto highway 80. It turned out to be a two-lane road filled with potholes. It began a slow climb into the foothills. Along the roadside were markers covered with flowers and ribbons. At first, I thought them to be memorial markers for dead drunk drivers. Then I realized there were no crosses, just bunches of trinkets and floral arrangements. Closer inspections showed that most of the flowers were plastic. The higher I went, the more shrines crowded the roadside until it looked like a lane to some strange fantasyland.

When I reached the compound wall, there was no sign, no guard gate – no gate at all. A white stucco arch curved over two thick posts decorated with multicolored tile mosaics. The post bases were crowded with mini shrines decorated with the same plastic flowers I had seen along the road. Many of them had plastic-covered photos of smiling people of all nationalities. One Mylar balloon danced like a drunken woman in a glittering party dress. THANK YOU printed on the side in splashy red letters. It reminded me of a Scorsese movie poster.

My brow furrowed in careful expectation while I slowly motored through the entrance. A winding drive curved up to what looked like an old mission. Cars, busses, motorcycles, and even bicycles crowded the dirt lot.

"This is interesting," I said.

I think I died here, David whispered.

I bumped my way over a rutted dip and found a place to park between an ancient VW Microbus and a brand new Cadillac Escalade. A six-foot white stucco wall surrounded the compound but, again, no gate. People wandered in and out of the arched front entrance, and everybody looked happy. I ran my hand over my head, adjusted my sunglasses, and left the car to make my way to the portal of redemption. It was then that I noticed they all wore yellow. Not in the creepy, they all wore the same yellow outfit – like a cult yellow. They just wore yellow clothes of all sorts. I felt out of place in my jeans and a gray T-shirt.

"Hello," a tall, skinny Mexican man said to me. His smile and his eyes were a bit too wide.

"Is it okay if I come inside and have a look around?"

"Of course, make yourself at home. Are you here for a reading or healing?"

I thought of Karen from 1937. "Neither. I heard about the compound and thought I'd check it out. Is that okay?"

"Absolutely. Visitors are always welcome. I only asked in case you needed some yellow."

"The clothes?"

"Yellow doesn't interfere with the diagnosis or healing."

"I see," I said. "No, I'm just visiting."

The tall man went to talk with someone else, and I took a look around. Hundreds of people wandered the grounds. The air was thick with the smell of flowers and burning incense. Another arched doorway opened into the main building. The heavy wooden door stood open, and a line of people slowly shuffled forward into the church. Everybody was either smiling or in what looked like a state of serene meditation. I became more conscious of my lack of yellow, but no one seemed to care. I stopped a woman walking by, holding a piece of paper.

"Excuse me," I said.

"Yes?"

"Do you know where I would go to see Charro?"

She pointed to the church door. "That's the line. It looks long, but it moves pretty fast. Do you need to see somebody about getting some yellow?"

"No thanks."

"Could I read you something? I just wrote it after seeing him."

I gave her an inviting smile. I mean, anything to fit in.

"It's about my bliss. I think you'll like it."

"Okay," I said.

"Hidden away from the world, I am alone but for the voices of desperation, anger, sadness, and loss. Together their collective message becomes a seductive lullaby that is impossible to resist. The urgent push takes me into soft darkness as gentle as down pillows. The void calls to me like a lover. I will find salvation in the sleep of oblivion."

"Is that about death?"

"No, about life." Then she offered me a blessing and walked away.

I was undeniably and profoundly freaked out. I half expected somebody to come around with a tray of Dixie cups filled with grape Kool-Aid. I reluctantly got in line and fingered the photo of David Franklin in my pant pocket. My neck became itchy in the damp heat, and dark rings formed beneath my arms. The line did move quickly, but inside, the building was as hot as outside. I could count about fifty people ahead of me, all waiting to see a man seated above the crowd. He wore a yellow woven shirt and was indeed the man on the website – Charro de Cristo.

Each person stood before him, and he put his hands on either side of their head. No more than thirty seconds later, he released them, raised his hands above his head, and spoke in Spanish. Translators repeated what he said in several languages. Every patient swooned, then supported by assistants dressed in yellow. In a state of euphoria, each visitor was taken outside, and the next person stepped up.

Between each reading or healing, Charro closed his eyes and took a deep breath. Over and over, he performed the same ritual. Each time he called out a different reading or diagnosis. The closer I got, the more euphoric I felt, almost giddy. I couldn't stop smiling. I wondered if the heat was getting to me. My next thought was there must be something narcotic in the incense they burned. I finally accepted that I was drawn into the collective revelry. Is this what cows feel like before the slaughter? My eyes were on Charro, and my mind was fuzzy with smoke and heat. I bumped the man in front of me. He turned and looked back, his eyes glazed with expectation.

"Hello, I'm Conrad," he whispered. "I'm here for my prostate."

"Good luck with that, Conrad," I said softly said.

"Thank you. You're not wearing yellow." Not an accusation, more from real concern.

"It's okay." I pulled the photo from my pocket. "I'm here for a friend."

Conrad's eyes grew misty. "You must care for him very much."

"He has a wife and kids."

Conrad gave me an explosive smile and turned around. I was next in line. Charro went through his routine, and Conrad had his head held, broke into tears, then escorted out. I waited while Charro took his breath.

We locked eyes, and I felt a lightness that was hard to explain, like somebody lifted a weight off my shoulders. I shivered despite the heat.

"Usted no está aquí para una lectura," Charro said. The translator echoed in English.

"You are not here for a reading?"

"No," I said.

Charro pointed at the photo. "Tiene una pregunta para mí?"

"You have a question for Charro?"

"Yes."

Charro gestured for me to come forward and looked at the photo of David. He gestured to an attendant, and they looked at it together. Charro handed back the picture. "Vaya por favor con ello."

Our fingers touched for a brief moment, and I experienced what felt like a mild shock.

He gestured to the door. "Sir, please follow me."

Charro suddenly put up his hand. "Uno memento. Por favor estancia donde usted es."

"He asks you to stay where you are and close your eyes."

Charro stepped up and gently cradled my head between his hands. I felt strangely happy, much like the kind of happy excitement I knew as a child on Christmas morning. Nearly delight. His hands left my skin, and I heard him say, "Dios, se compadece de por favor este niño suyo y cura su cuerpo y su alma!"

I needed no translation; I knew he was blessing me.

"Please come," the translator said.

He led me by the elbow out of the building to the shaded courtyard where he suggested I sit in a chair beneath a broad tree. I felt dizzy. "My name is Jose, I will stay with you until you feel stable."

I smiled like an idiot. "That was interesting."

"It is powerful."

"He said he knew I wasn't there for a reading. Was that because I wasn't wearing yellow?"

Jose smiled. "Charro just knows."

"Why did he bless me?"

"He must have sensed something."

A stabbing pain bloomed in my elbow, and I pulled up my sleeve to examine the mechanism of my prosthetic. The pain made me hiss, and I felt movement beneath my skin. A small pimple formed, the flesh bulged and then broke open. To my amazement, the single buckshot pellet exited my skin. Dumbfounded and giddy, I picked it off my arm.

"That's interesting."

Jose crossed himself. "Wonderful."

I gave him a skeptical look. "But…"

"Just accept it. So what did you need to ask about this man's photo?"

I looked at the pellet in my blood-stained fingers. The spot on my elbow was already scabbing over, and my mind muddled with post-Charro mojo. I finally managed to respond. "I wanted to ask if this man came to see Charro."

"Yes."

"David Franklin was here? When?"

"We did not know him by that name. He came as a pilgrim, maybe two months ago," Jose said. "He offered money and was very desperate. Of course, we do not charge for God's grace. He was very sick, and Charro treated him."

"He had pancreatic cancer," I said, my mind clearing.

"Yes, he was dying."

"So he died in your care?"

Jose gave me an ironic grin. "This man did not die. God cured him."

My heart jumped, but I also suspected my leg might be getting pulled. I had just witnessed something I could not understand, but to cure stage four pancreatic cancer? It was tough to swallow. "You're telling me this man is alive?"

"Yes."

"You wouldn't happen to know where he is now?" I rolled the buckshot between my thumb and index finger. The pain was gone from my elbow, and my mind felt clear and settled. This man could have punched me in the face, and I would have smiled at him.

"He lives in the village north of here," Jose said. "He works for the new library built by one of Charro's grateful pilgrims, a wealthy man from Australia. Charro accepts gifts to the village."

"This man works in your library?"

"Yes. He told us he had no family and no hope. We gave him some."

"How do I get there?"

"At the bottom of the drive, you make a left, and the village is a short drive. The library is on the left-hand side of the road past the Mercado. You can't miss it."

"Thank you."

Jose patted my leg, blessed me, and went back to work. I put the piece of shot in my pocket and stood up on my wobbly legs. Then I made my way back to the front of the building, smiling at everyone I saw.

I felt wonderful.

I hoped it wasn't permanent.

"Goodbye," the tall man that first greeted me called out. I waved back.

Driving was interesting because everything seemed slowed down a bit. I took lots of opiates after my accident and drank on top of them. That's what this felt like. I smiled down the hill and kept smiling when I made the left and drove into the village.

Just as Jose had said, the library squatted like an overweight tourist just past a small market. Compared to the rest of the town, it was pristine. While I parked, I imagined the wealthy patient who built it out of appreciation for his miracle. The heat seemed less intense while I walked the stamped concrete sidewalk and pushed through the double doors into the air-conditioned library. It was empty except for a solitary worker behind the counter. I stopped in my tracks.

Standing behind the counter, his hair thinner and his face serene, was a man who looked like David Franklin. He was thinner and grayer at the temples, but it was him.

I feel his need to reconcile what is left of him, Karen's voice whispered. You cannot destroy the spirit.

He thumbed through papers and looked up as I approached. My face must have betrayed me because he took a small step back. Then he folded his hands on the edge of the counter. I saw the thumb missing from his left hand.

"Como estas?" he said.

"Hello, David."

His cheeks flushed just a bit, but his eyes stayed steady. He did not attempt to run. "I'm sorry, my name is not David. Can I help you?"

I dropped the photo on the counter. "Oh, David, I know it's you."

He stared at the folded, creased, and now crumpled picture, and for a moment, I saw something pass in his face, like a man looking at his lost first love in an old high school yearbook.

I tapped the photo with my hook. "That's you."

"Yes, there is a likeness," he said. "I'm sorry, but I am not this man."

"I think your wife and kids would be heartbroken if they heard you say that."

"I've never been married," he said. "I have no family."

"No family? Claire and Brandon and Kelly don't ring a bell?" I intentionally used the wrong child's name and looked for a reaction. I got nothing.

"I'm sorry," was all he said.

"House in San Mateo, a job at an advertising agency?"

He slowly shook his head. "No."

It was odd. While I tried to interrogate him, my tone and thoughts were too gentle. I tried to shake the Charro touch, but the serenity was too strong. To come so far, risk so much, and not have the intimidation factor of scary Bobbi Jacobi? That would have pissed me off if I could have found that emotion. A deep divot surrounded by scar tissue marred his forearm above the missing thumb. It looked just like a poorly healed gunshot wound.

"I don't know those people. I have no idea what you're talking about," he said. "I am sorry I can't help you."

"David, this is you. I've followed a chain of clues and hunches from San Francisco to hell and back looking for you. The Bayside Consolidated Insurance Corporation paid out half a million dollars to your wife after they declared you dead, but I had a hunch it was fraud."

"Sir," he said and unclasped his hands. "I can appreciate that you are on some sort of mission, but I am not the person you are looking for. Please, I– "

I cut him off. "You came down here because you had cancer."

"Yes, I was dying, and I went to see Charro as a last resort. I am currently in remission, so I stay here to be close to him."

"And away from America," I said. "Otherwise, you'd have to explain to your wife and children why you abandoned them. Not to mention facing insurance fraud and having to give back the money."

He took another small step back. "That sounds very interesting, but you have the wrong person."

"Oh yeah? Tell me, how did you lose that thumb and injure that arm?"

"Farm accident when I was a kid living in Ohio," he said.

Now I was the one to step back. I opened and closed my hook. For three years, I had responded to everyone who asked with countless sarcastic, false explanations of how I lost my hand, just to be an asshole. This man stood before me and sincerely lied for what he thought was a noble reason. I felt shame for a brief moment and then opened my mouth to call him a liar.

"How'd you lose that hand?" The librarian asked.

"Uh," I said and realized I was about to lie to him. My face flushed and I felt cornered somehow.

"Are you all right?" he asked me. "You suddenly looked ill."

I took a deep breath. "I'm fine. I used to be a cop. A kidnapper shot my hand off with a shotgun. We saved the girl, and my partner shot the perpetrator and killed him."

"That's an intense story. It must have been painful."

"It's nothing compared to what you went through. How did you cut off that thumb?"

"I'm sorry," he said and shook his head. "I was so young, I hardly remember."

"Listen, David." I looked him in the eye. Or was it really him? I was beginning to doubt myself. "All I have to do is get a strand of hair, and I can prove who you are."

"Sir, you're becoming agitated, and I'm not comfortable with this."

"Just admit it," I said. "Then I can do my job."

"This is becoming upsetting to me, and I have work to do. Please leave, or I'll have to call the police."

I wanted to dare him to call the cops so he could explain why he ran out on his family and faked his death. I wanted to demand that he tell the truth about his deception and betrayal and confess the hurt and grief he caused and the money he stole. I wanted to do all of that, but I didn't. When I looked at him, I saw a man who did everything he could to keep his family from the streets, from prolonged heartache and the nightmare of his slow death. I wanted to be mad, but instead, I almost cried.

"I see," was all I managed.

What now? To force him back was kidnapping. I'd never make it out of Mexico. Extradition would take forever, and I'd have to have concrete grounds for requesting it. That was next to impossible without proof, and that required tissue samples for matching. Do I take a pound of flesh home in a cooler?

"Sir," he said. "I am struggling between calling for help or offering it. You look pale and weak. Are you all right?"

My shoulders sagged. "Okay, I'll have to do this another way. You should expect some visitors from the good people at Bayside Consolidated Insurance Corporation."

He smiled. "No, I won't. It looks like your arm is bleeding."

Indeed it was. The small hole where the buckshot climbed from its resting place had opened up. I dabbed at it with my thumb, and he handed me a tissue.

"Thanks," I said.

"Can I ask you a question? If a man like you was willing to cross the world to track down a man like David, then you were willing to forsake your own life and leave behind friends and family to find this man. What makes you think he would not be willing to take a chance and make a sacrifice for a much greater reason than money?"

"It's always about the money, one way or another," I said.

"You just said this man's family has accepted his fate and mourns him, and the insurance company has declared him dead. If this David is even a shade of a decent man, he would not want to upset the process of his family's healing. I would think he would never do anything to hurt his family more than his original act of selfless sacrifice. From what you tell me, he did none of this for himself. How can that be a crime?"

"It's still fraud," I said.

"Can you be that blind?"

"No matter how this is spun, it's fraud, and I have a responsibility to bring the guilty party to justice. It's my job."

"Did your boss send you here?" The librarian asked.

"No," I heard myself say.

"Has the family demanded that he should be returned?"

"Maybe if they knew he was still alive."

"Is the insurance company demanding restitution? Tell me, Mr. Jacobi, if the family accepts this David's death, and the insurance company has settled, who sent you to look for this man?"

"I'm working to prove the truth," I argued.

"At what cost?"

"Meaning what?"

"To tear open the wounds of a healing family, to embarrass a company for its mistake, to draw sensationalism into the lives of people who are only trying to finally return to normal? You say you want the truth. Who is to say how truth is defined? Many people believe in God with nothing more than blind faith. Is the law your God?"

"Wait a minute," I said.

He put up his hand and stopped me. "And imagine this David himself. What punishment could be worse than his own imposed seclusion and the knowledge his cancer was cured, but he must allow his family to believe he's dead. To live with the fact he will never see them again in light of his recovery? What is more terrible – for a family to lose a patriarch or the man to live knowing they all believe him to be dead?"

"It's not that easy," I said.

"No, it's not easy at all. It would be the hardest thing this David would ever have to endure."

All I could do is shake my head. But the more I looked at the librarian, the less he looked like the photo of David Franklin. Before long, they looked nothing alike.

"Please," the librarian said. "Let this man live in the prison of his own making. Face it. God certainly has a sense of humor."

"Then answer me one thing," I said. "Are you David Franklin?"

"Mr. Jacobi," he said. "I'm not sure who I am. Can I put a bandage on that for you?"

I stood still while he gently applied a dressing on my elbow.

"Now, if you'll excuse me, I have books to check-in."

I went back to the car in a bizarre state of acceptance. On the drive back to Guadalajara, I thought about going back and demanding a blood sample so I could have it tested to prove Franklin was alive. I vacillated between that thought and the knowledge that the people at Bayside Consolidated Insurance Corporation probably didn't give a good goddamn.

I found myself hating the many ambiguous layers of questionable bureaucracy that had nothing to do with life or death.

Just take in and payout.

By the time I reached the airport I was myself again. Maybe not completely, my mind wouldn't stop fingering the itch of stunned awareness I felt. Something had happened to me, and I was afraid I would never be the same again. Not that the old me was all that great, but I was used to it.

While turning in the rental car, I surrendered to something profound; I realized that going back and proving the truth would hurt more people than it helped. Between Karen Carlson and Charro del Christo, I was having a life-shifting change of heart regarding miracles. Odd, while I was seeking night and day in my professional life, my personal life had me wandering into someplace between dawn and twilight.

Then it hit me. When I got home, I would quit the job, call Buddy and take his offer. If I was to entertain spiritual ambiguity, then I needed clarity in my work life. Carl would understand, and Janice would be heartbroken, but that's the way of the world. Karen's voice whispered in my heart, and I thought of Gina, the wedding in my future, and I laughed out loud. People around me gave me some distance.

Lookout – it's a big crazy bald guy with a hook for a hand!

That made me laugh again while I happily went through airport security and cared nothing about the secondary pat-down. Along the wall, white telephones advertised per-minute international calls. I knew it was expensive, but I could afford it. With the receiver tucked under my chin, I called Gina and prayed for her to pick up.

"Hello?" she said.

"Hi, it's me."

"Are you home?"

"No, I'm in the airport in Mexico. I'm waiting for my flight to be called."

Gina said nothing.

"Hello?"

"I'm here."

"It's over. Really. As crazy as coming down here was, it was exactly what I needed to clear my head. I'm coming home, the man you and I both know and love. I promise."

"I'll know that when I see you. You sound like yourself."

"I'm better than myself. I'm happy and ready to come home and marry you and spend the rest of my life making you deliriously happy."

"Are you drunk?"

"No, why?"

"You sound giddy," Gina said with a laugh. "It's kind of scary. You sure you're not drunk?"

"Sober as a judge and happy as a pig in shit."

"So what happened?"

"Babe, this is costing me a fortune. Let's just say I found God, in a way."

"Okay. I'll see you when you get home. And Bobby?" I held my breath. "I love you."

"I love you more. Bye."

I stared at the ring on my finger, put there to tell the world I was taken, married to a Goddess, and forever committed to her in every way. I looked forward to my new life. Besides, working private investigations might be fun. Maybe a bit tawdry, but it had closure. It all felt right.

Once I was in the terminal, I found a seat. I fished the buckshot from my pocket and rolled it between my fingers. I would eventually adjust to the concept that there are things beyond my comprehension, beyond the world's small way of thinking, and more than the flesh hanging on our bones. I took a deep breath and dropped the small metal pebble on the floor in an act of overt symbolism.

I thought of David and looked at my missing hand and understood it was the lesser of two losses. His entire existence was amputated from what he loved. I had lost only a hand for an ideal I no longer embraced. There was no prosthetic for Franklin's life.

Once I was on the plane, I sat beside a family of American tourists with a daughter and a son. I thought of Claire, and my heart ached for a moment.

The young boy noticed my hook. "That's cool."

"Kevin, that's not appropriate," his mother said. "I'm so sorry."

"It's no problem." I waved it in the air.

"Were you in the military?" the father asked.

"No. I lost it when I was riding in the rodeo."

Kevin beamed. "Wow. Bulls or broncs?"

"Bulls," I said in my best Texas twang.

"Cool."

I felt no guilt for the lie. After all my recent enlightenment, it still felt good to fuck with the world a bit. Besides, nobody would recognize me if I were suddenly a completely new man.

I put on my seatbelt and prepared for takeoff. The captain gave us the obligatory speech, the attendants showed us how to use our seatbelts and explained how to use our seats as flotation devices. They showed us facemasks and pointed out the exits. Then we taxied away from the terminals and took our place in line for takeoff. I smiled at the symbolism of it. We were always in line for the next adventure of our lives, weren't we?

The captain moved us forward, positioning the aircraft on the field, and I stifled a laugh at the pure insanity of what was to come. A plane full of people sat in innocent faith that the man behind the controls was sane enough and skilled enough to take us safely home.

Is that not the same as believing in God? Karen had pushed me toward the void of faith, and Charro had shown me the power of true surrender. I now understood that was the basis of a spiritual life. Somebody else was at the controls and about to carry us through the sky, and we trusted that they would get us there. Okay, I thought, take me home.

The engines roared, the plane screamed down the runway, and we lifted off the ground with a stomach-dropping sway of tons of fuel-driven machinery. I sat back and smiled and truly surrendered for the first time. Bring it on. Give me life, and let me enjoy it beyond the veil of tangible bullshit.

Soon we were soaring through the clouds. The attendants came around and handed out drinks and snacks. I reclined my seat back, folded my hand in my lap, and held the cold curve of my hook in the cradle of my flesh and bone fingers.

A smile came across my face. If I found myself stuck and needing help when working as a private dick, I knew I could call on Karen Carlson. She said my future depended on it. What self-respecting P.I. didn't have his sources and resources to help him do his job? It suddenly sounded like a whole lot of fun.

With my head calm and my heart full, I thought of Gina and the rest of my life. Funny, I thought, when I got home, and Joe asked if I caught anything fishing, I could tell him I caught a big one and decided to let it go.

And it would be the truth.

– THE END

ACKNOWLEDGMENTS

Thanks to my colleague, Andrew McAllister, who helped me stay on track with my story. Thanks Dale for the input on Life Insurance facts and the way things work. I'll never look at my premium bill the same again.

I owe an immense debt of gratitude to my early reader group. A big thank you to West Coast Don from Men Reading Books, Tony Neal, Glen Freemont, and Christopher Reich. Your input helped this book find its way and stay on track.

Thanks to Jerry Shapiro for his never-ending faith in me.

Thanks to my son, Ian. Your creative strategy meetings with me helped this story come to fruition. Your help means more to me than you'll ever know.

Finally, and most importantly, this book would not exist without the support of my wife Stacy. Thank you for believing in me!

Sample Chapter of:

PARALLEL LINES
A Bobby Jacobi Mystery

NIGHT TRAIN

Every hour on the hour, the rails along the coast between San Diego and San Clemente, California sing with metal wheels carrying passengers. Beginning before dawn and screaming down the two rail highway until after sunset, the Surfliner trains make round trips, stop picking up and drop off intrepid travelers and slip into sidings so sister trains can access the tracks. Through the windows, riders stare at the passing Pacific Ocean, bluff side towns, and expensive homes. Winding up with the beast's momentum, then jerked into action along with the cars, they surged with determined mass until the next grinding stop to allow more to climb aboard or scuttle off.

At the controls, John Samuels watched his speed and monitored the track lines with the automated and unconscious precision of a well-seasoned veteran. Twenty years behind at the helm, seven

299

with Surfliner, he had ten to go, and the rails would be behind him instead of beneath him. Ten more years.

"Comin' up on Solana Beach." He hit two short blasts on the horn, followed by a long wail. Solana station was closed at this hour and they sailed through the man-made canyon below Coast Highway and out onto the flats through the marshlands. Night wind whipped the windows, and the machine's rumble blocked out the sound of evening waves on the sand. Hillside homes cast stretches of yellow light across the inlet. John sat back and listened to the train's monotonous song of steel on steel.

Encinitas was the next stop, and so he could let the beast roll through Del Mar and Costa Mar stations.

John felt the shift from the elevated run over the water to the flexing hard pack of the sandy bluffs. Each terrain had a different feel, and he knew them all. Rock rattled your bones, sand quieted the rumble, and the city stretch had a dangerous feeling like the rails were too shallow and the asphalt too hard to let the hulking snake move as it should.

The Costa Mar bluffs crowded the train on its course, and John always laughed that folks dropped millions for the beachfront property with vast Ocean Views and paid the additional price of the rattle and rumble of the regular trains passing in front of their expansive views. He imagined fine china chattering in the kitchen cupboards and crystal glasses chattering across glass tables. Many of these homes looked close enough to slap on the pass by.

Besides the close proximity of the properties, there was always the danger of automobile collisions at the crossings and people on the tracks. John knew the numbers, and it was unavoidable. Every engineer and crew had the experience eventually, and the disasters numbered around one a month. Most were pedestrian fatalities, usually drunks or suicides. Though that sounded like a lot, when John considering the number of trains running the rounds day after day, the incidents were actually few. When it did happen, despite the unfortunate wreckage and carnage, it meant paid time off during the investigation. Rarely was it their fault.

"Hugging the hill," John called out when the engine and five cars roared around the point and headed for the coastal bluffs. Even after dark, surfers were bobbing in the waves, and people walked the gravel trail beside the tracks. Most waved or gawked when they charged past and then turned to watch the fading sunset. In the small burg of Costa Mar, the old streets ran like steep gullies between the rows of bungalows, rental shacks, and mansions perched by the water. Each street ended with a barrier where illegal paths were cut to allow the surfers and beachgoers access to the sand. Every time they stepped across the tracks, they broke the law. Nobody cared, and the rails we rarely patrolled this far down. John checked the front camera and listened for any chatter about debris, but the rails were open.

"Clear to punch through," he said.

At the bottom of Catalina Street, where the steep embankment acted as the precarious access to the gravel path along the rails, John saw nothing in the dark shadows. With no reason to slow before the Cardiff By The Sea road crossing, he sipped his coffee and swayed with the machine.

In the dark of the hollow at the embankment base at the bottom of Catalina Street, the movement went unseen. The shift in the night was unnoticed. The train's massive momentum barely felt the impact of the man's body when he lurched in front of the locomotive. Like a moth striking the windshield of a semi-truck, the body was crushed instantly, and the corpse knocked thirty feet down the rails. It came to land in a broken heap in the tall grass beside the tracks.

Charging away like an angry Rhinoceros, the train kept its pace. The surfers bobbed, and the walkers returned home with the darkening skies. The body lay still next to the settling tracks. It was the last run of the night, and after the final stop on San Juan Capistrano, John and the crew trudge north to the train yard adjacent to Camp Pendleton Marine Corps Base. There they waited their turn and dropped cars, rolled onto the wheel, and backed the locomotive into the barn. Once docked and secure, John said goodnight and walked to his truck, unaware of the dead man crumpled in the dark.

He would not be found until morning.